The Crimson Gardenia and Other Tales of Adventure

BY

REX BEACH

AUTHOR OF
"HEART OF THE SUNSET"
"THE SPOILERS" ETC.

ILLUSTRATED

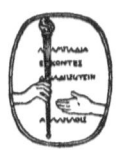

HARPER & BROTHERS PUBLISHERS

NEW YORK AND LONDON

BOOKS BY

REX BEACH

THE CRIMSON GARDENIA AND OTHER
    TALES OF ADVENTURE. Illustrated. Post 8vo
HEART OF THE SUNSET. Illustrated. Post 8vo
THE AUCTION BLOCK. Illustrated. Post 8vo
THE IRON TRAIL. Illustrated. Post 8vo
THE NET. Illustrated. Post 8vo
THE NE'ER-DO-WELL. Illustrated. Post 8vo
THE SPOILERS. Illustrated. Post 8vo
THE BARRIER. Illustrated. Post 8vo
THE SILVER HORDE. Illustrated. Post 8vo
GOING SOME. Illustrated. Post 8vo

HARPER & BROTHERS, NEW YORK

CONTENTS

ILLUSTRATIONS

THE
CRIMSON GARDENIA

I

THE royal yacht had anchored amid a
thunder of cannon, and the king had gone
ashore. The city was bright with bunting; a
thousand whistles blew. Up through the festooned streets His Majesty was escorted between
long rows of blue-coated officers, behind which
the eager crowds were massed for mile upon mile.
Thin wire cables were stretched along the curbs,
to hold the people back, but these threatened to
snap before the weight of the multitude.

In the neighborhood of the raised pavilion where
the queen and her maids of honor waited, the
press was thickest; here rows of stands had been
erected that groaned beneath their freight, while
roof-tops and windows, trees and telegraph-poles,
were black with clustered humanity.

The king was tall and dark; a long beard hid
his face. But the queen was young and blushing,

and her waiting-women were fairer than spring-time flowers. To a crashing martial air, she handed him a sparkling goblet in which he pledged her happiness, while the street rocked to the roar of many voices, and in the open spaces youths, grotesquely costumed, danced with goblin glee.

Mr. Roland Van Dam secretly thought it all quite fine and inspiriting, but he was too highly schooled to allow himself much emotion. He had been hard put to obtain seats, and had succeeded only through the efforts of a friend, the Duke of Cotton; therefore, he felt, the members of his party might have shown at least a perfunctory appreciation. But they were not the appreciative kind, and their attitude was made plain by Eleanor Banniman's languid words:

"How dull! It's nothing like the carnival at Nice, and the people seem very common."

Her father was dozing uncomfortably, with his two lower chins telescoped into his billowing chest; Mrs. Banniman complained of the heat and the glare, and predicted a headache for herself. Near by, the rest of the party were striving to conceal their lack of interest by guying the crowd below. Van Dam had been the one to suggest this trip to New Orleans for the Mardi Gras, and he felt the weight of entertainment bearing heavily upon him. In consequence, he assumed a sprightly interest that was very far from genuine.

"This sort of thing awakens something medieval inside of one, don't you know," he said.

THE CRIMSON GARDENIA

Miss Banniman regarded him with a bland lack of comprehension; her mother moaned weakly, the burden of her complaint being, as usual:

"Why *did* we leave Palm Beach?"

"All those dukes and things make me feel as if it were real," Van Dam explained further. "They say this Rex fellow is a true king during Mardi Gras week, and those chaps in masks are quite like court jesters. Maybe they sing of wars and love and romance—and all that rot."

"I dare say life was just as uninteresting in olden days as it is now," Eleanor remarked. "Love and romance exist mainly in books, I fancy. If they ever did exist, we've outgrown them, eh, Roly?"

Being a very rich and a very experienced young woman, Miss Banniman prided herself upon her lack of illusion. To be sure, she occasionally permitted Roland to kiss her in celebration of their engagement, but such caresses left her unperturbed; her pulses had never been stirred. She looked upon marriage as a somewhat trying, although necessary, institution. Van Dam, being equally modern and equally satiated by life's blessings, shared her beliefs in a vague way.

Manifestly, no lover could allow such an assertion as this to go unchallenged, so he rose to the defense of romance, only to hear her say:

"Nonsense! Do be sensible, Roly. Such things aren't done nowadays."

"What things aren't done?"

"Oh, those crude, primitive performances we

5

read about in novels. Nice people don't fall in love overnight, for instance. They don't allow themselves to hate, and be jealous, and to rage about like wild animals any more."

"The idea! Your father is a perfect savage, at heart," said Mrs. Banniman. She nodded at her sleeping husband, who was roused at that moment by a fly that had strayed into his right nostril. Mr. Banniman sneezed, half opened his eyes, and murmured a feeble anathema before dozing off again. It was plain that he was not greatly enjoying the Mardi Gras.

"All men are primitive," said Roly, quoting some forgotten author, at which Eleanor eyed him languidly.

"Could you love at first sight and run off with a girl?"

"Certainly not. I'd naturally have to know something about her people—"

"Were you ever jealous?"

"You've never given me an occasion," he told her, gallantly.

"Did you ever hate anybody?"

"Um-m—no!"

"Ever been afraid?"

"Not exactly."

"Revengeful?"

"Certainly not."

She smiled. "It's just as I said. Respectable people don't allow themselves to be harrowed by crude emotions. I hate my modiste when she fails

6

THE CRIMSON GARDENIA

to fit me; I was jealous of that baroness at the Poinciana—the one with all those gorgeous gowns; I'm afraid of flying-machines; but that is as deep as such things go, nowadays—in our set."

Van Dam was no hand at argument, and he had a great respect for Miss Banniman's observation; moreover, he had been discussing something of which he possessed no first-hand knowledge. Therefore, he said nothing further. No one had a greater appreciation of, or took a keener pleasure in, life's unruffled placidity than the young society man. No one had a denser ignorance of its depths, its hidden currents, and its uncharted channels than he; for adventure had never come his way, romance had never beckoned him from rose-embowered balconies. And yet, as the world goes, he was a normal individual, save for the size of his income. He had not lost interest in life; he was merely interested in things which did not matter. That, after all, is quite different.

There were times, nevertheless, when he longed vaguely for something thrilling to happen, when he regretted the Oslerization of romance and the commercializing of love. Of course, adventure still existed; one could hunt big game in certain hidden quarters, if one chose. Van Dam detested stuffed heads, and it took so much time to get them. These unformed desires came to him only now and then, and he felt ashamed of them, in an idle way.

Now that the parade had passed, the visitors

7

lost no time in leaving, and a dignified stampede toward the hotel occurred, for the gentlemen were thirsty and the ladies wished to smoke. It was due to their haste, perhaps, that Van Dam became separated from them and found himself drifting along Canal Street alone in a densely packed crowd of merrymakers. A masked woman in a daring Spanish dress chucked him under the chin; her companion showered him with confetti. A laughing Pierrot whacked him with a noisy bladder; boys and girls in ragged disguises importuned him for pennies. A very, very shapely female person, in what appeared to be the beginnings of a bathing suit, laughed over her shoulder, inviting him, with eyes that danced.

"My word!" murmured the New-Yorker. "This is worth while."

Ahead of him, he caught a glimpse of Miss Banniman's aigrettes and the ponderous figure of her father. But the gaiety of the carnival crowd had infected him, and he was loath to leave it for the Grunewald, whither his friends were bound with the unerring directness of thirsty millionaires. It was a brilliant, gorgeous afternoon; the streets were alive with color. Somewhere through this crowd, the young man idly reflected, adventure— even romance—might be stalking, if such things really existed. So he decided to linger. To be quite truthful, Van Dam's decision was made, not with any faintest idea of encountering either romance or adventure, but because a slight indigestion made the thought of a gin-fizz or a julep unbearable at the moment.

As he continued to move with the throng, the butt of badinage and the target for impudent glances, he felt a desire to be of it and in it. He yielded himself to a most indiscreet impulse. Assuring himself that he was unobserved, he stepped into a store, purchased a plain black domino and mask, donned them, and then fell in with the procession once more, dimly amused at his folly, vaguely surprised at his impropriety.

But now that he was one of the revelers he was no longer an object of their attentions; they paid no heed to him, and he soon became bored. He engaged himself in conversation with an old flower-woman, and, as she had only a solitary gardenia left in her tray, he bought it in order that she might go home. He pinned the blossom on the left breast of his domino, and wandered to the nearest corner to watch the crowds flow past.

He had been there but a moment when a girl approached and stood beside him. She was petite, and yet her body beneath its fetching Norman costume showed the rounded lines of maturity; at the edge of her mask her skin gleamed smooth and creamy; her eyes were very dark and very bright. As Mr. Van Dam was a very circumspect young man, not given to the slightest familiarity with strangers, he confined his attentions to an inoffensive inventory of her charms, and was doubly startled to hear her murmur:

2 9

"You came in spite of all, m'sieu'!"

A French girl, he thought. No doubt one of those creoles he had heard so much about. Aloud, he said, with a bow:

"Yes, mademoiselle. I have been looking for some one like you."

Her eyes flashed to the white gardenia on his breast, then up to his own. "You were expecting some one?"

"I was. A girl, to guide me through the carnival."

"But you are early. Did you not receive the warning?"

"Warning?" he answered, confused. "I received no warning."

"I feared as much," she said, "so I came. But it was unwise of you; it was madness to risk the streets." Her eyes left his face, to scan the crowds.

He fancied she shrank from them, as if fearing observation. Van Dam was puzzled. Her voice and manner undoubtedly betrayed a genuine emotion, or else she was a consummate actress. If this were some Mardi Gras prank, he felt a desire to see the next move. If it proved to be anything more, he fancied that he was too sophisticated to be caught and fleeced like a countryman. But something told him that this was no ordinary street flirtation. The words "warning," "risk" seemed to promise entertainment. If, as he suspected, she had mistaken him for some one else, a brief masquerade could lead to no harm. He decided to see how far he could carry the deception.

"What warning could serve to prevent my seeing you?" he asked in a hollow voice; then was surprised at the flush that stole upward to the girl's dainty ear.

"You are indeed insane to jest at such a time," she breathed. "I would never have known you without the flower. But come—we are in danger here. Some one—is waiting. Will you follow me?"

"To the ends of the earth," he replied, gallantly.

Again she gave him a startled glance, half of pleasure, half of deprecation; then, as he made a movement to accompany her, she checked him.

"No, no! You must let me go ahead. They are everywhere. They may suspect even my disguise. I—I am dreadfully afraid."

Van Dam scarcely knew how to answer this. So, like a wise man, he held his tongue.

"Listen!" she continued. "I will walk slowly, and do you remain far enough behind for your own safety—"

"My safety is as nothing to yours," he told her, but she shook her head impatiently.

"Please! Please! They will never select you out of a thousand dominos, and I am not sure they suspect me. But should they try to lift my mask, you must escape at once."

"Would they dare?" Mr. Van Dam inquired, shocked at such a breach of carnival etiquette.

"They would dare anything."

"But I couldn't allow it, really," he persisted.
"If any hand is to lift your mask, I insist that
mine be the favored one."

She darted a doubtful look at him, being plainly
perturbed at his tone, then shook her head. "She
told me you were reckless, but you are quite—
insane."

For a second time he discovered that delicious
color tingeing her neck and laughed, which dis-
concerted her even more. She hesitated, then
turned away and he fell in behind her.

But distance served only to enhance the girl's
charms. Roly saw how beautifully proportioned
she was, how regally she carried herself, how light
and springy was her step. Although he had not
seen her face, he somehow felt agreeably certain
that she possessed a witching beauty.

The circumspection with which she avoided the
densest crowds made him wonder anew at the
character of the danger that could overhang a
masked maiden at mid-afternoon on a carnival day,
for by this time he had forgotten his first suspicion. He thought not at all that the peril could
be serious, or in any way involve him, for the
magic of the Van Dam name protected its owner
like invisible mail. The effect of that patronymic
was really quite wonderful; policemen bowed to it,
irate strangers allowed their anger to ooze away
before it. It smoothed the owner's way through
difficulties and brought him favors when least

expected; rage changed to servility; indignation, opposition, even jealousy altered color in the shadow of the Van Dam millions. Nothing really unpleasant ever happened to Roly, and so it was that he had become *blasé* and tired at twenty-six.

He followed his masked guide across Canal Street and into the foreign quarter of the city, where the surroundings were unfamiliar to him. He gazed with mild repugnance at the squalid old houses, moldering behind their rusted iron balconies. Dim, flag-paved hallways allowed him a glimpse of flowered courtyards at the rear; cool passages went twisting in between the buildings. Over hard-baked, glaring walls there drooped branches laden with bloom and fruit. The streets were narrow, the houses leaned intimately toward one another, as if exchanging gossip; little cafés with sanded floors opened upon the sidewalks. Here the carnival crowd was more foreign in character; people were dancing to orchestras of guitar and mandolin; youths turned somersaults for pennies; ragged negroes jigged and shuffled with outstretched hats.

Through this confusion the Norman girl took her way, now seeking some deep doorway to allow a particularly boisterous group to pass, now flitting through the open spaces with the swift irregularity of a butterfly winging its course through sunlit stretches. But her caution, her birdlike, backward glances, told Van Dam that she was in constant dread of discovery, and in-

13

voluntarily he lessened the distance between them.

It was well, perhaps, that he did so, for just then a man in a domino like his own accosted the girl. Roly saw his guide shrink away, saw her turn and signal him with a swift, imperious gesture of warning. Instead of heeding it, he moved forward in time to intercept the stranger. The fellow was laughing loudly; he assumed a tipsy air and lurched against the girl; then, with a quickness that belied his pose, he snatched at her mask and bared her features. She cried out in terror, and with the sound of her voice Mr. Van Dam flew to action. He knew that until six o'clock disguises were inviolate, and that it was against the strictest of police regulations to unmask a reveler; therefore he yielded to a righteous impulse and struck the man in the domino squarely upon the jaw. Beneath Roly's rounded proportions was a deceptive machinery of bone and muscle that had been schooled by the most expensive instructors of boxing. He had known how to hit cleanly since he was twelve years old, and although he had never struck a man in anger until this moment, his fist went true. The fellow rocked stiffly back upon his heels and fell like a wooden figure, his head thumping dully on the pavement, and Roly gave vent to a most ungentlemanly snort of surprise and satisfaction. It had been much easier than he had expected, and feeling that the man should have every opportunity for fair play Roly began

promptly to count, "One, two, three—" Then
he felt the girl's hand upon his arm, and turned in
time to catch a fleeting glimpse of a dimpled chin
as she drew her mask down. "Rotten trick, that!"

"Heaven above!" she gasped. "You must flee
—quickly!"

People were crossing the street toward them,
drawn by the sight of the fallen man.

"Run away and leave you?" queried Roly.
"Hardly!"

"Then"—the breath caught in the girl's throat
—"come!"

She clutched his hand and they fled, side by side,
pursued by half a score of shouting merrymakers.
Around the first corner they scurried, into a crowd,
then out of it and into the next thoroughfare,
doubling and turning until the girl's breath was
gone.

"Why—did—you do—it? Ah!—why?" she
gasped, still hurrying him along.

"Drunken loafer!" Van Dam said, vindictively.

"He was not drunk! Don't you understand?
Didn't you guess? It was the Black Wolf!"

Roly did not understand, and he had no opportunity to guess who or what the Black Wolf
might be, for his companion paused, crying:

"God help us! They are coming."

From the street behind rose a babble of angry
voices.

"He saw me! He knows!"

She cast a despairing glance about, and, spying

a narrow alley close at hand, darted toward it, dragging Van Dam with her.

Retreat carries with it a peculiar panic, and the young man felt the stirring of an utterly new sensation within him. He was running away! What was more, he wanted to keep running, even though he had not the faintest idea of what menaced him. It was quite remarkable. He seemed to feel, for some unknown reason, that this sprightly young person beside him was indeed risking her safety for him. Therefore, he began to share her apprehensions, but as to what it meant or whither the adventure was leading he had not a suspicion. He did wonder, however, where the Black Wolf got his name.

The alley was damp and slippery, being no more than a tunnel-like passage between two buildings, and it led into a large courtyard full of carts and wagons. A low shed ran along one side of the inclosure; at the rear was a two-story structure used as a stable.

"There! I guess we've given them the slip," Van Dam sighed, with relief.

But his companion shook her head. "No, no! We must hide. The Black Wolf has the cunning of Satan, and now that he knows—" She sped through the confusion of vehicles to the stable door, with Roly following. An instant more and they were in an odorful, dim-lit place divided into stalls out of which the heads of several horses were thrust in friendly greeting. The girl closed the door and leaned panting against it, one hand to her heaving bosom. Her head was bowed and her ears were strained for sounds of pursuit. In the silence Van Dam heard his own heavy breathing, the swish of the horses' tails, an impatient stirring of hoofs, and a gentle whinny. He discovered that his pulse was hammering in a very unusual manner and that he was agreeably excited.

The girl uttered an exclamation. "I feared so! Hurry!" She slipped past him to a rickety stairway that led upward. "Ah—h—! this mask is smothering me!" She disengaged it hastily, and he saw it dangling in her hand as he mounted the steep stairs behind her. He saw also a pair of dainty silken ankles, swelling into delicious curves that were hidden in the foamy whiteness of lingerie. Being an extremely respectful gentleman, Mr. Van Dam lowered his eyes, anticipating with curious eagerness the pleasure of beholding her countenance, once they had gained the loft. The desire to see behind her mask became really acute. He had missed one opportunity by so narrow a margin as to quicken his desires.

They came out upon a rough landing, and Van Dam caught the whisk of her skirts disappearing through a door that led into the haymow. As he followed, the door closed and he found himself in utter darkness. He heard her fumbling with the lock. Their hands came together as he turned a rusty key and he felt her figure close

17

against his; her fragrant breath fanned his cheek.

"Make no sound, as you value our lives."

As she whispered this, Van Dam swore mildly at the luck that prevented him from appraising his companion's good looks, now that her mask was off. From the courtyard below sounded voices. The girl clutched him nervously; her hand was shaking. He could feel her shiver, so he slipped an arm about her waist. He did this merely to steady her, he told himself. He reasoned further that such a familiarity could scarcely be offensive in the dark. As she yielded gratefully to his embrace, her soft body palpitating against his own, he ceased reasoning and drew her closer. It was very agreeable to discover that she made no resistance; he could not recollect any sensation quite like this! As yet he had done nothing improper, in view of the fact that it was every gentleman's bounden duty to succor beauty in distress. He wondered if his friends at the Grunewald had missed him, then realized with relief that Miss Banniman never allowed his presence or his absence to interfere in the slightest with her arrangements. They were probably finishing their drinks by now. This would make an entertaining story, later in the evening; they would never guess what he was doing.

"Who is that speaking?" he inquired.

"François, the Spider," whispered the girl. "Eh, God! How they all have come to hate you!"

THE CRIMSON GARDENIA

Roly reasoned from these words that his enemies numbered more than one or two, and involuntarily he asked: "Hate me? What for?"

The girl trembled. "As if you did not know."

"And what would happen if they found me—us?" he persisted, feeling vaguely for some hint.

"Ah!" Her breath caught. "Hush!" She laid her fingers over the lips of his mask.

Van Dam yielded to an ungovernable impulse and kissed them through the stiff, harsh cloth, whereat she said in wonderment:

"Heaven guard us! You are actually laughing. That you are wild, I knew; but—you are—you act very strangely, m'sieu."

"Perhaps I'm intoxicated," he murmured, and pressed her slender waist meaningly; whereupon she seemed to feel his arm for the first time. She drew away, but as she disengaged his embrace her hand encountered his.

"It is wet — bloody — where you struck the Black Wolf."

"That was a good wallop, wasn't it?" Van Dam chuckled, with satisfaction, while she felt for her handkerchief and dabbled at his bruised knuckles. "I wondered if I could put him out."

Then they ceased whispering, for some one was entering the stable beneath them. After a time the stairs creaked to a heavy tread, a hand tried the door, and they could feel a presence within arm's-length. They stood motionless, not daring even to shift their weight upon the crazy floor, until the fellow began to explore the other portion of the loft.

"That is the Spider himself," breathed the girl, close to Van Dam's ear. "He thinks he has me in his web; but—"

"Yes?"

"I would die before I married him."

A sudden dislike for spiders in general awoke in Roly's breast.

"I hate him. I would kill him if I dared, but he frightens me—" She broke off and caught at her companion, gasping: "God! What are you doing?"

He had turned the key softly and was opening the door. To be quite truthful, Roly Van Dam did not know exactly what he intended doing, but some reckless impulse moved him to action. He was invaded by a sudden desire to lay hands upon this Spider person who went about terrorizing pretty girls. Having been reared to a habit of doing exactly as impulse dictated, he felt no hesitation now. Away back in his mind, however, something told him calmly that he had gone quite mad, that the magic of adventure had sent his wits a-flying and had played havoc with his common sense. And a change really had come over him with the very beginning of this enterprise, although he had not stopped to notice it. The flaring rage that had answered to the Wolf's assault upon the girl, the joyful sensation of setting his fist into the fellow's face, the excitement of the flight and the pursuit, had all combined to upset his equilibrium. Then, too, the presence of this bewitching creature close beside him in the darkness, the pressure of her body in his arms, the scent of her warm breath—all this helped to completely electrify him. He felt the dawning of new and utterly absurd desires. Away with discretion! To the winds with prudence! This maiden's cause was his. Here was the one glad moment of his life.

"François!" he called in a low voice. He slipped the girl's hand from his arm, thrust her back into the shadows, and stepped out upon the landing.

"*Oui!* In a moment!" The Spider came stumbling toward him. "She is not here." Van Dam saw a tall man in a domino like his own. "*Sacré!* She has disappeared; and that devil's spawn is with her. You found no trace in the yard below?"

"Sst! Listen," breathed Roly. He sank his fingers into his palms and measured the distance carefully. Then, as François turned his head attentively, Roly braced himself and swung. It may have been due to the uncertain light, or to the narrow eyelet-holes through which he peered; at any rate, Van Dam's blow went short.

The Spider uttered a cry of fury and surprise. Roly felt himself hugged by a pair of thin, iron-muscled arms; then his hands felt in beneath the man's disguise, and the cry changed to a gurgle.

They strained and rocked against each other briefly; the floor sagged and creaked; the door behind them flew open. François was groping with one free hand at his waist; but his domino was like a shirt, and he could not find that for which his hungry fingers searched. As for Van Dam, a delicious ferocity was flaming through his veins. Here was an enemy bent upon his quick destruction. No game he had ever played was half so exhilarating as this. He could feel the fellow writhe and the breath bursting through beneath his fingers; he could feel the man's cords harden until they were like wire. Strange to say, with every wrench and every surge his own abysmal fury increased. But the Spider was no weakling; he fought desperately until, in a burst of blind anger that was like some diabolic glee, Van Dam lifted him bodily and hurled him at the opening in the floor. The fellow missed his footing, clawed wildly, then fell backward headlong into the light below. The next instant Van Dam, too, had lost his balance and followed, bumping from step to step until he fetched up at the foot with a jar that drove the breath out of him.

He sat up in a moment, still dazed; then he heard a rustle, and beheld above him a pair of frightened, dark eyes gazing into his. Although he could see nothing of the girl's face—she had replaced her mask—he knew that she was racked with anxiety.

"Are you killed?" she queried.

THE CRIMSON GARDENIA

"No; just abominably twisted," he said. Then, with a wry face: "Ouch! That was an awful bump." As he felt himself over gingerly he stopped short at the sight of his mask lying crumpled beside him. He realized that the jig was up and began to formulate an explanation of his deception, only to hear her exclaim, tremulously:

"God be praised! You are unhurt."

He sat still, staring at her, amazed that no outburst followed her glimpse of his face.

"How did you dare—?" She turned to the figure of François, which Roly discovered motionless an arm's-length away.

The Spider was sprawled loosely in the litter. His head was twisted upon his shoulders in a peculiar way, and his mask, having slipped to the back, stared upward with a placid, waxlike smile that was horrible under the circumstances.

Still lost in wonderment, Van Dam arose, dusted off his clothing, and picked up his own disguise. Was it possible that she did not know the person she had gone to meet? It seemed so, indeed, for she was hanging upon him anxiously, as if still doubting his safety, while she half sobbed her admiration of his bravery and her gratitude at his escape. Roly began to fear he had been imposed upon, after all, else how could she fail to realize that he was an utter stranger? But the girl's honesty was compelling; he found that he could not doubt the sincerity of her gaze.

He felt an unaccountable lack of compunction regarding the Spider. In fact, he experienced a sense of satisfaction at the completeness of his victory over the ruffian, and she seemed to share the feeling.

He heard her urging him to make haste, and before he had fully regained his wits he found himself following her out into the sunlight. Underneath the wagon-shed she guided him, around behind it and into a narrow three-foot space, the left side of which was bounded by a board fence about head-high.

"Quick!" she cried, eagerly. "Once we are on the other side we may escape. The others are somewhere close by."

II

VAN DAM, being accustomed by this time to a certain obedience, lifted the girl up to the top of the fence, scrambled over it himself, and held up his arms to her. He was in another yard, much cleaner than the one he had just quit. There were trees and flowers in it, and looking down on them were shuttered windows which seemed empty. As she surrendered her weight to him he gave rein to the license which was in his blood and pressed a warm kiss back of her mask where the hair lay in wispy ringlets against her neck.

"*Mon Dieu!* What a man!" she laughed, struggling gently to free herself. "You had better put on your mask. We haven't far to go, but there may be observing eyes."

"Am—I—er—quite the person you pictured?" he queried, as he adjusted the false face.

"Not at all."

"You have never seen me before to-day?"

"Of course not! How could I?"

"I have seen you often."

"Impossible! Where?"

"Dreams!" said Van Dam, vaguely, yet with some degree of truth. "This all seems like a dream, as a matter of fact. I'm afraid I'll turn over, and you'll change into an old lady with hoop-skirts, or a flock of purple snowbirds, or a friendly crocodile with gold spectacles."

She pondered this for a moment as they made their way across the yard, being careful in the mean while to see if they were observed. After a moment she halted.

"Wait!" she said. "I—am not sure we dare risk going farther, for the streets are alarmed and the Wolf is in the neighborhood with all his pack. I had thought to take you straight home, but now they will be watching. It would be madness to try it." Again she fell silent, only to exclaim: "I have an idea. Come!" She turned abruptly to the right.

"Where are we going now?" he inquired, mildly.

She pointed to a house the back yard of which

abutted upon the one that they were crossing. "Yonder is your cousin Alfred's house. He is away at business, the servants are out watching the carnival, and so it is empty. Do you dare venture it?"

"Just the thing!" he said, amiably. "I owe Alfred a call."

The girl laughed shortly. "Ah! He would die of rage—or fright—if he knew; but you can wait there while I go—"

"Oh, I say! You're not going to leave me?" queried Roly in genuine alarm.

"Of course, silly! Some one must bring her."

Van Dam fell silent, speculating upon this last remark. After a moment he said, "You're sure Alfred won't return?"

"Who knows? We must run some hazards. The key will be under the step, I think. Come!"

They gained ingress to the next inclosure through a cedar hedge. Then, as they neared the back door, a distant commotion sounded from the stable-yard, warning them that the Spider's friends had stumbled upon him. But the girl's ready fingers found the key where it was hidden, and an instant later they were in a spotless creole kitchen ornamented with shining pots and pans. A cat rose from a sleepy window-ledge, arched its back, and stretched.

With a warning gesture Van Dam's guide bade him wait, then disappeared, returning in a moment.

26

THE CRIMSON GARDENIA

"It is as I thought—the house is empty." She beckoned him, and he followed her past a pantry, down a hall, and into a study furnished with a considerable degree of elegance. Drawn blinds shut out the glaring heat; it was dim and cool and restful.

The maiden heaved a sigh of relief and steadied herself against one of the massive mahogany chairs, showing by her attitude that the recent strain had told upon her.

"Heaven be praised! You are safe here, for a time at least," she managed to say.

"Nice, comfy place, this," remarked Van Dam, with an appreciative glance at the surroundings. "We can sit here and—and get acquainted—eh?"

"Hm-m! I think I have learned to know you quite well in the past half-hour," she laughed.

"True! But we've had very little chance to talk calmly and rationally; now, have we? Of course you're accustomed to such things, perhaps; but it has been a trifle strenuous for a person of my easy ways. I don't mind telling you that I'm positively winded. Let's rest a bit before you leave."

But the girl shook her head at his suggestion. "You forget how she has waited and longed for this hour. She has been very ill; nothing seemed to interest her until you promised to come on the last day of the *fiesta*. Since then she has been like another woman. She is counting the moments now until she feels your arms about her."

27

Roly stirred uncomfortably, for here was something he had not counted upon. One woman at a time was ample; he had no desire to hold another to his breast. He was shocked, too, that this girl should suggest such a thing after what had passed between them. It was unseemly. He felt tempted to confess his deception and to demand an explanation of the whole affair, but some sense of shame held him back. Besides, his companion was undoubtedly sincere, and he could not bring himself to cause her dismay.

Another reason that urged him to hold his tongue and to let the adventure run its course was that as yet he had not seen her face. The desire to do so was becoming insufferable. He was about to claim the privilege when she changed the current of his thoughts.

"You must not be shocked if she does not recognize you. She has been ill, very ill, since you—proved so great a—trial to her. You understand?"

"Perfectly!" he said, thankful that she could not detect his signs of bewilderment.

"Very well, then. You will make free of your cousin Alfred's hospitality while I am gone." She laughed nervously. "La! There is irony for you."

"Suppose he should return in the mean time?"

She shrugged. "You seem quite capable of caring for yourself, m'sieu'. I should not wish to be in his shoes, that is all. But there is little danger. And now I must leave you."

THE CRIMSON GARDENIA

"Just a moment," he said, taking her two hands in his. "You have seen my face. Don't you think I wish to see yours?"

Her breath caught at the tone of his voice. "Not yet. Please! When I return—when you have held her in your arms and made your peace. Then, perhaps, if you wish—but not until then." She pressed his fingers meaningly, and he thrilled.

"You haven't spoken my name, either," said he. "Won't you tell me that you—like me?"

"I—like you, Cousin Emile," said she; then, in a voice that told him she was blushing rosily, "and what name do you give to me?"

Roly's wits came to his rescue barely in time; with an air of deepest tenderness, that was not all assumed, he said: "I haven't dared acknowledge the name my heart has given you, even to myself. It is—"

"No, no!" she laughed, tremulously. "Call me Madelon."

"Madelon, Desire of my Dreams." He raised her hand to his lips. "Until you give me leave to lift your mask I kiss these dimpled fingers."

It was plain that his boldness did not altogether displease her, for she paused reluctantly upon the threshold. Her eyes were shining, although her mask smiled at him vacuously as she said:

"You are a most unusual young man. You awaken something strange within me. I cannot despise you as I should, for you have taken away my reason. That is disturbing, is it not? Now, then, avail yourself of the hospitality of the man who has robbed you. I shall return as fast as ever my feet will bring me." She waved him a kiss and was gone.

He heard the front door close. Then he endeavored to piece out some theory as to the cause of this situation, but the more he considered the clues in his possession the more bewildered he became. One thing only stood out with alarming certainty—his cousin Madelon had gone to fetch a woman who loved him. So long as the adventure had concerned him only with the masked girl herself he had been eager to continue it. Now that it threatened to involve a second woman, he decided it was time to go.

She would return and find him gone. It would be a disappointment, perhaps, but not so great as his own at parting from her and leaving this mystery unsolved. He was somewhat proud of his exploits thus far, for in an hour's time he had met and bested two of his enemies and had changed a maiden's heart. No mean accomplishment for an idler! But why did she feel that she ought to despise him? Why had she risked so much for a man beloved by another? Why, under these circumstances, had she welcomed his advances and promised him a sight of her face— a kiss, perhaps? Above all, who were the Black Wolf, the Spider, and Cousin Alfred? He gave up puzzling over the affair and determined to get out of this stranger's house without delay.

THE CRIMSON GARDENIA

It was evident that Cousin Alfred was a person of substance, for the study was furnished in rich old Santo Domingo mahogany, blood-red and flaming where the light struck it; the books were bound in uniform levant; the paintings were valuable; the bric-à-brac in irreproachable taste. An inlaid ivory humidor was filled with coronas at exactly the right degree of moisture. He removed the ground-glass stopper from an etched decanter and sniffed of the contents. The aroma brought a smile to his face, and, reflecting that the owner had robbed him, he took time to pour out a drink and to light a fragrant cigar. All gentlemanly housebreakers did the like, he reflected. Then he yielded to a whimsical notion and fumbled in his pocket, thinking to leave the price of his refreshments on the tray.

Midway in this purpose he paused. The breath hung in his throat, the hair at the back of his neck seemed to rise. He had heard no one enter the house, there had been no faintest stir since Madelon had left, he detected no sound whatever, and yet he was positive that eyes were boring into his back—that he was no longer alone. It was ridiculous, and yet— A gentle cough sounded behind him!

With a swift gesture he settled his mask back in place and, whirling around, beheld the most evil-appearing human being he had ever seen. The man was little and stooped and undersized, all but his head, which was unusually large. His face was fleshless and covered with a tight skin of unusual pallor. He was bowing at Van Dam, but his smile was mocking and his eyes glittered malignantly.

"Good day, Monsieur Black Wolf," said the stranger, harshly. "Making yourself at home with my wines, as usual, eh?"

Van Dam felt the cold sweat leap out upon his body; he cursed the deliberation that had betrayed him. With an assumption of indifference he mumbled something and waved his cigar carelessly.

"How often must I tell you to come here only at night?" snarled the old man. "Already the police are suspicious. Fortunately, it is carnival day—I dare say no one suspected you in that disguise."

The speaker deposited his hat upon the table with a sour glance; then, when his caller said nothing, he snapped:

"Well, well? What is it?"

Van Dam was at a loss for words; he was panic-stricken; but swift upon his consternation came a reckless determination to take advantage of the old gentleman's first mistake and to try to brazen the matter through. There was nothing to be gained by explanation; no one would believe his story. He spoke out boldly.

"The Wolf is hurt, and the Spider, I think, has his neck very neatly broken. I came to tell you that your cousin Emile is in the city."

THE CRIMSON GARDENIA

The effect of these words was amazing, electric. Cousin Alfred turned a corpselike green; he froze in his tracks; his eyes rolled in their sockets.

"Emile! Here!" His teeth chattered, he plucked at his collar as if he were strangling. "Then—you? Who are you?"

Roly shrugged. "I am one of the others. I was sent to warn you." He recognized now the character of the old fellow's emotion. It was cowardice, terror, but of such utter foulness as to be disgusting.

Evidently this Emile, whoever he was, had a reputation. Roly multiplied his host's discomfiture by adding:

"Yes; he struck down the Wolf in the street; then dropped the Spider on his head from the top of a staircase."

"God help us!" stammered Cousin Alfred. "He will take me next! Oh, he has threatened me—" He cast a frightened glance over his shoulder, as if expecting the sanguinary Emile to appear at any moment. Then he began to whine: "I know him, I know him. And the servants gone! I—I am an old man; he would like nothing better than to find me alone. But how—how dared he come? Wait! It was Félice. Ho! I'll wager she sent for him; and he would not refuse, the scoundrel!" The speaker's lips were wet and loose, his gaze was very evil as he mumbled along.

Félice must be the other girl, the one for whom Madelon had gone, Roly decided. In view of

33

Alfred's evident hatred, it did not seem right to allow Madelon to bring the other girl without some warning. One glance at those working features convinced the young man that such a meeting would be dangerous; and yet he was quite at a loss how to prevent it. His host was running on.

"It was only yesterday that she appealed to me, she and Madelon, and all the time they knew he was coming." He ground his teeth. "I have been a fool to spare them so long."

"This Félice," Van Dam ventured, groping blindly for some clue, "your cousin Emile is fond of her, I judge."

"Damnation! He would pass through fire for her. And she would sacrifice her soul for him." Alfred poured himself a drink with shaking hand. The glass rattled against the decanter; he spilled the wine over his waistcoat as he gulped it.

"So they planned to catch me napping, eh? But we shall see. Yes, yes! We shall see." After a moment, during which he pulled himself together, he continued: "You shall remain here with me. When he comes we shall afford him a surprise." He slid open a drawer in the big desk and took from it a revolver, at which Roly exclaimed:

"I say—whatever makes you think he'll come here?"

"Oh, he will come! There is no doubt of it. He has promised me that much. Those were his last words—"

"Er—why don't you clear out? You don't have to stay and see him."

But the old man's eyes were red and vindictive as he shook his head. "You don't understand. So long as he lives we are none of us safe, not even you. Besides, he would return again; he hangs upon me like a leech. I—I dream about him."

"Well, what are you going to do?"

"If I—if I should kill him, the law would say nothing. I could kill him very easily and nothing would be said. You understand?" Cousin Alfred's lips were watery; little drops of moisture gleamed upon his sallow face; he eyed the pistol with a shrinking fascination. "I—I—" He fell to trembling weakly, as his first desperation cooled.

Van Dam watched him curiously. He looked up, at length, to meet Roly's gaze. His own eyes were wavering; his face was distorted with mingled fear and eagerness. He stretched his neck, as if he already felt on it the fingers of his cousin Emile. When Van Dam did not offer to help him he whined: "He has always intended to even up the score; but I am an old man. My hand is unsteady. Perhaps you— It would be worth something to escape those dreams! I could afford to pay well, as you know. You are a strong man. You have no nerves; your hand is sure—" The old villain's expression was crafty; he was gnawed by a fierce desire that he was loath to put into words.

"You mean you'd like to have me make away with him?" queried Van Dam, as if in a dream.

"Yes, yes! The law would say nothing."

"How so? It's not so easy to kill a man and—"

"But the reward—two thousand dollars! You would get that. I will double it. Eh? Come now, is it a bargain?" The speaker was trembling, but when he received no answer he went on: "I will take the blame upon myself. I will say that I did it; and you will get the money—four thousand dollars. Let us say five thousand, eh? A tidy sum for a moment's work with no risk. We are alone in the house. No one but the Wolf knows you are here. Even I don't know— By the way, I—I haven't seen you yet."

"Under the circumstances, I think I'll keep my mask on," Van Dam answered. "Perhaps the less you know about me, the better."

"Then you agree?" queried the other, all ashake.

Roly declined with a gesture.

"Eh, God! Five thousand dollars! A fortune, indeed! Think of it! Heaven knows I am not a Crœsus, and yet—I might increase even that a little. What do you say? Six thousand, then, all cash?"

"This is the money you stole from Emile, I believe," said Van Dam. "You could afford even more—"

"Seven thousand five hundred!" chattered Alfred. "Not another cent, or I shall do it my-self."

"Good! You do it!" Roly exclaimed; whereat the tempter writhed and shivered in an ague of fear. With a wail that came like a sob and with a final wrench of his miserly soul, he exclaimed:

"Wait, then! I will pay you ten thousand dollars if you kill him. The money is there. It will bankrupt me; but— God above! Ten thousand dollars! It is scarcely worth it—such a little job!"

"How do I know you'd make good?" inquired the young man. "You robbed him. You might rob me."

"I have promised! It is there—in the safe. The moment he is dead—"

"Bah!" Mr. Van Dam managed a mocking laugh, although his heart was pounding. "Your word is worth nothing to me."

Alfred made answer by slipping across the room and kneeling before the steel safe. He spun the knob swiftly to right and to left, then gave a wrench, and the massive door opened.

"Come here!"

Van Dam obeyed.

"Look!"

He saw legal documents, deeds, mortgages, and blue envelopes, all neatly marked, then a cash-drawer crowded full of symmetrical packages of crisp, new ten-dollar bills, each with its bank band plainly labeled "$1000."

"Eh? Are you satisfied?" The owner was staring craftily up at him, careful to keep his body between Van Dam and the treasure.

"Jove!" Roly exclaimed in astonishment. "You'll be robbed some night."

"Is it a bargain?"

"I'm no business man." The masker hesitated with an air of extreme suspicion. "Will you pay in advance?"

At this, Cousin Alfred uttered a bleat of dismay, but Roly was firm.

"I'm not sure you'd open the safe again, don't you see? Besides, it would take time, and—I'd prefer not to wait; really I would, for I'm always a bit nervous after a job of this kind."

"Listen, then," exclaimed the old man. "I will close the safe, but I will leave the combination off. See! We must each run some risk in this matter, I suppose; but—I trust you. Once it is over, there will be no delay. A moment and you can be away with ten thousand dollars in your pocket—and with me to do the explaining."

Why he had allowed the affair to run to so extraordinary a length Van Dam hardly knew, except that he wished to gain time. He had no idea that the mysterious Emile would really come to the house, for Madelon had as much as told him that a far different reason lay behind the young man's presence in the city.

What did concern Roly, however, the more he considered it, was the possible consequence if the two girls returned. Thus far he had been able to meet each new surprise, each fresh situation, with a resource that amazed himself, but if they came face to face with him and Alfred, his own masquerade would end at once and disastrous explanations would certainly follow. Nevertheless, he could not run away and leave them in an awkward position. As he looked back over the fantastic occurrences of the past hour or more it amused and amazed him to realize how nicely he had fitted into the puzzle—and puzzle it surely was; for the whole sequence of events that had followed the purchase of the white gardenia that lay above his heart was now more bewildering than ever.

That there was something more than mere roguery afoot he had ample proof. He felt himself groping along the edge of something vague and black and sinister. But what it was, what were the issues, or who were the people involved, he had not the slightest conception. Of one thing only was he sure, Madelon had no place in this elaborate web and woof of crime. She had impressed him more deeply even than he had realized, and his main anxiety now, outside of a desire to protect her from the venom of this poisonous old man, was to see her face, to lift with his own fingers the mask that had so tantalized him.

The owner of the house was busily arranging the plans for Emile's destruction when the doorbell rang. He clutched his guest nervously by the arm and thrust the revolver into his hand, whispering:

"It is he! The scoundrel has arrived! Quickly now—behind the door!"

But Roly stepped to a front window and, cautiously drawing the curtain aside, peered out. He saw what he had feared—the figure of a petite Norman maid, and beside it that of a masked woman in a long, dark robe.

"Well, now! Who can it be?" he heard Alfred whisper, and discovered the senile villain peering past his shoulder.

"It is Madelon and Félice," Roly explained.

"*They!* Here? Wait! I will give them a cursing to remember." But before the speaker could move he found his arms pinioned behind him and his own weapon pointed at his head. He uttered a squeak of amazement and terror. "*Mon Dieu!* What is this?"

"Shut up!" Roly dragged the old man from the window, stripped a thick curtain cord from its hook, and knotted his wrists together.

Alfred offered no resistance; a horrible fear had him by the throat; he hung like a sack in the younger man's grasp. His eyes alone retained their activity. These followed Van Dam in a horrified stare; they seemed about to emerge from their sockets.

Roly deposited his limp captive in a chair and, stepping to the window, tapped sharply. When Madelon looked up he signaled her to wait. The hall portières furnished another cord for Cousin Alfred's ankles, and a handkerchief served as a gag. As this was being adjusted, however, the captive quavered, hoarsely:

"Who—are you?"

"I?" Roly laughed. "Why, I am your cousin Emile!"

The householder voiced a thin shriek and began to plead for his life. Then the remnants of his strength escaped, leaving him a spineless heap in the great leather chair.

Van Dam bore him in his arms down the hall, searching for a place of concealment. This he found in a closet, the door of which he closed. Then he hastened back to the front entrance.

"You kept us waiting sufficiently," Madelon said, as he stepped aside for the two women to enter.

Roly's eyes were glued upon the taller of the two figures, but Félice seemed to take no heed of him. He heard her murmuring in a sick, eager voice:

"Emile! My own beloved! Emile!"

Madelon raised her hand in a warning gesture and the young man shrank closer into the shadows.

"Courage, dear!" she said to her companion. "We have arrived at last. A moment now and he will come." She half led, half supported the taller woman into the library. The next instant she was back at Van Dam's side. Drawing him into the parlor, across the hall, she exclaimed in a voice which showed that tears were in her eyes: "Thank Heaven, no one recognized us! But I was weak with fright. Oh! It was pitiful! I have wept at every step. She has been calling you like that, night and day. Go—quickly!" She removed his mask and thrust him into the hall.

This was the most embarrassing moment Van Dam had experienced thus far. He had been prepared to face eventual discovery, and had decided to make a clean breast of his part in this comedy when the necessary moment arrived, but—this was altogether different. Félice was ill, half-demented. What might be the effect upon her of this disclosure? There was nothing to do, however, but to face it out and to make the truth known as quickly and as gently as possible.

But as he entered the study he received a surprise that robbed the adventure of all its entertainment, that changed this comedy into a tragedy and humbled the man's reckless spirit.

III

VAN DAM saw that which filled him with an aching pity; for, instead of a girl, he found awaiting him a frail, sweet-faced old woman whose fingers were locked as if in prayer, whose lips were murmuring the name of her son. Her hair, softer and finer than silken floss, was silvery white; her wistful, wrinkled countenance was ablaze with a glad excitement that made it glorious and holy. That which caused Van Dam's heart to melt and to turn away completely, however, was the fact that she was blind.

She had heard his step, muffled as it was in the inch-thick carpet, and rose with a tender cry, pausing with her arms outstretched, her body shaken by an ecstasy of yearning.

"Emile! Emile!" she whispered, and came toward him. Her sightless eyes were wet; she was trembling terribly.

Van Dam experienced a desire to flee. He tried to speak and to warn her off, but as the feeble figure swayed toward him, the age-old, appalling tragedy of mother love caused his throat to tighten. Then he took her hands in his; his arms enfolded her. She lay against his breast, weeping softly, gladly, while he bowed his head reverently over hers. Had his life depended upon his speaking, he could not have done so. He merely waited, with a sick feeling of dread, the instant of her awakening. He was vaguely surprised as moment followed moment and it did not come. Then he discovered the explanation. Grief had set her wits to wandering; days and weeks and months of yearning had burned away some part of her faculties, leaving her possessed by such a reasonless hunger that almost any object would have served to fill her want. He had heard of demented mothers whose minds had been saved by the substitution of a living for a dead child, and it seemed that this was a similar case; for she was flooded now with a supreme content and appeared to experience no suspicion of fraud.

The touch of her fluttering fingers on his cheek was like the caress of butterfly wings; her voice was soft; her words, though wandering, were tender and filled with such a heaven-born adoration that his distress was multiplied. This was her hour, he reflected. Perhaps an all-wise Providence had selected him to fill this part and to bring glory to her withered heart. At any rate, he would have been unspeakably cruel to disillusionize her.

He led her to a chair, then knelt and bowed his head to her straying fingers, murmuring those terms of endearment which cause a mother's breast to thrill. When he looked up to Madelon, at last, she saw that he was crying—quite like a little boy.

From the disconnected words that fell from the blind woman's lips he began, after a time, to piece the truth together.

Emile had been an only son, a paragon of manly virtues, the keeper of his mother's soul. There had come a great shock and a great disgrace that had evidently conspired to unseat her reason. She spoke indirectly of them, as a child marked by some prenatal influence recoils at contact with the cause of its infirmity. Then, it seemed, Madelon had come to watch over and to comfort her, filling a son's place with a daughter's devotion.

THE CRIMSON GARDENIA

There had been persecution, want, the loss of
property through an enemy of whom the mother
spoke ramblingly. Van Dam recollected the
dried-up villain in the closet down the hall, and
felt a flame of rage mount through him. He
longed mightily to ask questions, to run the
matter down without delay, but dared not, for
he was in momentary dread that the imposture
would be discovered. So he spoke as infre-
quently as possible, and substituted for words
those gentle caresses and endearing attentions
that are far more welcome to a starving heart.
Madelon remained close by, adding a grain of
comfort and encouragement now and then, and
regarding Van Dam with a strangely bewildered
attention.

But the mother was far from strong. Her excitement had wearied her, and now, with the re-
laxation of contentment, fatigue stole over her.
She lay back among the soft cushions, her restless
hands moving more slowly, her gentle voice stilled.
She dozed at last, her face serene and beatific.

Madelon motioned to Van Dam, and he rose.
Noiselessly they stole across the hall and into the
drawing-room, leaving the placid figure in repose.

She turned upon him, saying, doubtfully:
"With every moment you surprise me, Emile.
You are not at all what I expected, not at all the
cousin of whom I have heard so much! Even in
looks you seem—how shall I say it?—strange."

"Are you pleased or disappointed?"

45

"Ah! Pleased! I—I feel that I must weep. You are so brave and strong, and yet so gentle, so sweet! Perhaps only a mother recognizes the good that is in one. That scene in yonder was very—touching. I—I can hardly credit my ears and my eyes."

"It's plain you have a wrong idea of me. I'm not at all a bad sort."

"So I begin to believe, in spite of everything. La! It is confusing. I am all in a whirl." She uttered a hesitating, silvery little laugh that proved her embarrassment.

"We must speak quickly," he said. "I am also greatly confused. You have opened up a great possibility for me, Madelon. The whole world is suddenly different. I—I think I am in love with you, my little cousin."

She flung out her hand to check him, crying: "No, no! I could never love you!"

Her voice was uncertain, and he imprisoned her outstretched palm. Then, with his free hand, he removed her mask. She made no resistance, she did not even draw away from him. His heart leaped wildly at the face he saw; for it was more perfect even than he had imagined. The eyes were deep brown, the skin was smooth and olive-hued, the lips were red and pouting with em-barrassment. She met his hungry gaze with a flaming blush of defiance; then she smiled pa-thetically, and without further delay he drew her to him and kissed her once, twice, again and again, until she lay, spent and shaken, in his arms. After a time, she said, wonderingly:

"What miracle is this? I have always hated you; I—hate you now when I think of the evil you have done. I shall continue to hate you."

"I hardly believe that."

"It is very sad that this has come to pass; it means nothing but unhappiness."

"How so?"

"Can you ask? You—a refugee, with a price upon your head!" She shuddered and buried her face against his shoulder. "Why have you made me love you?"

"It was fate, my little witch. If you will trust me, all will come out right in the end. But there is a great deal here that I don't understand. For instance, how came you two to be in want?"

"Surely you know as well as I."

"I do not."

"But I wrote—"

"Letters go astray. Tell me."

"There is little to tell. We hardly know ourselves, except that we trusted in our good cousin Alfred, as you trusted. He is a snake!" She clutched Roland fiercely by the folds of his domino. "Oh! It is too bad that I did not know you sooner, Emile! I would have saved you from those evil men; for I am very wise. But now you must suffer the punishment for your crime; and I must suffer also. It is hardly just, is it?"

"Suppose I told you—er—I am innocent?"

47

"Please!" One rosy palm closed his lips. "You must never lie to me, even to promote my happiness. No! When a woman loves, she loves blindly, without reason, regardless of her lover's unworthiness. You have brought misery to me as you brought it to—her. Perhaps you, too, will suffer, as a punishment."

"And why have you devoted yourself to my mother?" he inquired.

"I love her. I am alone in the world. We are poor together. Cousin Alfred has my money, too, you understand."

Van Dam was tempted, as upon several former occasions, to tell her the truth, but a sudden idea occurred to him—an idea so inspiring, so brilliant, that it brought an exclamation to his lips.

"Wait here for a moment," he said, and, leaving her, he stole into the library. With an eye upon the sleeping figure, he knelt before the safe and turned the knob. It opened noiselessly; and the sight of the close-packed cash-drawer filled him with a tremendous merriment. It was exhilarating, it was God-like to be endowed with the power of restitution and retribution. He greatly enjoyed the feel of the crisp new bank-notes as he emptied the compartment and assembled the packages into a bundle. He was amazed at the amount represented. There must have been twenty thousand dollars, all in those smooth, unsoiled ten-dollar bills. Evidently the old miser preferred lock and key to a banker's vagaries.

THE CRIMSON GARDENIA

Naughty Alfred, to rob widows and orphans! Well, he had been warned of the danger of robbery. Van Dam predicted apoplexy for the owner when he discovered his loss.

The girl was waiting where he had left her, but when she discovered the nature of the gift he bore, she drew back in amazement.

"Come! Come!" he said. "It belongs to you and—Félice."

"But— *Mon Dieu!*"

"I have prospered. A lucky speculation—a gift from the gods, as it were! You need have no hesitation in accepting it, for it is yours. And no one can take it from you, not even Cousin Alfred."

She was still protesting, when they heard the mother call.

"This money—another miracle!" Madelon exclaimed. "It is wonderful! I feel that I am dreaming. But come! We have overstayed; we may be discovered at any moment."

He took her in his arms again and whispered his adoration. "I am coming to find you, Madelon. I have the power to work miracles, you see."

"No, no! If you care for me, you must guard yourself. Perhaps after many years—perhaps when you have shown yourself worthy, and the world has forgotten—then—" She shivered at thought of the weary wait ahead of her; her lips quivered pathetically.

There were many things he wished to ask her; the hunger to retain her in his arms was almost unbearable. But now that she had been reawakened to the perils of their situation she allowed him no opportunity. She tore her lips reluctantly from his; she held him off in an agony of pleading, and when the mother's voice sounded a second time they returned hand in hand to the study.

There followed a touching farewell as the blind woman clung shakingly to the gentle impostor, praying for his safety, imploring him piteously to be a good man and to walk in the shadow of righteousness. Then came a lingering, heart-breaking caress, and once more the three were at the front door.

Van Dam seized the girl's fingers and kissed them, while the look in his eyes brought tears to hers. Then they were gone; and he stood alone in the hall of the house he had robbed.

He remained motionless for a time, lost in a blissful intoxication. Was this strange, new-born delirium—love? It must be, it could be, nothing else. It was quite amazing, utterly bewildering. He had never dreamed of anything at all like it. He felt a desire to cry aloud the news of this marvel; he was melting with pain and gladness; something inside him was singing gloriously. At thought of Madelon's deep, wide eyes, of her tender lips, dewy with the birth of passion, his muscles swelled and the whole world seemed to applaud. But it was so new—so unbelievable! The swift rush of this afternoon's events had left him in a dizzy whirl. An hour ago he had been deaf, dumb, and blind, but he had suddenly regained his every sense.   He was no longer *blasé;* he was awake with yearnings and appreciations.   Madelon had taught him the greatest secret of the universe. Madelon— But who the devil was Madelon?

Van Dam brought himself abruptly out of his reverie.   There had been enough mystery for one day.   Now for the solution of this puzzle.   Back yonder, gagged and bound, was a cringing human rat who knew everything Van Dam desired to know, and who would talk, if forced to do so. Roly decided to have the inmost details of this affair, if it became necessary to roast the soles of Cousin Alfred's feet over a slow fire in order to loosen his tongue.   Time had flown, but there was a little margin left.

He hurried down the hall, flung open the door behind which his captive lay, then recoiled, with mouth agape.   The closet was empty!

"Alfred!" he called.   "Alfred!"   But his voice echoed lonesomely through the empty rooms. Not a sound broke the silence.   There on the floor lay the handkerchief and the two tasseled curtain cords.   He felt a chill of apprehension, for unseen eyes were observing him, he was certain.   With that vindictive little ruffian at large, the situation altered; each door might hide a menace, each moment add to his peril.

· The thought of that rifled safe, and the consequences of discovery, convinced Van Dam that this was no place for a respectable New York society man, so he clapped on his mask and darted down the hall toward the rear of the house.

Past the pantry and into the kitchen he fled, his precipitate haste nearly causing him to collide with another masked figure that had just entered from the garden. Instinctively the two men recoiled. Van Dam saw that the stranger wore a black domino like his own, and that a white gardenia was pinned over his heart—it was a twin to the flower that reposed upon his own breast.

"Emile!" he exclaimed.

With a start the new-comer swept his mask downward, and simultaneously he conjured an automatic revolver from some place of concealment. The face that he exposed was not pleasant to look upon, for it was coarsened by dissipation, and the eyes were both violent and furtive. Underneath his heavy, passionate features, however, lay a marked resemblance to the blind mother who had just left.

"Yes. I am Emile," he panted; then, with a snarl, he raised his weapon until it bore upon Van Dam's breast. "And you are one of the gang, eh?"

"Here! Don't point that confounded thing at me. It might go off." Roly brushed the mask from his own face, explaining, "I'm not one of the gang; I'm a friend."

Emile eyed him intently before lowering his weapon. "I never saw you before."

"Of course not. But—come. We've both got to get out of here."

"Indeed! I came to see my cousin Alfred. It is a little call I promised him."

"I know everything; and, believe me, you have no time to lose."

"How do you come to know so much?" demanded Emile, suspiciously. "And what is that?" With the muzzle of his weapon he indicated the waxen white flower upon Roly's domino.

"There's no time to explain everything—but I know why you are here. The old man has gone—"

"Gone! Bah! That is a lie. I have followed him all through the city. I've been to his office, and they told me he was here. I've a little matter to settle with him. It will only take a moment."

"I tell you he's gone."

"Who the devil are you, anyhow? I have no friends."

"I am Madelon's fiancé," Van Dam said, boldly.

"Another lie! She has no fiancé." The speaker's face darkened. "If she marries any one, it shall be me."

An unfamiliar pang smote Van Dam suddenly, but he disregarded it.

"Don't be a fool," he insisted. "I know why you came here, but you're too late. Your mother and Madelon were here, too, a moment ago—"

"Here?" exclaimed the youth, incredulously.

"Yes! Alfred heard you were in the city and he planned to ambush you; I tied him up and threw him into a closet. Then I robbed his safe and gave the money to Madelon and your mother."

Emile's face was a study at this amazing intelligence.

"When I came to look for the old fellow, a moment ago, I found he'd escaped. I don't know where he has gone. That's why we'd better cut and run for it, before he sets up an alarm."

"Run!" Emile shook his head. "I have been running — with the Black Wolf at my heels. I thought they had me cornered more than once. They're after me now, the whole pack."

"Do they know you're here?"

"I dare say; they were right behind me." He cursed violently. "And to think that I missed Cousin Alfred, after all!"

"You had no business in the city. You must get out again."

"It's too late now. Why, it's nearly six o'clock. I could never get away before it's time for masks off."

"Nevertheless, you must try," Van Dam said, decisively. "If you stay here, you're lost. We'll climb the fence at the rear of the next yard and slip out through the stable way."

Emile pondered for a moment. "I hadn't thought of that. It's a chance, but you can't go with me. I sha'n't allow it."

"Nonsense!"

"You don't know the Wolf! If I were seen it would mean the death of both of us."

"Very well, then, I'll leave by the front way. Now go!"

THE CRIMSON GARDENIA

Van Dam half shoved the young man toward the door.

"Thanks," murmured the fugitive. "You seem to be the right sort. If I live, I sha'n't forget." The next instant he was gone.

Roly watched him race across the yard, squeeze through the hedge; then, an instant later, saw his form as he mounted the fence to the wagon inclosure where the Spider had gone to his destruction earlier in the afternoon. It was a risky route to safety, he reflected, but, in view of what Emile had said about his pursuers, it was infinitely preferable to any other.

Why he had helped the fellow Van Dam scarcely knew, unless it was because of his sympathy for the under dog. Whatever the boy had done, he possessed a reckless bravery that was commendable, and he still held his mother's love.

Roly was about to close the door when he saw a second man, in a long, black domino, briefly silhouetted above the fence. Then he heard a whistle. The fellow dropped over into the tracks of Emile, leaving the New-Yorker amazed at the apparition. A sickening fear clutched Van Dam, but he knew it was useless to cry out. Could it be that he had sent the young fellow to his death?

When a moment, then another, had passed with no sound from that quarter, he closed the kitchen door and retraced his steps swiftly to the front of the house.

As he came to the library entrance he found it

closed, and, from inside, he heard a tinkle as if a
telephone hook was being violently agitated. In-
clining his ear, a low, agonized voice came to
him:

"... Le Duc again.... Why haven't you sent the
police? ... Robbery.... My cousin Emile ...
murder me.... God above! They are slow! ...
He will escape...."

Van Dam tried the door. It was locked.
Then he called, sweetly: "Alfred! My dear cousin
Alfred!"

The voice at the telephone ended in a shriek.
There came a crash as the instrument fell from
the old man's fingers.

So the police were on their way! Escape, then,
must be but a matter of moments. With his
heart pounding, Van Dam stepped into the drawing-room and reconnoitered from a front window.
What he saw did not reassure him, particularly
in view of Emile's words; for, directly opposite,
he beheld a masked man in a black domino who
looked very much like the Black Wolf. Scattered up and down the block were others, all idling
about in a seemingly objectless manner. Evidently the house was surrounded. He dared not
risk the back way, after what he had seen. He
could not remain. From the library again came
that faint, frantic tinkling.

Van Dam dropped his mask, tore the flimsy robe
from his back, and strode to the front door.
Under any other circumstances he would have pre-

ferred to remain and to take the consequences, but for Madelon's sake he dare not risk an explanation to the police. Besides—how could he explain that twenty thousand dollars, in clean, crisp ten-dollar notes, that she had in her possession? He flung the portal wide, stepped out, then turned and bowed as if to some one inside. "Good-by!" he called, cheerily. "Had a delightful afternoon." The door closed with a click, and he was in the open air. He extracted a cigarette from his jeweled case, noting from the corner of his eye that, with one accord, the maskers were closing in upon him. Descending the steps, he turned to the left, walking briskly.

His one chance now depended upon whether these men knew Emile by sight. If so, he felt that he was reasonably safe. If not—

He was approaching two of them. They separated to let him pass between. From beneath their fatuously smiling masks he saw eyes staring at him curiously. The flesh along his spine crinkled and rippled, but he did not turn his head or falter, even when he knew they had halted. He could feel the puzzled gaze of many eyes upon him, and imagined the mystification his appearance had excited. In the midst of their indecision there sounded the faint clamor of a gong. It grew rapidly until, with wild clangor, a patrol-wagon reeled into the street and drew up in front of the house Van Dam had just quitted. He turned as a half-dozen blue-coats tumbled out of it and rushed up the steps; incidentally, he saw that the black-clad figures were melting away in various directions.

Roly did not wait to observe what followed. He turned the first corner, then quickened his gait, at the next corner swinging once more to the left. His pulses were jumping, his ears were roaring, he found the muscles of his jaw were aching from the strain. A close call, surely! But he had come through it all safely; he was whole, and on his way out of this mysterious neighborhood. Once more his promptness and resource had saved him. Here was the very street up which he and Madelon had fled; yonder was the entrance to the blind alley that led into the stable-yard.

He noticed that a little crowd was congregated there, many of its members in the costume of merrymakers. He reflected that Emile might have found their presence awkward in making his escape. They seemed greatly excited or shocked over something, he noted, as he approached. They completely blocked the alley entrance. In among them he forced his way, then paused, staring down with startled eyes at what he saw. A babble of voices smote his ears, but he heard nothing. He was elbowed aside, but his gaze remained riveted upon the body of a man in a black domino. It lay sprawled in the dirt, and covering the face was a mask which smiled placidly up at the beholders; on the left breast was pinned a solitary gardenia, crimson with blood. It had been pierced with a dagger, and out of it had trickled a bright-red arterial stream.

Van Dam continued to stare at the gruesome sight while his wits whirled dizzily. Why, it was but a moment ago that this boy had left him, in the full flower of his youth! The body was still warm. It seemed inconceivable that the grim reaper could have worked this grisly change in so short a time! How had it happened? He recalled that somber figure as he had seen it scaling the fence; he recalled that warning whistle. At the memory he turned sick. Was it possible that he had been to blame for this? He shook the notion from him, reflecting that Emile's fate would have been the same, or worse, had he chosen any other course. Arrest, he knew, would have been no more welcome than this.

Roly felt a great desire to shout the truth at these people who stood about so stupidly; he longed to set them on the trail of the Black Wolf and his pack, but he refrained. How little he really knew, after all! Who was the Black Wolf? Who was this Emile? What had the young scapegoat done to place himself not only outside the law, but outside the good graces of those conspirators? What intricate network of hatred and crime was here suggested? The desire to know the truth overcame all thought of his own safety, so he began to question those around him, heedless of the fact that he was being hunted in this very block.

THE CRIMSON GARDENIA

The crowd was growing. An officer returned after sending a call for an ambulance, and began to force the people back.

Van Dam discovered a voluble old woman, evidently a shopkeeper, who seemed better informed than the others, and to her he applied himself.

"Do I know him, indeed?" she cried, shrilly, in answer to his question. "And who should know him better than I, Emile Le Duc—a fine boy, sir, of the very best family. Think of it! To be murdered like this! Ah! That's what comes of a bad life, sir. But right at my own doorstep, as you might say, and in the light of day! Well! Well! What can you expect? He must have been mad to return, with the whole city knowing him so well." She was greatly excited, and her voice broke under the stress of her feelings. "It doesn't help the neighborhood, you understand, to have such things happen," she ran on, "although nobody can say it's not as quiet and respectable hereabouts as the next place. You've noticed as much yourself, I dare say. Nothing ever happens. A misfortune to all of us, I call it. Why, it's barely two hours ago that they brought a poor fellow out of this very alley with his head lolloping around like a ball on a string. He fell and hurt himself, I hear, although he looked perfectly dead to me. Think of that! Two in one day. Oh, it doesn't help the neighborhood, although there's nobody in the whole block as would do another an injury, unless it might be that poor boy's cousin, the old rip who lives in the fine house through yonder. He's a bad one, far worse than Emile, if I do say it who never speaks ill of my neighbors. And there's others besides me who'll be sorry it isn't him instead of the young man who lies there with a hole through his ribs. Why, I thought he was some masquerader, up to his carnival pranks, or drunk, perhaps, until I noticed him all over blood."

Van Dam drew the speaker into her shop, which was near by, then handed her a bank-note. "Come! I want you to tell me all you know."

"Ho! A detective, eh? Not that I wouldn't tell you all I know without this— Ten dollars, is it? Peace and love! You *are* generous! Well, then, he has stood right in your tracks, in this very store, many's the time. Law! What a lad he was! Nothing bad about him, but just reckless, we used to think. Of course that was before we learned the truth."

"What do you mean?"

"You must be a stranger. Why, the whole world knows the scandal. It made a commotion, I can tell you. But the poor lad! He's paid for all his evil deeds. Why, sir, he was dead when he walked out into the street. He must have been a corpse even when I took him for a merry-maker. Strange things do happen on these carnival days. They must have finished him with one stroke. Ugh!"

"They? Whom do you mean?"

The old woman winked, and wagged her head sagely. "Oh! You'll never learn who, but we know. You think the gang was broken up when Emile went to prison, but where do all these counterfeits come from, eh? Answer me that. There's not a week goes by that one of them doesn't find its way into my store. They're perfect, or nearly so; it would take a bank-teller to find a flaw. I'm always frightened to death till I work them off again. For all I know, this very ten-dollar bill you gave me is bad, but I'll risk it. Some people don't seem to mind them at all, and so long as there's a chance to get rid of them, why, I don't object. But that's how it all came about— through counterfeit money, sir. They used Emile for a cat's-paw, so I've heard, but when he was caught they let him take his punishment. It was his cousin, Alfred Le Duc, who got him to confess, under promise of a light sentence. They do say the old rascal fooled him into it, for what reason nobody ever knew. Anyhow, they sent Emile away for ten years. He threatened to turn state's evidence, and perhaps he would have done so if he hadn't escaped."

"Ah! So he broke jail?"

"Exactly! And they've been hunting him ever since, with a reward on his head, and all the time the counterfeits are still coming in, and the police are as far from the truth as ever. Poor boy! There he lies, dead, with a flower over his heart.

THE CRIMSON GARDENIA

And I saw him fall! This will kill his mother. She's blind, you know, and very feeble."

"He has a cousin, Madelon, I believe," Roly ventured.

"Eh? Then you know her? A blessed angel, with a face like a picture and a heart of pure gold. Hark!" The old lady listened. "There go the clocks striking six. That means masks off and the end of the carnival. Too bad! Too bad! And Emile with a flower over his heart."

Like one in a dream Roland Van Dam emerged from the foreign quarter into the broad reaches of Canal Street. He had been gone nearly three hours. The pavements were strewn with confetti and the litter of a Mardi Gras crowd, but nowhere was a masker to be seen. Directly ahead of him loomed the Grunewald, a splendid tower of white brick and terra-cotta. Inside were his friends, awaiting him, perhaps. He realized, with a sinking sensation, that Eleanor Banniman was among them and that he had asked her to be his wife. What a change three hours had brought to him! Why, in that brief interval he had lived through all those very emotions the existence of which they had both denied earlier in the day. Life had opened for him, and he had seen it in the raw. On his hands was the blood of a fellow-man; on his lips the fragrance of a kiss that set his veins afire.

"I say, Roly, where *have* you been?" Miss

63

Banniman's strident voice demanded, as he entered the café.

"Bless my soul!" exclaimed her father, waving his prospective son-in-law to a chair with a pudgy hand. "We thought you were lost in the tall grass. You missed tea, but you're in time for a cocktail. Eleanor is quite cranky if she misses hers."

"Beastly stupid place, don't you think?" Miss Banniman inquired of her sweetheart.

"Um-m! I haven't found it so," Roly said, with a sigh of relief. "Fact is, I've been quite entertained."

"You have *such* absurd tastes. A dash of absinthe in mine, if you please, waiter. Papa has ordered the car attached to the evening train, and we're dining aboard. What d'you say to Pinehurst and a week of golf?"

Roly felt a sudden distaste for Pinehurst, for golf, for all the places and people he had known. "Lovely!" he managed to say; then, summoning his courage: "I'll join you later, perhaps. Sorry to break up the party, but I've a little business here that will take a day or so."

"Business? *You?* How funny!" exclaimed Eleanor.

"Too bad!" her father said. "It's blooming hot here, and the flies are awful."

The others joined in commiserating the young man. When they arose to go up-stairs and prepare for the train, Roly fell in behind them with Miss Banniman.

"See here, Eleanor, are you sure you love me?" he asked.

She lifted her brows slightly. "Not at all. What put such an idea into your head? You're a charming boy, even if you are a bit romantic. But love—I thought we understood each other."

"I've been thinking—something unusual for me—and I don't believe we're either of us quite ready to take the fatal plunge. How does it strike you?"

"I'm in no hurry," Miss Banniman said, indifferently. "Let's call it off for the present. We can try it on again in the autumn, if we feel like it."

"Mighty sensible of you," Van Dam told her, with relief.

"Oh, that's all right! Don't let this keep you away from Pinehurst, however. The season's nearly over, and we'll need you for a foursome." She extended her hand, and Van Dam took it gratefully.

Her father called from the elevator: "See you in a few days, Roly. Good luck with your business, and don't take any bad money." Mr. Banniman's use of slang was neither brilliant nor original, but he was chuckling as the car shot up out of sight.

Van Dam hastened to the desk and called for a city directory, then ran through it to the L's.

"*L-a, L-e*—" Ah, there it was! "Le Duc, Félice —wid. res. 247 Boule St."

THE CRIMSON GARDENIA

He made a note of the address, then settled his hat upon his head, lit a cigarette, and walked jauntily out into the evening and turned toward Canal Street. It was growing cool; the street lights were gleaming; long rows of them were festooned for blocks in all directions, blazing forth in fanciful designs. In a short time now the Rex parade would be under way, with its countless floats depicting "The Age of Romance."

"Romance, indeed!" smiled Mr. Van Dam, contentedly. Why *this* was the age of romance. Something recalled Mr. Banniman's parting words to him—"bad money!" The young man paused abruptly. "Bad money!" What a coincidence! He pictured a safe sunk into a library wall, an open cash-drawer jammed with neatly pinned packages of crisp, new ten-dollar bank-notes. Then he recalled the story of the garrulous old shop-woman.

Roly came to himself with a jerk. He began to laugh.

"Good Lord!" said he, aloud. "I wonder if Cousin Alfred's money was counterfeit!"

He was still smiling as he bought a white gardenia and placed it in his buttonhole.

ROPE'S END

ROPE'S END

I

AROUND moon flooded the thickets with gold and inky shadows. The night was hot, poisonous with the scent of blossoms and of rotting tropic vegetation. It was that breathless, overpowering period between the seasons when the trades were fitful, before the rains had come. From the Caribbean rose the whisper of a dying surf, slower and fainter than the respirations of a sick man; in the north the bearded, wrinkled Haytian hills lifted their scowling faces. They were trackless, mysterious, darker even than the history of the island.

Beneath a thatched roof set upon four posts was a table, spread with food, and on it a candle burned steadily. No wind came out of the hot darkness; the flame rose straight and unwavering. Under a similar thatched shed, a short distance away, a group of soldiers were busy around a smoldering cook-fire. There were other huts inside the jungle clearing, through the dilapidated walls of which issued rays of light and men's voices.

Petithomme Laguerre, colonel of tirailleurs, in the army of the Republic, wiped the fat of a roasted pig from his lips with the back of his hand. Using his thumb-nail as a knife-blade, he loosened a splinter from the edge of the rickety wooden table, fashioned it into a toothpick, then laid himself back in a grass hammock. He had expected to find rum in the house of Julien Rameau, but either there had been none or his brave soldiers had happened upon it; at any rate, supper had been a dry meal—only one of several disappointments of the day. The sack of the village had not been at all satisfactory to the colonel; one yellow woman dead, a few prisoners, and some smoldering ruins—surely there was no profit in such business.

Reclining at ease, he allowed himself to admire his uniform, a splendid creation of blue and gold which had put him to much pains and expense. It had arrived from Port au Prince barely in time to be of service in the campaign. As for the shoes, they were not so satisfactory. Shoes of any sort, in fact, cramped Colonel Petithomme Laguerre's feet, and were refinements of fashion to which he had never fully accustomed himself. He wore them religiously, in public, for a colonel who would be a general must observe the niceties of military deportment, even in the Haytian army, but now he kicked them off and exposed his naked yellow soles gratefully.

On three sides of the clearing were thickets of guava and coffee trees, long since gone wild. A

ruined wall along the beach road, a pair of bleaching gate-posts, a moldering house foundation,
showed that this had once been the site of a
considerable estate.

These mute testimonials to the glories of the
French occupation are common in Hayti, but
since the blacks rose under Toussaint l'Ouverture
they have been steadily disappearing; the greedy
fingers of the jungle have destroyed them bit by
bit; what were once farms and gardens are now
thickets and groves; in place of stately houses
there are now nothing but miserable hovels.
Cities of brick and stone have been replaced by
squalid villages of board and corrugated iron,
peopled by a shrill-voiced, quarreling race over
which, in grim mockery, floats the banner of the
Black Republic inscribed with the motto, "Liberty, Equality, Fraternity."

Once Hayti was called the "Jewel of the
Antilles" and boasted its "Little Paris of the
West," but when the black men rose to power it
became a place of evil reputation, a land behind
a veil, where all things are possible and most
things come to pass. In place of monastery
bells there sounds the midnight mutter of voodoo
drums; the priest has been succeeded by the
"papaloi," the worship of the Virgin has changed
to that of the serpent. Instead of the sacramental
bread and wine men drink the blood of the white
cock, and, so it is whispered, eat the flesh of "the
goat without horns."

As he picked his teeth, Colonel Petithomme
Laguerre turned his eyes to the right, peering
idly into the shadows of a tamarind-tree, the
branches of which overtopped the hut. Suspended from one of these was an inert shape,
mottled with yellow patches where the moonbeams
filtered through the leaves. It stirred, swayed,
turned slowly, resolving itself into the figure of an
old man. He was hanging by the wrists to a rawhide rope; his toes were lightly touching the earth.

"So! Now that Monsieur Rameau has had
time to think, perhaps he will speak," said the
colonel.

A sigh, it was scarcely a groan, answered.

"Miser that you are!" impatiently exclaimed
the colonel. "Your money can do you no good
now. Is it not better to part with it easily than
to rot in a government prison? You understand,
the jails are full; many mulattoes like you will be
shot to make room."

"There is no—money," faintly came the voice of
the prisoner. "My neighbors will tell you that
I am poor."

Both men spoke in the creole patois of the
island.

"Not much, perhaps, but a little, eh? Just a
little, let us say."

"Why should I lie? There is none."

"Bah! It seems you are stubborn. Congo,
bring the boy!" Laguerre spoke gruffly.

A man emerged from the shadows at the base

of the tree and slouched forward. He was a negro soldier, and, with musket and machete, shuffled past the corner of the hut in the direction of the other houses, pausing as the colonel said:

"But wait! There is a girl, too, I believe."

"Yes, monsieur. The wife of Floréal."

"Good! Bring them both."

Some moments later imploring voices rose, a shrill entreaty in a woman's tones, then Congo and another tirailleur appeared; driving ahead of them a youth and a girl. The prisoners' arms were bound behind them, and although the girl was weeping, the boy said little. He stepped forward into the candle-light and stared defiantly at the blue-and-gold officer.

Floréal Rameau was a slim mulatto, perhaps twenty years old; his lips were thin and sensitive, his nose prominent, his eyes brilliant and fearless. They gleamed now with all the vindictiveness of a serpent, until that hanging figure in the shadows just outside turned slowly and a straying moon-beam lit the face of his father; then a new expression leaped into them. Floréal's chin fell, he swayed uncertainly upon his legs.

"Monsieur—what is this?" he said, faintly.

The girl cowered at his back.

"Your father persists in lying," explained Laguerre.

"What do you—wish him to say?"

"A little thing. His money can be of no further use to him."

6   73

"Money?" Floréal voiced the word vacantly. He turned to his wife, saying, "Monsieur le Colonel asks for money. We have none."

The girl nodded, her lips moved, but no sound issued; she also was staring, horror-stricken, into the shadows of the tamarind-tree. Her arms, bound as they were, threw the outlines of her ripe young bosom into prominent relief and showed her to be round and supple; she was lighter in color even than Floréal. A little scar just below her left eye stood out, dull brown, upon her yellow cheek.

Laguerre now saw her plainly for the first time, and shook off his indolence. He swung his legs from the hammock and sat up. Something in the intensity of his regard brought her gaze away from the figure of Papa Rameau. She saw a large, thick-necked, full-bodied black, of bold and brutal feature, whose determined eyes had become bloodshot from staring through dust and sun. He wore a mustache, and a little pointed woolly patch beneath his lower lip. Involuntarily the girl recoiled.

"Um-m! So!" The barefoot colonel rose and, stepping forward, took her face in his harsh palm, turning it up for scrutiny. His roving glance appraised her fully. "Your name is—"

"Pierrine!"

"To be sure. Well then, my little Pierrine, you will tell me about this, eh?"

"I know nothing," she stammered. "Floréal

speaks the truth, monsieur. What does it mean
—all this? We are good people; we harm nobody.
Every one here was happy until the—blacks rose.
Then there was fighting and—this morning you
came. It was terrible! Mamma Cleomélie is
dead—the soldiers shot her. Why do you hang
Papa Julien?"

Floréal broke in, hysterically: "Yes, monsieur,
he is an old man. Punish me if you will, but my
father—he is old. See! He is barely alive. These
riches you speak about are imaginary. We have
fields, cattle, a schooner; take them for the Republic, but, monsieur, my father has injured no one."

Petithomme Laguerre reseated himself in the
hammock and swung himself idly, his bare soles
scuffing the hard earthen floor; he continued to
eye Pierrine.

Now that young Rameau had brought himself to
beg, he fell to his knees and went on: "I swear to
you that we are not traitors. Never have we
spoken against the government. We are 'colored,'
yes, but the black people love us. They loved
Cleomélie, my mother, whom the soldiers shot.
That was murder. Monsieur—she would have
harmed nobody. She was only frightened." The
suppliant's shoulders were heaving, his voice was
choked by emotion. "She is unburied. I appeal
to your kind heart to let us go and bury her. We
will be your servants for life. You wish money.
Good! We will find it for you. I will work, I
will steal, I will kill for this money you wish—I

swear it. But old Julien, he is dying there on the rope—"

Floréal raised his tortured eyes to the black face above him, then his babbling tongue fell silent and he rose, interposing his body between Pierrine and the colonel. It was evident that the latter had heard nothing whatever of the appeal, for he was still staring at the girl.

Floréal strained until the rawhide thongs cut into his wrists, his bare, yellow toes gripping the hard earth like the claws of a cat until he seemed about to spring. Once he turned his head, curiously, fearfully, toward his young wife, then his blazing glance swung back to his captor.

The silence roused Laguerre finally, and he rose. "Speak the truth," he commanded, roughly, "otherwise you shall see your father dance a bamboula while my soldiers drum on his ribs with the cocomacaque."

"He is feeble; his bones are brittle," said the son, thickly.

"As for you, my little Pierrine, you will come to my house; then, if these wicked men refuse to speak, perhaps you and I will reach an understanding." Laguerre grinned evilly.

"Monsieur—!" With a furious curse Floréal flung himself in the path of the black man; the wife retreated in speechless dismay.

Petithomme thrust young Rameau aside, crying, angrily: "You wish to live, eh? Well, then, the truth. Otherwise—"

"But—she? Pierrine?" panted Floréal, with a twist of his head in her direction.

"I may allow her to go free. Who can tell?" He led the girl out across the moonlit clearing and to the largest house in the group. He reappeared, making the door fast behind him, and returned, stretching himself in the hammock once more.

" Now, Congo," he ordered, " let us see who will speak first." Taking a pipe from his pocket, he filled it with the rank native tobacco and lighted it. The tirailleur he had addressed selected a four-foot club of the jointed cocomacaque wood, such as is used by the local police, and with it smote the suspended figure heavily. Old Julien groaned, his son cried out. The brutality proceeded with deliberation, the body of old Julien swung drunkenly, spinning, swaying, writhing in the moonlight.

Floréal shrank away. Retreating until his back was against the table, he clutched its edge with his numb fingers for support. He was young, he had seen little of the ferocious cruelty which characterized his countrymen; this was the first uprising against his color that he had witnessed. Every blow, which seemed directed at his own body, made him suffer until he became almost as senseless as the figure of his father.

His groping fingers finally touched the candle at his back; it was burning low, and the blaze bit at them. With the pain there came a thought, wild, fantastic; he shifted his position slightly until the flame licked at his bonds. Colonel Laguerre was in the shadow now, watching the torture with approval. Maximilien, the other soldier, rested unmoved upon his rifle. Floréal leaned backward, and shut his teeth; an agony ran through his veins. The odor of burning flesh rose faintly to his nostrils.

"Softly, Congo," directed the colonel, after a time. "Let him rest for a moment." Turning to the son he inquired, "Will you see him die rather than speak?"

Floréal nodded silently; his face was distorted and wet with sweat.

Laguerre rose with a curse. "Little pig! I will make your tongue wag if I have to place you between planks and saw you in twain. But you shall have time to think. Maximilien will guard you, and in the morning you will guide me to the hiding-place. Meanwhile we will let the old man hang. I have an appetite for pleasanter things than this." He turned toward the house in which Pierrine was hidden, whereat Floréal strained at his bonds, calling after him:

"Laguerre! She is my wife—by the Church! My wife."

Petithomme opened the door silently and disappeared.

"Humph! The colonel amuses himself while I tickle the sides of this yellow man," said Congo in some envy.

"I don't believe there is any money," Maximilien observed. "What? Am I right?" He turned inquiringly to Floréal, but the latter had regained his former position, and the candle-flame was licking at his wrists. "To be sure! This is a waste of time. Make an end of the old man, Congo, and I will take the boy back to his prison. It is late and I am sleepy."

The speaker approached his captive, his musket resting in the hollow of his arm, his machete hanging at his side. "So, now! Don't strain so bitterly," he laughed. "I tied those knots and they will not slip, for I have tied too many yellow men. To-morrow you will be shot, monsieur, and Pierrine will be a widow, so why curse the colonel if he cheats you by a few hours?"

Congo was examining his victim, and uttered an exclamation, at which Maximilien paused, with a hand upon Floréal's shoulder.

"Is he dead?"

"The club was heavier than I thought," answered Congo.

"He brought it upon himself. Well, the prison at Jacmel is full of colored people; this will leave room for one more—"

Maximilien's words suddenly failed him, his thoughts were abruptly halted, for he found that in some unaccountable manner young Rameau's hands had become free and that the machete at his own side was slipping from its sheath. The phenomenon was unbelievable, it paralyzed Maximilien's intellect during that momentary pause

79

which is required to reconcile the inconceivable
with the imminent. It is doubtful if the trooper
fully realized what had befallen or that any danger
threatened, for his mind was sluggish, and under
Rameau's swift hands his soul had begun to tug
at his body before his astonishment had disappeared. The blade rasped out of its scabbard,
whistled through its course, and Maximilien
lurched forward to his knees.

The sound of the blow, like that of an ax sunk
into a rotten tree-trunk, surprised Congo. A
shout burst from him; he raised the stout cudgel
above his head, for Floréal was upon him like the
blurred image out of a nightmare. The trooper
shrieked affrightedly as the blade sheared through
his shield and bit at his arm. He turned to flee,
but his head was round and bare, and it danced
before the oncoming Floréal. Rameau cleft it,
as he had learned to open a green cocoanut, with
one stroke. On the hard earth, Maximilien was
scratching and kicking as if to drag himself out of
the welter in which he lay.

Floréal cut down his father and received the
limp figure in his arms. As he straightened it
he heard a furious commotion from the camp-
fire where the other tirailleurs were squatted.
From the tail of his eye he saw that they were
reaching for their weapons. He heard Laguerre
shouting in the hut, then the crash of something
overturned. As he rose from his father's body
he heard a shot and saw the soldiers of the Repub-

As Floréal rose from his father's body he heard a shot
and saw the soldiers of the Republic charging him.

lic charging him. They were between him and
Pierrine. He hesitated, then slipped back into
the shadow of the tamarind-tree, and out at the
other side; his cotton garments flickered briefly
through the moonlight, then the thicket swallowed
him. His pursuers paused and emptied their guns
blindly into the ink-black shadows where he had
disappeared.

When Colonel Laguerre arrived upon the scene
they were still loading and firing without aim, and
he had some difficulty in restoring them to order.
Blood they were accustomed to, but blood of their
own letting. This was very different. This was a
blow at the government, at their own established
authority. Such an appalling loss of life seldom
occurred to regular troops of the Republic; it was
worse than a pitched battle with the Dominicans,
and it excited the troopers terribly.

Perhaps he had been mistaken and there was no
money, thought the colonel, as he returned to his
quarters after a time. Of course the girl still
remained, and he could soon force the truth from
her, but she was the only source of information
left now that Floréal had escaped, for Laguerre
had noted carelessly that the body of Julien had
hung too long. It was annoying to be deceived
in this way, but perhaps the day had not been
without some profit, after all, he mused.

The road to the Dominican frontier was rough
and wild. All Hayti was aflame; every village
was peopled by raging blacks who had risen against

their lighter-hued brethren. Among the fugitives who slunk along the winding bridle-paths that once had been roads there was a mulatto youth of scarcely twenty, who carried a machete beneath his arm. In his eyes there was a lurking horror; his wrists were bound with rags torn from his cotton shirt; he spoke but seldom, and when he did it was to curse the name of Petithomme Laguerre.

II

FLORÉAL took up his residence across the border. The countries had long been at war, so he found reason to change his name. He likewise changed his language, although that was not so easily accomplished, and then, since he had been born of the sea, he returned to it. But he could not bring himself to utterly forsake the island of his birth, for twice a year, when the seasons changed, when the trades died and the hot lands sent their odors reeking through the night, he felt a hungry yearning for Hayti. During these periods of lifeless heat his impulses ran wild; at these times his habits changed and he became violent, nocturnal. As he thought of Petithomme Laguerre he bit his wrists in an agony of recollection. Women shunned him, men said to one another:

"This Inocencio is a person of uncertain temper. He has a bad eye."

82

"Whence did he come?" others inquired. "He is not one of us."

"From Jamaica, or the Barbadoes, perhaps. He has much evil in him."

"And yet he makes no enemies."

"Nor friends."

"Um-m! A peculiar fellow. A man of passion —one can see it in his face."

Hayti had become quiet once more—as quiet as could be expected—and the former colonel of tirailleurs had prospered. He was now "General Petithomme Laguerre, Commandant of the Arrondissement of the South," and the echo of his name crept eastward along the coast, even to Azua.

The bitterness of this news finally sent Inocencio seaward in a barkentine, the business of which was not above suspicion. He cruised through the Virgin Islands, on around the Leewards and the Windwards, seeing something of the world and tasting of its wickedness. A year later, at Trinidad, he fell in with a Portuguese half-breed, captain of a schooner bound on hazardous business, and, inasmuch as high wages were promised, he shipped. Followed adventures of many sorts, during which Inocencio became a mate, but made no friends.

One night when the moon was full and the schooner lay becalmed there was drinking and gambling in the little cabin. It was the change of the seasons, before the rains had come; the air was close; the ship reeked with odors. Inocencio played like a demon, for his heart was fierce, and the cards befriended him. All night he and the Portuguese half-breed shuffled and dealt, drank rum, and cursed each other. When daylight came the schooner had changed hands.

Colon sits on the southern shore of the Caribbean, and through it drifts a current of traffic from many seas. It is like the riffle of a sluice or the catch-basin of a sewer, gathering all the sediment carried by the stream, and thither Captain Inocencio headed, drawn on the tide. It was at the time of the French fiasco, when De Lesseps's name was powerful, and when Colon was the wickedest, sickest city of the Western Hemisphere.

Into the harbor came Inocencio's schooner, pelting ahead of the stiff trade-winds that blew like the draught from an electric fan, and there the Haytian stayed, for in Colon he found work that suited him. There he heard the echo of tremendous undertakings; there he learned new rascalities, and met men from other lands who were homeless, like himself; there he tasted of the white man's wickedness, and beheld forms of corruption that were strange to him. The nights were ribald and the days were drear, for fever stalked the streets, but Inocencio was immune, and for the first time he enjoyed himself.

But he was solitary in his habits; the festering town, with its green-slimed sewers and its filthy streets, did not appeal to him, so he took up his abode on the shore of a little bay close behind, where a grove of palm-trees overhung a sandy beach. Just across a mangrove swamp at his back was the city; before him lay his schooner, her bowsprit pointing seaward. Day and night it pointed seaward, like a resolute finger; pointed toward Hayti and—Pierrine.

In time the mulatto acquired a reputation and gathered a crew of ruffians over whom he tyrannized. There were women in his camp, too, 'Bajans, Sant' Lucians, and wenches from the other isles, but neither they nor their powdered sisters along the back streets of Colon appealed to Inocencio very long, for sooner or later there always came to him the memory of a yellow girl with a scar beneath her eye, and thoughts of her brought pictures of a blue-and-gold negro colonel and an old man hanging by the wrists. Then it was that he felt a slow flame licking at his tendons, and his hatred blazed up so suddenly that the women fled from him, bearing marks of his fingers on their flesh.

Sometimes he sailed away and was gone for weeks. When he returned his crew told stories of aimless visits to the Haytian coast in which there appeared to be neither reason nor profit, since they neither took nor fetched a cargo. These journeys came at regular intervals, as if there arrived upon the hurrying trades a call that took him northward, just before the seasons changed.

His helpers retailed other gossip also, rumors of a coming revolution in the Republic, tales of the great general, Petithomme Laguerre, who had aims upon the Presidency. Inocencio's ears were open, and what he heard stirred his rage, but he was not a brilliant man, and his brain, unused to strategy, refused to counsel him. For five years he had studied the matter incessantly, nursing his hate and searching for a means to satisfy it. Then, as if born of the lightning, he saw his way.

He consulted a French clerk in the Canal offices, and between them they contrived a letter which ran as follows:

To His Excellency, General Petithomme Laguerre, Commandant of the Arrondissement of the South, Jacmel, Republic of Hayti.

GENERAL,—The bearer, Inocencio Ruiz, of Cartagena, master of the schooner *Stella*, will consult you upon a matter of extreme delicacy which concerns the sale of two hundred rifles. These arms, of latest model, were consigned to this port, but under the existing relations of amity between the French and Colombian governments they cannot be used. Knowing your patriotism and the zeal with which you safeguard the welfare of your country, the writer makes bold to offer these arms to you, as agent of the Haytian government, at a low figure. Captain Ruiz, a man of discretion, is empowered to discuss the matter with you at greater length.

In full appreciation of your supreme qualities as a soldier and statesman, it is with admiration that I salute you.

Respectfully,

ANTOINE LEBLANC.

ROPE'S END

When the letter was finally read to Inocencio he nodded; but the French clerk said, doubtfully:

"This Laguerre is a man of force, I believe. I should not care to trifle with him in this way."

"I, too, am a man of force," said the mulatto.

"He is your enemy?"

"To the death."

The white man shook his head. "Danger lurks along the Haytian coast; many things happen there, for the people are barbarians. I should prefer to forgive this Petithomme rather than oppose him, even though he were my enemy."

Inocencio scowled. "When I die I shall have no enemies to forgive, for I shall have killed them all," he said, simply.

Jacmel lay white in the blazing sun as the *Stella* dropped anchor. The trades were failing, and the schooner drifted slowly under a full spread of canvas. Near where she came to rest lay a Haytian gunboat, ill-painted, ill-manned, ill-disciplined, and Inocencio regarded her with some concern, for her presence was a thing he had not counted upon. It argued either that Laguerre had won the support of her commander or that she had been sent by the government as a check upon his activities. In either event she was a menace.

A band was playing in the square, and there were many soldiers. Inocencio did not go ashore. Instead he sent the letter by a member of his crew, a giant 'Bajan whom he trusted, and with it he sent word that he hoped to meet His Excellency, General Laguerre, that evening at a certain drinking-place near the water-front.

The sailor returned at dusk with news that set his captain's eyes aglow. Jacmel was alive with troops; there had been a review that very afternoon and the populace had hailed the commandant as President. On all sides there was talk of revolution; the whole south country had enrolled beneath the banner of revolt. The gunboat was Laguerre's; all Hayti craved a change; the old familiar race cry had been raised and the mulattoes were in terror of another massacre. But the regular troops were badly armed and the perusal of Inocencio's letter had filled the general with joy.

Captain Ruiz was early at the meeting-place, but he waited patiently, drinking rum and listening to the chatter of the street. His Spanish accent, his identity as the master of the schooner in the offing, and, above all, his threatening eyes, won him a tolerance which the warlike blacks did not accord to Haytians of his color; therefore he was not molested. He soon confirmed his sailor's story; revolution was indeed in the air; the country was seething with unrest. Many houses already had been burned—sure token of an uprising. The soldiers had had a taste of pillage and persecution. The streets were thronged with them now; merchants were on guard before their shops; from every side came the sounds of revelry and quarreling.

ROPE'S END

Laguerre arrived, finally, a huge, forbidding man of martial bearing, and he was heralded by cheers. He was much older and infinitely prouder than when Inocencio had seen him. His uniform had been blue at that time, but now it was parrot-green; his epaulettes were broader, the golden braid and dangling loops were heavier, and he was fat from easy living. With age and power he had coarsened, but his eyes were still bloodshot and domineering.

"Captain Ruiz?" he inquired, pausing before the yellow man.

"Your Excellency!" Inocencio rose and saluted. The seaman's eyes were smoldering, but his lips were cold, for he felt the dread of recognition.

Time, it seemed, had dulled the sharp outlines of Laguerre's memory as it had changed the younger man's features, for he continued, unsuspectingly:

"You are the agent of Monsieur Leblanc, I believe."

"The same."

"Good! Now these rifles—you have them near by?"

"Within gunshot, Excellency. They are in the harbor at this moment."

Laguerre's face lighted. "Ha! A man of business, this Leblanc. You will fix the price, as I understand it."

There followed a certain amount of bickering, during which the general allowed himself to be

7   89

worsted. He agreed weakly to Inocencio's terms, having already decided to appropriate the God-sent cargo without payment. The latter had counted upon this, and, moreover, he had right-fully construed the light in those bloodshot eyes.

"Monsieur le Général must see these rifles for himself, to appreciate them, and he must count them, too, else how can he know that I am not deceiving him? We must observe caution, for there may be spies—" Inocencio spoke craftily.

"Pah! Spies? In Jacmel?"

"Nevertheless, there is a gunboat in the harbor and she flies the flag of the Republic. My skiff is waiting; we will slip out and back again—in an hour the inspection will be completed. You must see those rifles with your own eyes, Excellency. They are wonderful—the equal of any in the world; no troops can stand before them. They are magnificent."

"Come!" said Laguerre, rising.

"But alone!" Inocencio displayed a worthy circumspection. "This is hazardous business. That war-ship with the flag of the Republic—my employer is a man of reputation."

"Very well." Laguerre dismissed an aide who had remained at a distance during the interview, and together the two set out.

"You arrived barely in time, for we march to-morrow," said the general; "at least we march within the week. My defiance has gone forth. My country cries for her defender. There will be

90

bloody doings, for I tell you the temper of the people is roused and they have no stomach for that tyrant at Port au Prince."

"Bloody doings!" Inocencio smiled admiringly upon his companion. "And who could cope with them better than yourself? You have a reputation, Excellency. The name of Petithomme Laguerre is known, even in my country."

" Indeed! " The black general's chest swelled.

"We have heroes of our own—men who have bathed in blood defending our rights—but our soldiers are only soldiers, they are not statesmen. We are not so fortunate as Hayti. We would welcome, we would idolize such a one. Would that we had him; would that we boasted a—Petithomme Laguerre."

The hearer was immensely gratified at this flattery and he straightened himself pompously, saying:

"But we are favored by God, we Haytians, and we have bred a race of giants. We have gained our proud position among the nations at the price of blood. Believe me, we are not ordinary men. Our soldiers are braver than lions, our armies are the admiration of the world, we have reached that level for which God created us. It requires strong hands to guide such a people. My country calls. I am her servant."

The moon was round and brilliant as they walked out upon the rotting wharf—all wharves in Hayti are decayed—the night had grown still, and through it came the gentle whisper of the tide, mingled with the babel from the town. Land odors combined with the pungent stench of the harbor in a scent which caused Inocencio's nostrils to quiver and memory to gnaw at him. He cast a worried look skyward, and in his ungodly soul prayed for wind, for a breeze, for a gentle zephyr which would put his vengeance in his hands.

He had dropped anchor well offshore, hence the row was long, but as they neared the *Stella* a breath came out of the open. It was hot, stifling, as if a furnace door had opened, and the yellow man smiled grimly into the night.

The crew were sleeping on the deck as the two came overside, but at sight of that glittering apparition of green and gold they rubbed their eyes open and stared in speechless amazement. They were reckless fellows, fit for any enterprise, but Inocencio had learned to keep a silent tongue, so they knew nothing of his present plans. They heard him saying:

"Into the cabin, Monsieur le Général, if you will be so good. It is dark, yes, but there will be a light presently, and then—a sight for any soldier's eyes! Something that will gladden the heart of any patriot!" They went below, leaving the sailors open-mouthed. "A miserable place, Excellency," came the soft voice, "but the Cause! For Hayti one would suffer— A match, if you will be so kind. The lamp is at your hand." The skylight glowed a faint yellow, then was brightly

illuminated. "For Hayti one would endure—
much."

There followed the sound of a blow, of a heavy
fall, then a loud, ferocious cry, and a subdued
scuffling, during which the crew stared at one another. The giant 'Bajan crept forward finally and
was met by Inocencio, emerging from the cabin.
The captain was smiling, and he carefully closed
the hatch before he gave orders to make sail.

The breeze was faint, so the schooner gathered
headway slowly, but as the lights of Jacmel and
of the anchored gunboat faded out astern Inocencio sat upon the deck-house and drummed with
his naked heels upon the cabin wall. He lit one
cigarette after another, and the helmsman saw
that he was laughing silently.

Dawn broke in an explosion of many colors.
The sun rushed up out of the sea as if pursued;
night fled, and in its place was a blistering day,
full grown. The breeze had died, however, and the
Stella wallowed in a glassy calm, her sails slatting,
her booms creaking, her gear complaining to the
drunken roll. The slow swells heeled her first
to one side, then to the other, the decks grew
burning hot; no faintest ripple stirred the undulat-
ing surface of the Caribbean. Afar, the Haytian
hills wavered and danced through a veil of heat.
The slender topmast described long measured arcs
across the sky, like a schoolmaster's pointer; from
its peak the halyards whipped and bellied.

"Captain!" The 'Bajan waited for recognition. "Captain!" Inocencio looked up finally. "There —toward Jacmel—there is smoke. See! We have been watching it."

The mulatto nodded.

"The smoke of a ship."

"Ah! A ship!" Inocencio smiled and the negro recoiled suddenly. All night long the master of the *Stella* had sat upon the deck-house, staring at the sea and smoking. At times he had laughed and whispered to some one whom the helmsman could not see, but this was the first time he had smiled at any member of his crew. In fact, it was the first time the sailor had ever seen him smile. The 'Bajan withdrew and went forward to consult with his fellows. They eyed their employer curiously, fearfully, for much had happened to alarm them, not the least of which had been a furious commotion from below. Frightful curses had issued from the cabin, threats which had caused their limbs to tremble, but they had affected the captain like soothing music. It was very strange. It caused the sailors to look with concern upon that thin, low streamer in the distance; it led them to go aft in a body finally and speak their minds.

"The smoke is growing larger," they declared, and Inocencio roused himself sufficiently to look. "It is the war-ship. We are pursued. Who is this big man below?"

"He is a—friend of mine, Petithomme Laguerre—"

ROPE'S END

"Laguerre!"

"What did I tell you?" exclaimed the 'Bajan, breathlessly.

"What shall we do?" one of them inquired in a panic. "That smoke! The wind has forsaken us." He shuffled his bare feet uncomfortably. "We will be shot for this."

Inocencio tossed away his cigarette and rose; he lifted his eyes aloft. The slim topmast arrested his attention as it swept across the sky, and he watched it for a moment; then to the giant sailor he said: "You will find a new rope forward. Make it fast to the end of this halyard and run it through yonder block." He slid back the hatch and descended leisurely into the cabin.

Laguerre was sitting in a chair with his arms and legs securely bound, but he had succeeded in working considerable havoc with the furnishings of the place as well as with his splendid uniform. His lips foamed, his eyes protruded at sight of his captor; a trickle of blood from his scalp lent him a ferocious appearance.

Inocencio seated himself, and the two men stared at each other across the bare table.

Laguerre spoke first, his tongue thick, his voice hoarse from yelling. Inocencio listened with fixed, unwavering gaze.

"You tricked me neatly," the former raved. "You are a government spy, I presume. The government feared me. Well, then, it was bold work, but you will listen to what I say now.

95

We will settle this matter quickly, you and I. I
have money. You can name your price."

The hearer curled his thin lips. "So! You
have money. You offer to buy your life. Old
Julien had no money; he was poor."

Petithomme did not understand. "I am too
powerful to remain in prison," he declared. "The
President would not dare harm me; no man dares
harm me; but I am willing to pay you—"

"All Hayti could not buy your life, Laguerre!"

Some tone of voice, some haunting familiarity
of feature, set the prisoner's memory to groping
blindly. At last he inquired, "Who are you?"

"I am Floréal."

The name meant nothing. Laguerre's life was
black; many Floréals had figured in it.

"You do not remember me?"

"N-no, and yet—"

"Perhaps you will remember another — a woman. She had a scar, just here." The speaker laid
a tobacco-stained finger upon his left cheek-bone,
and Laguerre noticed for the first time that the
wrist beneath it was maimed as from a burn. "It
was a little scar and it was brown, in the candle-
light. She was young and round and her body
was soft—" The mulatto's lean face was suddenly distorted in a horrible grimace which he
intended for a smile. "She was my wife, Laguerre,
by the Church, and you took her. She died, but
she had a child—your child."

The huge black figure shrank into its green-and-

gold panoply, the bloodshot eyes rested upon
Inocencio with a look of terrified recognition.

"I have no children, Laguerre; no wife; no
home! I am poor and you have become great.
There was an old man whom you stretched by the
wrists, in the moonlight. Do you remember him?
And the old woman, my mother, whom one of
your soldiers shot? Maximilien did it, but I killed
him and Congo! And now there is only you."

"That was—long ago." The prisoner rolled
his eyes desperately; his voice was uncertain as he
whined, "I am rich—richer than anybody knows."

"Others had more money than we, eh?"

The general nodded.

"Pierrine is dead, and you would have been
the President. It is well that I came in time."
Again Captain Ruiz smiled, and the corpulent
soldier was shaken loosely as by an invisible hand.
"Come now! Your friends are approaching and
I must prepare you to greet them."

He untied the knots at Laguerre's ankles, then
motioned him toward the cabin door.

That streamer of smoke had grown; it was a
black smudge against the sky when the two gained
the deck, and at sight of it the general shouted:

"My ship! The gunboat! Ho! If harm comes
to me—"

Inocencio took one end of the new rope which
had been run through the block at the mast-
head, and knotted it about his prisoner's wrists,
then with his knife he severed the other bonds.

"Give way!" he ordered.

The crew held back, at which he turned upon them so savagely that they hastened to obey. They put their weight upon the line; Laguerre's arms were whisked above his head, he felt his feet leave the deck. He was dumb with surprise, choked with rage at this indignity, but he did not understand its significance.

"Up with him! In a rush!" cried the captain, and hand over hand the sailors hauled in, while upward in a series of jerks went Petithomme Laguerre. The schooner listed and he swung outward; he tried to entwine his legs in the shrouds, but failed, and he continued to rise until his feet had cleared the crosstree.

"Make fast!" Inocencio ordered.

Laguerre was hanging like a huge plumbob now, and as the schooner heeled to starboard he swung out, farther and farther, until there was nothing beneath him but the glassy sea. He screamed at this, and kicked and capered; the slender topmast sprung to his antics. Then the vessel righted herself, and as she did so the man at the rope's end began a swift and fearful journey. Not until that instant did his fate become apparent to him, but when he saw what was in store for him he ceased to cry out. He fixed his eyes upon the mast toward which the weight of his body propelled him, he drew himself upward by his arms, he flung out his legs to break the impact. The *Stella* lifted by the bow and he cleared the spar by a few inches. Onward he rushed, to the pause that marked the limit of his flight to port, then slowly, but with increasing swiftness, he began his return journey. Again he resisted furiously and again his body missed the mast, all but one shoulder, which brushed lightly in passing and served to spin him like a top. The measured slowness of that oscillation added to its horror; with every escape the victim's strength decreased, his fear grew, and the end approached. It was a game of chance played by the hand of the sea. Under him the deck appeared and disappeared at regular intervals, the rope cut into his wrists, the slim spar sprung to his efforts. In the distance was a charcoal smear which grew blacker.

After a time Laguerre heard Inocencio counting, and saw his upturned face.

"Ha! Very close, Monsieur le Général, but we will try once again. Ship's timber is not so hard as cocomacaque, but sufficiently hard, nevertheless. And the rope bites, eh? But there was old Julien— What? Again? You were always lucky. His flesh was cold and his bones brittle, yet he did not kick like you. If Pierrine were here to see this! What a sight — the liberator of his country—God's blood, Laguerre! The sea is with you! That makes five times. But you are tiring, I see. What a sight for her—the hero of a hundred battles dangling like a strangled parrot. It is not so hard to die, monsieur, it— Ah-h!"

A cry of horror arose from the crew who had

gathered forward, for Petithomme Laguerre, dizzied with spinning, had finally fetched up with a crash against the mast. He ricocheted, the swing of the pendulum became irregular for a time or two, then the roll of the vessel set it going again. Time after time he missed destruction by a hair's-breadth, while the voice from below gibed at him, then once more there came the sound of a blow, dull, yet loud, and of a character to make the hearers shudder. The victim struggled less violently; he no longer drew his weight upward like a gymnast. But he was a man of great vitality; his bones were heavy and thickly padded with flesh, therefore they broke one by one, and death came to him slowly. The sea played with him maliciously, saving him repeatedly, only to thresh him the harder when it had tired of its sport. It was a long time before the restless Caribbean had reduced him to pulp, a spineless, boneless thing of putty which danced to the spring of the resilient spruce.

They let him down finally and slid him into the oily waters, overside, but the breeze refused to come and the *Stella* continued to wallow drunkenly. The sky was glittering, the pitch was oozing from the deck, in the distance the Haytian mountains scowled through the shimmer.

Inocencio turned toward the approaching gunboat, which was very close by now, a rusty, ill-painted, ill-manned tub. Her blunt nose broke the swells into foam, from her peak depended the banner of the Black Republic, symbolic of the motto, "Liberty, Equality, Fraternity." The captain of the *Stella* rolled and lit a cigarette, then seated himself upon the cabin roof to wait. And as he waited he drummed with his naked heels and smiled, for he was satisfied.

INOCENCIO

INOCENCIO

CAPTAIN INOCENCIO prepared to let himself over the side of the schooner. Outside, the Caribbean was all agleam, save where the coral-reef teeth gnashed it into foam; inside, a sand beach, yellow in the moonlight, curved east and west like a causeway until the distance swallowed it. Back of that lay the groves of cocoanut-trees, their plumes waving in the undying undulations that had never ceased since first the trade-winds breathed upon them. Beneath the palms themselves the jungle was ink-black, patched here and there with silver. The air was heavy with the slow rumble of an ever-restless surf and, all about, the sea was whispering, whispering, as if minded to tell its mysteries to the moon, not yet two hours high.

It was the sort of night that had ever wakened wild impulses in Captain Inocencio's breast. It was on such a night that he had first felt the touch of a woman's lips; it was on such another night that he had first felt a man's warm blood upon his hands. That had been long ago, to be sure, in far Hayti, and since that time both of those sensations had lost much of their novelty, for he had lived fast and hard, and his exile had plunged him into many evils. It was on such a night, also, that he had begun his wanderings, fleeing southward between moonrise and moonset; southward, whither all the scum of the Indies floated. But, even to this day, when the full of a February moon came round with the fragrant salt trades blowing and the sound of a throbbing surf beneath it, the sated, stagnant blood of Captain Inocencio went hot, his thin mulatto face grew hard, and a certain strange exultance blazed within him.

His crew had long since come to recognize this frenzy, and had they now beheld him, poised half nude at the rail, his fierce eyes bent upon the forbidden shore, they would have ventured no remark. As it happened, however, they were all asleep, all three of them, and the captain's lips curled scornfully. What could black men know about such subtleties as the call of moonlight? What odds to them if yonder palm fronds beckoned? They had no curiosity, no resentfulness; otherwise they, too, might have dared to break the San Blas law.

It was four years now since he had begun to sail this coast, and even though he was known on every *cay* and bay from Nombre de Dios to Tiburon, and even though it was recognized that the Señor "Beel Weelliams" paid proper price for cocoa and ivory nuts, his head trader had never beaten down the people's distrust. On the contrary, their vigilance had increased, if anything, and now, after four years of scrupulous fair dealing, he, Captain Inocencio, was still compelled to sleep offshore and under guard, like any common stranger.

It had made the Haytian laugh at first; for who would wish to harm a San Blas woman, with the streets of Colon but a hundred miles to the west? Then, as the months crept into years, and for voyage after voyage he never saw a San Blas woman's face, he became furious. Next he grew angry, then sullen, and a sense of injury burned into him. He set his wits against theirs; but invariably the sight of his schooner's sails was a signal for the women to melt away—invariably, when night came, and he and his blacks had been herded back aboard their craft, the women returned, and the sound of their voices served to fan the flame within his breast.

Night after night, in sheltered coves or open river-mouths, the captain of the *Espirita* had lain, belly down, upon the little roof of the deckhouse, his head raised serpent-wise, his gloomy eyes fixed upon the cook-fires in the distance. And when some woman's figure suddenly stood out against the firelit walls, or when some maiden's song came floating seaward, he had breathed curses in his bastard French, and directed a message of hate at the sentinel he knew was posted in the jungle shadows. At times he had railed at his crew of spiritless Jamaican "niggers," and lusted for a following of his own kind—men with the French blood of his island in their veins, men who would follow where the moonlight flickered. He had even gone so far, at one time, as to search the water-fronts from Port Limon to Santa Marta in quest of such fellows; he had winnowed the off-scourings of the four seas gathered there, but without success. They were villainous chaps, for the main part, crossed with many creeds and colors, and ready for any desperate venture; but he could not find three helpers of sufficient hardihood to tamper with the San Blas virgins. Instead, they had retold him the tales he already knew by heart; tales of swift and sudden retribution overtaking blacks and whites; retribution that did not halt even at the French or the hated *Americanos*. They told him that, of all the motley races gathered here since earliest Spanish days, the San Blas blood alone retained its purity. It was his boss, the Señor Williams, who had gone back farthest into history, and it was he likewise who had threatened him with prompt discharge if he presumed to trespass. The Señor Williams was not one to permit profitable trade relations to be jeopardized by the whim of a Haytian mulatto.

Inocencio had listened passively; then, when alone, smiled. He owed no loyalty. He had no law. Even the name he went by was a fiction.

INOCENCIO

He continued to make his trips and, when he came driving in ahead of the humming trade-winds, his schooner laden with the treasures of the islands, the back streets of Colon awoke to his presence and prepared to greet him. But however loud the music in the *cantinas*, however fierce the exaltation of the liquor in him, however wild the orgy into which he plunged, he could never quite drown the memory of those sleepless vigils far to the eastward. Ever in his quiet moments he heard the faint song of San Blas women wafted by the breath of the sea, ever in his dreams he saw the slim outlines of girlish figures black against a flaring camp-fire.

Four years this thing had grown upon him, during which he haunted the San Blas coast. And then, one night, he slipped overside and swam ashore. It was not so dangerous as it seemed, for, once he had gained the shelter of the jungle, no less than a pack of hounds could have followed him, inasmuch as the thickets were laced by a network of trails that gave forth no sound to naked soles, and the rustling branches overhead, played upon by the never-ceasing breeze, drowned all signal of his presence. Once he had defied the tribal law, he knew no further peace. It was like the first taste of blood to an animal. Thereafter Inocencio, the outlaw, whose name was a symbol of daring, became a jackal prowling through the midnight glades, tasting the scent of the villages, and staring with hungry eyes from just beyond the shadow's edge.   Rather he became a panther, for in his caution was no cowardice, only a feline patience.   Village after village he hunted until he had marked his prey.   Then he waited to spring.

To be sure, he had never spoken with the girl, nor even seen her clearly, but the sound of her voice made him tremble.

To accomplish even this much had taken many trips of the *Espirita*, had meant many sleepless nights and some few tense moments when only the shadows saved him from betrayal.   There had been times, for instance, when the quick simulation of a wild pig's grunt or the purr of *el tigre* had served to explain the sound of his retreat; other times when he had stood motionless in the shadows, the evil rust-red blade of his machete matching the hue of his half-nude body.

To-night he crouched behind the deck-house and ran his eye over the schooner in one final glance of caution.   It was well that all should be in readiness, for the moment of his spring might come within the hour, or, if not to-night, then to-morrow night, or a week, a month, a year from to-night, and then a tackle fouled or a block jammed might spell destruction.

He thrust his head through a loop of the leathern scabbard, and swung the huge knife back until it lay along the crease between his shoulders; then he seized the port stay and let himself softly downward overside.   The water rose to his chin.

INOCENCIO

Without a ripple, he glided into the moonlight astern, and a moment later his round, black head was no more than a piece of bobbing drift borne landward by the current.

Down past the village he swam, noting the rows of dugouts on the beach. He saw a blot in the big mahogany *cayuca*, a great canoe hewn from one priceless trunk, and recognized it for the sentinel. On he floated, then worked his way ashore behind the little point. Once he felt the hard, smooth sand beneath his soles, he waited until a cloud obscured the moon, and when the light broke through again he was dripping underneath a wide-leaved breadfruit-tree at the jungle's edge. Removing the machete from his neck, he wrung the water from his cotton trousers. Over his head a night-bird croaked hoarsely.

The girl was at her father's house, tending a fire on the dirt floor. It was a large house, for the old man was rich in daughters, and, by the San Blas rule, their husbands had come to live with him. He had waxed fat long ago on their labors, and now only this youngest one remained unmarried. But the ceremony was set. Inocencio had heard the news upon his arrival three days before, and had grudgingly bought a big store of tortoise-shell from the groom-to-be, knowing full well that the money was intended for the wedding celebration. Markeeña was the fellow's name, a straight, up-standing youth who more than once had excited the Haytian's admiration for his skill with a canoe. But since that day the latter had regarded him with smoldering eyes.

The big thatched roof with its bark-floored loft stood on posts blackened by the smoke of many feasts;. there were no walls. The jungle crept close to it from the rear, and hence the watcher could witness every movement of the girl as she passed between the hammocks or stooped to her task. He could see, for instance, the play of her dark round shoulders above the neck of her shift. He ground his yellow teeth and gripped the moist earth with the soles of his naked feet, as a tiger bares its claws before the leap.

It was very hard to wait. For an hour he stood there. Once a dog came to him and sniffed, then, recognizing a frequent visitor, returned to the house and resumed its slumber beside the fire. From the houses beyond came the sound of voices, of a child crying querulously, and of a woman quieting it. People came and went. An old hag began pounding grain in a mortar, crooning in a broken voice. The girl's father came rolling into view, and, after a word to her, struggled heavily up the ladder to his bed. He was snoring almost before the structure had ceased to creak beneath him. In the thicket a multitude of nocturnal sounds arose, the insect chorus of the night.

And then, before Inocencio realized what she was up to, the girl had stolen swiftly out and past him, so close that he could hear the scuff of her sandals on the beaten path. The next instant he had glided from cover and fallen in behind, his pulses leaping, his long, lithe muscles rippling; but he moved as silently as a shadow.

Had he been a less accomplished bushman he might have lost her, for she plunged into the jungle unhesitatingly. However, he had long ago learned these trails by daylight, and knew them better than the lines of his own palm; hence, every moonlit turn, every flash of her white slip, found him close upon her track.

It puzzled him at first to discover her reason for this unexpected sally, but soon he decided she must be bent upon some mission. Then, when he saw that she purposely avoided the village and was bending toward the open palm-grove abreast of his anchorage, he knew she must be going to a tryst. So Markeeña was the sentinel! That fellow in the mahogany *cayuca* was her lover! Inocencio, the dissolute, felt a flame of rage suffuse him. When, at last, his quarry emerged into the mysterious half-light under the high roof of palms, and paused, he strode after her. She gave the melancholy call of the night-bird that had sounded in the breadfruit-tree over his head earlier in the evening; then, seeing him close beside her, uttered a little cry of pleasure. Not until he was too near for flight did she discover her mistake, and then she seemed to freeze. Her utter silence was more menacing than a scream.

INOCENCIO

It was the instant for which he had schooled himself, so he spoke to her in her own tongue.

"Make no outcry! I will not harm you."

She drew back, at which he laid his great, bony hand upon her, his eyes blazing. She was deathly frightened, being little more than a child.

"I have waited for you many nights," he explained. "I feared you would never come." Then, as she continued to stare up at him uncomprehendingly, he ran on: "I am Inocencio, the trader. Every night I have watched you at your work. I want you for my woman."

Her voice had forsaken her utterly, but she struggled weakly, so he tightened his grip until his fingers sank into her flesh. She began to gasp as if from a swift run; the open neck of her garment slipped down over one shoulder; her eyes were distended until he saw them ringed about with white. The terror of this tall yellow man with the hungry eyes robbed her of power, and she let him drag her toward the lapping water as if she were no more than some weak, wild thing that he had trapped.

Of course she knew him, for, while the San Blas law may banish women, it cannot blind them, and she, too, had studied him from concealment. Although his words had made no impression whatever upon her, his grasp and the direction he was drawing her had at last translated what was in his mind. Then she burst into life. But she made no outcry, for it takes strength to scream, and every atom of her force was directed against his. She began to moan. Her every muscle writhed. With her free hand she tore at his entwining fingers, but they were like jungle creepers that no human strength could serve to loosen. And all the time he drew her with him, speaking softly.

Then she felt him pause, and her distracted vision beheld another figure entering the shadows from the shore. She called to her lover hoarsely, and saw him halt at the strange note, peering inward for a sight of her. She voiced words now for the first time, crying:

"The stranger! The stranger!"

Then, hearing the scrape of her captor's machete as he drew it from its scabbard, she renewed her struggle more fiercely.

Captain Inocencio held the girl at his left side until the last moment, balancing the great knife-blade as if to try his arm; then, when the Indian was close upon him, coming straight as a dart, he freed himself. A slanting moonbeam showed Markeeña's ferocious visage and his upraised weapon, but the Haytian met the falling blow with a fierce upward stroke that once before had done him service. It was the stroke that had made him an exile years before.

Inocencio's physical strength had ever been his pride, if also his undoing. Above all things, he prided himself upon the dexterity and vigor of his wrist. His early training on that blood-red Caribbean isle, and a later life in thicket and swamp, had served to transform the cumbrous native weapon into a thing of life at his hands. More than once, for instance, he had harried a serpent until it struck, for the mere satisfaction of severing its head in midcourse, and now he felt the wide blade enter flesh. Before his antagonist could cry out twice he had slashed again, this time downward as if to split a green cocoanut. The next instant he had seized the girl as she fled into the jungle.

But she had found her voice at last, and he was forced to muffle her with his palm. When they were out into the moonlight, however, with the dry sand up to their ankles, he let her breathe; then, pointing with his machete to the *Espirita* lying white and ghostlike in the offing, he drove her down into the warm sea until it reached her waist.

"Swim!" he ordered, and, when she would have renewed the alarm, he raised his blade, grimly threatening to call the sharks with her blood.

"Swim!" he repeated, and she struck out, with him at her shoulder.

But the village was roused. A confused clamor betrayed its bewilderment, and before the swimmers had won more than half-way to the schooner, figures came running along the shore. Inocencio cautioned the girl to hold her tongue, and she obeyed, thoroughly cowed by his roughness. She turned upon her side and swam with her face close to his, her eyes fixed upon him curiously, wonderingly. Her easy progress through the water showed that her fright had largely vanished, and showed likewise that, had the Haytian been no uncommon swimmer himself, she might have distanced him. All the way out to the boat she stared at him with that same fixed look, maintaining her position at his side. The moon and the salt brine in his eyes played him tricks, else he might have fancied her to be half smiling, as if in some strange exaltation akin to his own.

Not until he finally dragged her, panting, to the deck of the *Espirita*, and her white-clad figure stood out clearly from the shore, did her tribesmen realize the nature of the alarm. Then the vibrant turmoil suddenly stilled for the space of a full minute while the enormity of the outrage made itself felt. They drew together at the edge of the sea, staring open-mouthed, amazed, before they raised their blood-cry.

The man and woman rested a moment, their eyes upon the shore, and where they stood twin pools of water blackened the deck. Then Inocencio turned to look upon his prey. The girl's flimsy cotton shift was molded to her figure, and he saw that she was even fairer than he had pictured. In spite of his need for haste, he paused to gloat upon the favor the moon and the salt sea had rendered him. As for her, she flung his glance back bravely until he wrenched open the cabin hatch and pointed to the dark interior. Then she weakened. But she had a will of her own, it seemed, for she refused to be locked inside.

He strode toward her, and she clutched the rigging
desperately, turning her glance to one of appeal.

"You may come up in a moment," he translated, but still she clung to the stay. "If you
try to escape—" He scowled upon her terribly, at
which she shook her head. Having already tasted
her strength, he knew there was no time to force
her, so he leaped at his crew.

The three blacks were snoring forward of the
deck-house, so he seized a bucket of water at the
rail and sluiced them into wakefulness, keeping
his eye upon the girl meanwhile. When he saw
that in truth she made no move he let his caution
slip and raged over the ship like a tiger, beating
his half-clad crew ahead of him with the flat of
his machete. By the time they had gained their
wits the tribesmen were massing at the canoes.
As the mainsail rose creaking he broke out the jib
with his own hand, then with one stroke of his
knife severed the manila mooring-rope, and the
Espirita fell off slowly ahead of the breeze.
Inocencio ran back to spur his befuddled "niggers"
to further activity, only to find the girl still
motionless, her eyes following his every movement.
Under the curses, the schooner slowly raised her
wings and the night wind began to strain at the
cordage.

But at last, when the Jamaicans were fully
awake to the state of affairs, they threatened
mutiny, whereat the mulatto flung himself upon
them so savagely that they scattered to arm them-

selves with whatever weapons lay at hand. Then they huddled amidship, rolling their eyes and praying; for out from the shore came a long mahogany *cayuca*, and it was full of straight-haired men.

It takes a sailing-craft some time to gain its momentum, and as yet the full strength of the trades had not struck the *Espirita;* hence the canoe overtook her rapidly. Inocencio called to one of his men and gave him the tiller, then took stand beside the girl, the naked blade of his weapon once more beneath his arm.

The schooner's helmsman gave himself to God, while the cordage overhead began to whine as the deck rose. It was upon the Haytian's lips to warn his pursuers off when one of them called to the girl, bidding her leap. Inocencio heard the breath catch in her throat, but she made no move, and the command was repeated.

This time she answered by some exclamation that he did not understand, whereat the canoemen ceased paddling, as if her word had paralyzed them. They hurled their voices at her savagely, but she remained motionless, the while the waters beneath her began to foam and bubble. The *Espirita's* crew ceased their prayers, and in the silence that ensued the sea whispered at the bow as the craft listed more heavily under the full force of the wind.

Inocencio could not fathom the meaning of the subdued colloquy among the San Blas men, so he shouted a warning, but, strangely enough, they made no answer. They only crouched, with paddles motionless, staring at the dimming figures facing them, until the *Espirita*, "wing and wing" ahead of the trades, was no larger than a seagull. As yet they had not learned of the other tragedy hidden in the shadow of the palms; had they suspected what lay weltering at the edge of a trampled moonlit glade behind them, no threat of Inocencio's, no plea of his new-found woman, could have held them back.

Once the schooner was under way, the Haytian led the girl to the deck-house and thrust her roughly inside, closing the hatch. Then with his own hands he took his craft through the reef and out into the leaping Caribbean. Not until the San Blas coast was a mere charcoal line upon the port quarter and the salt spray was driving high did he deliver over the helm. At last, however, he gave his crew instructions for the night and went below, closing and bolting the hatch behind him. When the smoky lamp that swung between the bunks was lit and its yellow gleam had illumined the interior he saw the girl's eyes fast upon him. He went toward her across the tilting floor and she arose to meet him, smiling.

II

SEÑOR BILL WILLIAMS was in a fine rage. "Didn't you like your job?" he questioned.

INOCENCIO

Inocencio shrugged languidly. "Oh yes! The job was good."

"You knew I'd fire you!"

"*Si!*"

The American tempered his indignant glare with a hint of curiosity. "You must love that San Blas girl."

"What do you say?"

"You must love her—better than your job at least?"

"*Si*, señor. I suppose so."

"What is she like, Inocencio?"

"Well, she is just like other women. All women are alike—only some are fat. One time I had a female from Martinique, and she acted just the same as this one."

"Humph! If she is like all the others, what the devil made you—do it?"

"Señor, you have plenty of money, and yet one night I saw you bet two thousand pesos on the *rouge*. Why did you do that, eh?"

"That is altogether different."

The Haytian smiled. "I am tired of these females at Colon. They are common people—very common. Then, too, those San Blas people, they are so scared that somebody is going to steal a woman! Maybe if they had left me asleep on shore I would never have noticed no woman at all. But they don't trust me, so, sure enough—I steal one."

"And you say she came willingly?" queried Williams, incredulously.

INOCENCIO

"Oh yes! When her people commanded her to jump from my schooner she refused them. I did not understand at the time, but by an' by she told me." He swelled his chest with pride. "I guess she never seen so brave a man as me before. Eh, señor?"

"Humph! I guess I never will *sabe* you niggers," acknowledged the American.

Inocencio corrected his recent employer, but without show of the slightest heat:

"I am no nigger, señor; I am Haytian. She is San Blas Indian. My father was not even so dark as me. Black men have thick heads and you have to beat them, but nobody ever beat me, not even a white man. When those niggers sleep I lie awake and study; I make schemes. That is why I left Hayti."

"Do you understand that you've got me into a hell of a fix? I've got to take a trip down there myself to square things."

Inocencio lighted a black cigarette and blew the smoke through his nose. Evidently other people's troubles did not concern him. Recognizing the futility of reproach or indignation, the former speaker continued:

"But see here, now! This girl! You can't keep her."

"Eh? Who's going to take her away?" interrogated the Haytian, quickly. "Bah! One man tried that, and—I killed him with my machete." His thin lips drew back at the memory, and for an instant his yellow face showed a hint of what had made his reputation.

"She won't stay with you."

"Oh yes, she will. She was wild, very wild at first, but—she will stay."

"And how about her people? They're bad *hombres*. Even the government lets them alone— fortunately for you."

"They won't make no trouble about that Markeeña. He is quite dead, I think."

"By Jove! You're a cold-blooded brute!"

"Señor! You told me once that nobody had ever married a San Blas female, eh?"

"Yes. Even the old Spaniards tried it, but the blood is clean, so far; something unusual, too, in this country."

Inocencio began to laugh silently, as if at a joke. "Some day, maybe, you will see a San Blas half-breed playing in the streets of Colon," said he.

"I don't believe it."

"I'll bet you my wages—two hundred pesos. Come! I'll show you."

"You get out of here," said the American, roughly. "That's something I don't allow anybody to joke about." And, when the mulatto had gone, he continued aloud: "By Heaven! this is sure a tough country for a white man!"

Inocencio strode through the streets toward the swamp that lies behind the town, oblivious to the grilling midday heat that smote him from above, from the concrete walks beneath, and from the naked walls on every side. It was before the days of the American occupation, and the streets were nothing more than open cesspools, the stench from which offended sorely. Buzzards flapped among the naked children at play in the mire beside the sewer ditches.

The place was filled with everything unhealthy, and had long been known as the earth's great festering sore. Neither the Orient nor the farthest tropics boasted another spot like Colon, or Aspinwall, as it had been called, with its steaming, hip-deep streets and its brilliant flowering graveyards. So hateful had it proved, in fact, that when seamen signed articles binding themselves to work their ships into any corner of the globe they inserted a clause exempting them from entering Aspinwall.

Now, however, the town was lively, for this was the dry season, when the fever was at its lowest, and the resorts were filled with the flotsam and jetsam of a tropic world. It was a polyglot town, moreover, set upon a fever-ridden mangrove isle serving as one terminus of the world's short cut, and in it had collected all the parasites that live upon the moving herd.

The French work of digging had but served to augment the natural population by a no less desperate set from overseas, and now from the open doors of their cubbyholes women of every color greeted the passer-by.

Inocencio, whose last exploit was already a

thing of gossip, received unusual attention, there being no color line in Colon town. White, yellow, and black women fawned upon him and bade him tarry, but he merely paused to listen or to fan their admiration by a word, then idled onward, pleased at the notice he evoked.

Once fairly out of the pest-hole, he threaded his way through the swamp toward the other shore of the island. Blue land-crabs scuttled among the mangrove roots at his approach; the place was noisy with the hum of insects; on every hand the heated mud gave forth a sound like the smack of huge moist lips. But on the other side he came into a different domain. Here the sea-breeze banished the hovering miasma, the shore was of powdered coral sand, a litter of huts drowsed beneath a grove of cocoa palms, while a fleet of *cayucas* lay moored to stakes inside the breakers or bleaching in the sun.

Captain Inocencio was a person of some importance here, for, besides his occupation as a trader, he exacted toll from a score or more of lazy blacks. They were a lawless crew, gathered from the remotest corners of the Indies, composed of Jamaicans, 'Bajans, and Saint Lucians, all reared to easy life and ripe for such an occasional crafty pilgrimage as Inocencio might devise. They had gathered around him naturally, paying him scant revenue, to be sure, yet offering a certain loyalty that had its uses. Although the village was but a mile from the town itself, Inocencio's word was law; when the Colombian soldiers were called upon to visit the spot, they came in numbers, never singly.

The girl was seated on the rickety porch of his cabin, her feet drawn under her, her chin upon her knees. The other women were gossiping loudly, staring at her from a distance, but her black eyes only smoldered sullenly. He swore at the curious negro wenches and sent the girl about her household duties, then stretched himself in the shade and eyed her complacently until he fell asleep.

It was a week later that one of his men came to him breathlessly to announce that the San Blas Indians were in the town.

"How many?" queried Inocencio.

"Four boat-loads."

"Did they come to trade?"

"Oh yes, boss."

This was no unusual thing, for they often displayed their little cargoes of nuts and fruits and vegetables upon the water-front. Inocencio rose lazily and stretched, then, calling the woman, explained the tidings to her.

"I will go see them," he announced, finally.

"Oh, boss," cried the black man, "they will kill you!"

He shrugged his brawny shoulders and, thrusting the machete beneath his arm, took the trail out through the mangrove swamp.

Straight to the Colon water-front he went, and there flaunted himself before the men from down the coast. Here and there he strolled, casting back their looks of hatred with a bravado that attracted all the idlers in the neighborhood. Wenches nudged one another and tittered nervously, pointing him out and telling anew the story of his daring. Men watched him with wondering admiration, and he heard them murmuring:

"Ah, that Inocencio!"

"*El diabolo!*"

"And so brave! He would fight an army."

"See the great arms of him, and the eye like a tiger."

It was the keenest pleasure he had ever tasted.

As for his enemies, they kept their silence. They bartered their stock and, having made their purchases, raised sail and scudded away down the coast whence they had come.

Inocencio got drunk that night—for who could withstand the lavish flattery that poured from every *cantina* up and down the length of Bottle Alley? Who could resist the smiles of the chalk-faced females of Cash Street, all eager to laud his bravery. Some time before morning he reeled into his shack beneath the palms, to find the woman waiting fearfully. He cursed at her for staring at him so, and fell upon his bed.

In the months that followed he seldom lost an opportunity of showing himself to the San Blas men when they came to town, but in time this pleasure palled as all others had, for the woman's kindred seemed incapable of resentment. Gradually, also, he became accustomed to her presence, and spent much of his time among the women of Cash Street. On one occasion he returned from an orgy of this sort to find her talking to one of his men, a young Barbadian with a giant's frame. It was only by accident, due to the liquor in him, that his hand went wild and he missed killing the fellow; then he beat the woman unmercifully.

Chancing to meet the Señor Williams on the street some time later, he said: "*Buenas dias*, señor! You see, Captain Inocencio is still alive and the woman has not run away."

His former employer grunted, as if neither phenomenon were worthy of comment.

"I've heard how you rub it into those San Blas fellows," Williams remarked. "I can't understand why they never avenged Markeeña."

"Bah! They have heard of me," said the Haytian, boastfully; then, with a grin, "You remember our bet, señor?"

"I never made you a bet," the American denied, hotly. "But I've a mind to. I've been here ten years, and I think I know those people."

"Two hundred pesos!"

"You'll never have a child by her. They won't allow it. They'll get her and you, too, in ample time. I tell you, their blood is clean."

"Two hundred pesos that she brings me a San Blas half-breed within two months," smiled the mulatto, insolently.

INOCENCIO

And Williams exclaimed: "I'll do it. It's worth two hundred 'silver' to see a miracle."

"*Bueno!* I'll bring him to you when he comes."

Thereafter Inocencio gave over beating the woman.

Back at the little settlement beyond the swamp the coming event did not pass without comment, and although the black women were kind to their straight-haired neighbor, she never made friends with them, nor did she ever accompany Inocencio to town. On the contrary, she seemed obsessed by an ever-present dread, and whenever she heard that her own people were near she concealed herself and did not appear again until they were gone. Bred into her deepest conscience was the certainty that her tribe would make desperate attempt to preserve its most sacred tradition, and hence, as the days dragged on and her condition became more pronounced her fears increased likewise. She began to look forward to the birth of the child as the crisis upon which her own life hinged. Inocencio did his best to dissipate her fears, explaining boastfully that the mere mention of his name was ample protection for her, and, did he wish it, not even the army of the Republic could take her from him. But still she would not be convinced.

And then, in the dark of the December moon, the expected came. It was that season when the rains were at their heaviest, when rust and rot might be felt by the fingers. A gray mold had crept over all things indoors; a myriad of insect pests burdened the air.

In the rare intervals between showers every faintest draught deluged the huts from the dripping palm leaves overhead. From the swamp arose a noxious vapor whenever the sun exposed itself; tree-toads shrilled incessantly. Outside, the turf maintained its sullen murmur; through the gloom of starless nights its phosphorescent outlines rushed across the reef like phantom serpents in parade.

In the dead of a night like this the visitors arrived.

Even the heavy animal slumber of the blacks was broken by the scream that issued from the hut of Captain Inocencio. And then the sound of such fighting! The negroes might have rushed to the assistance of their leader had it not been for the echo of that awful woman-cry hovering over the village like a shadow. It filled the air and hung there, saturating the breathless night with such unnamable terror that the wakened children began to whimper and the women buried their heads in the ragged bedding to keep it out. Death was among them and the bravest cowered while through the quivering silence there came the sounds of a mighty combat lasting for such an interminable time that the listeners became hysterical.

At length they discovered that the night was dead again, save for the sudden patter of raindrops on the thatches when the palm fronds

stirred. One of them called shrilly, another answered, but they did not venture forth. Afterward they fancied they had heard the thrust of
paddles in the lagoon and strange voices dwindling
away to seaward, but they were not sure. Eventually, however, the stillness got upon them more
fearfully than the former noises, and they stirred.
Then, in time, they heard the voice of Inocencio
himself cursing faintly, as if from a great distance.
A light showed through the cracks of a hut, and
Nicholas, the least timid, emerged with a lantern
held on high. He summoned the rest around him,
then went toward the black shadow of Inocencio's
dwelling with a score of white-eyed, dusky faces
at his shoulder.

The door was down, and from the threshold they
could see what the front room contained. It was
Nicholas who, with clattering teeth and nerveless
fingers, dragged a blanket from the bed and covered the woman's figure. It was he who traced the
feeble voice to the wreck of a room behind, and
strove to lift Inocencio out of the welter in which
he lay. But the Haytian blasted him with curses
for opening his wounds; so they propped him
against the wall by his direction, and bound him
about with strips torn from the mattress. Then
he called for a cigarette, and its ashes were upon
his breast when the French doctor arrived from
the hospital on the Point.

When the white man's work was done, the
mulatto addressed him weakly:

"Will m'sieu' do me a great favor?"

"Certainly."

"M'sieu' is acquainted with the American, Señor Williams?"

"*Oui.*"

"Will *m'sieu' le docteur* please to tell him that Captain Inocencio has won his wager?"

"I don't understand."

"Listen! In the room yonder, under the bed, m'sieu' will find a little boy baby rolled up in a blanket. The woman heard them at the door, and she was just in time. Oh, she knew they would be coming."

The French doctor nodded his comprehension. "But—your wife herself?" said he. "Perhaps when you are well again you can have your vengeance. The soldiers will—"

"Bah! What is the use?" interrupted Inocencio. "The world is full of women." Then, strangely enough, he bared his yellow teeth in a smile of rarest tenderness. "But this boy of mine! They came to kill him, m'sieu', and to show that the San Blas blood cannot be crossed; but the woman was too quick of wit. They did not find him, praise God! *Le docteur* has seen many children, perhaps, but never a child like this." He ran on with a father's tender boastfulness. "M'sieu' will note the back and the legs of him. And see, he did not even cry, poor little man! Oh, he is like his father for bravery! He will be my vengeance, for he has the San Blas blood in him; he will be a man like me, too. Bring him to me quickly; I must see him again." He was still babbling fondly to the negroes about him when the doctor reappeared, empty-handed.

"The child is dead," said the white man, simply.

In the silence Inocencio rose to a sitting posture. His fierce eyes grew wild with a fright that had never been there until this moment. Then, before they could prevent him, he had gained his feet. He waved them aside and went into the room of death, walking like a strong man. A candle guttering beside the open window betrayed the utter nakedness of the place. With one movement of his great, bony hands he ripped the planks of the bed asunder and stared downward. Then he turned to the east and, raising his arms above his head, gave a terrible cry. He began to sway, and even as the doctor leaped to save him he fell with a crash.

It was Nicholas who told the priest that the French doctor would not let them move him; for he lay upon his face at the feet of the San Blas woman, his arms flung outward like the arms of a cross.

THE WAG-LADY

THE WAG-LADY

HER real name was June—well, the rest doesn't matter; for no one ever got beyond that point. It was the Scrap Iron Kid who first bore news of her coming to the Wag-boys. Knowing him for a poet, they put down his perfervid description as the logical outpouring of a romantic spirit.

Reddy summed it up neatly by saying, "The Kid has fell for another quilt, that's all."

"I 'ain't fell for no frill," the Kid stoutly declared. "I've saw too many to lose me out. This gal's a thoroughbred."

"Another recruit for Simons, I suppose," Llewellyn yawned. "I'll drop in at the theater and look her over."

"An' she ain't no actor, neither," Scrap Iron declared. "She's goin' to start a hotel."

"Bah! If she's as good-looking as you claim, some Swede will marry her before she can buy her dishes."

"Sure! They must all pull something like that to start with," said the Dummy, who was a woman-hater; "then when you've played 'em straight

they h'ist the pirate's flag and go to palmin' per-
centage checks in some dance-hall."

But again the idealistic Scrap Iron Kid came
stubbornly to the defense of the new-comer; and
the argument was growing warm when Thomasville and the Swede entered with two caddies of
tobacco which they had managed to acquire during the confusion at the water-front, thus ending
the discussion.

There were six of the Wag-boys, six as bold and
unscrupulous gentlemen as the ebb and swirl of the
Northern gold rush had left stranded beneath the
rim of the Arctic, and they had joined forces,
drawn as much, perhaps, by their common calling
as by the facilities thus afforded for perfecting any
alibis that a long and lonesome winter might
render necessary. Nor is it quite correct to state
that they were stranded; for it takes more than
the buffets of a stormy fate to strand such men
as the Dummy and George Llewellyn and the
Scrap Iron Kid and their three companions.

Llewellyn was the gentleman of the outfit, owing
to the fact that the polish of an early training had
not been utterly dulled by a four years' trick at
Deer Lodge Penitentiary. The Dummy had
gained his name from an admirable self-restraint
which no "third-degree" methods had ever served
to break; Thomasville was so called because of a
boyish pride in his Georgia birthplace; while
Reddy and the Swede— But this is the story of
the Wag-lady, and we digress.

THE WAG-LADY

To begin with, June was young, with a spring-time flush in her cheeks, and eyes as clear as glacier pools. Yet with all her youth and beauty, she possessed a poise that held men at a distance. She also had a certain fearlessness that came, perhaps, from worldly innocence and was far more effective than the customary brazenness of frontier women. She went ahead with her business, asking neither advice nor assistance, and, almost before the Wag-boys knew what she was up to, she had leased the P. C. Warehouse near their cabin and had carpenters changing it into a bunk-house.

In a week it was open for business; on the second night after it was full. Then she built a tiny cabin near her "hotel," and proceeded to keep house for herself, sleeping daytimes and working nights.

"Say, she's coinin' money!" the Scrap Iron Kid advised his companions some time later. "She's got fifty bunks at a dollar apiece, and each one is full of Swede. You'd ought 'o drift by in business hours—it sounds like a sawmill."

"If she's getting the money so fast, why don't you grab her, Kid?" inquired Llewellyn.

"You cut that out!" snapped the former speaker. "There ain't nobody going to grab that dame. I'd croak any guy that made a crack at her, and that goes!"

Seeing a familiar light smoldering in the Kid's eyes, Llewellyn desisted from further comment, but he made up his mind to become acquainted with June at once.

Now, while he succeeded, it was in quite an unexpected manner; for before he had formulated any plan Thomasville came to him with a proposition that drove all thoughts of women from his mind and sent them both out to the mines shortly after dark, each provided with a six-shooter and a bandana handkerchief with eyeholes cut in it.

Jane had returned to her cabin the following morning, and was preparing for bed, when she heard a faltering footstep outside. She glanced down at her money-sack filled with the night's receipts of her hotel, then at the fastenings of her door. She knew that law was but a pretense and order a mockery in the camp, but the next instant she slid back the bolt and let in a flood of morning sunlight.

There, leaning against her wall, was a tall, dark young man whose head was hanging loosely and rolling from side to side. His hair beneath the gray Stetson was wet, his boots were sodden and muddy, one arm was thrust limply into the front of his coat as if paralyzed. She saw that the sleeve was caked with blood. Even as she spoke he sagged forward and slid down at her feet.

She was not the sort to run for help, and so, taking him under the armpits, she had him on her bed and his sleeve cut away before he opened his eyes. It was but an instant's work to heat a basin of water; then she fell to bathing the wound.

When she drew forth the shreds of cloth that had been taken into the flesh by the bullet, the man's face grew ghastly and she heard his teeth grind, but he made no other sound.

"That hurt, didn't it?" she smiled at him, and he tried to smile back. "How did it happen?" she queried.

"Accident."

"You have come a long way?"

He nodded.

"Why didn't you ask for help?"

"It—wasn't worth while."

She looked at him wonderingly, admiring his gameness; then was surprised to hear him say:

"So you're June!"

"Yes."

He closed his eyes and lay still while she poured some brandy for him; then he said:

"Please don't bother. I must be going."

"Not till you've eaten something." She laid a soft, cool palm upon his forehead when he endeavored to rise, and he dropped back again, watching her curiously.

He had barely finished eating when another footstep sounded outside and a heavy knock followed.

"Hey, June!" called a voice. "Are you up?"

It was Jim Devlin, the marshal, and the girl rose, only to stop at the look she saw in the wounded man's face. His dark eyes had widened; desperation haunted them.

"What is it, Mr. Devlin?" she answered.

"Have you seen anything of a wounded man within the last half-hour?"

She flashed another glance at her guest, to find him staring at her defiantly, but there was no appeal in his face. "What in the world do you mean?"

"There was a hold-up at Anvil Creek, and some shooting. We're pretty sure one of the gang was hit, but he got away. Pete, the waterman, says he saw a sick-looking fellow crossing the tundra in this direction. I thought you might have noticed him."

Again June's eyes flew back to the pale face of the stranger. He had risen now and, seeing the frank inquiry in her gaze, he shrugged his shoulders and turned his good hand palm upward as if in surrender, whereupon she answered the marshal:

"I'm sorry you can't come in, Mr. Devlin; but I'm just going to bed."

"Oh, that's all right. I'll take a look through your bunk-house. Sorry to disturb you."

When the footsteps had died away the stranger moistened his lips and asked, "Why did you do that?"

"I don't know. You are brave, and brave men aren't bad. Besides, I couldn't bear to send any person out of God's sunshine into the dark. You see, I don't believe in prisons."

When Llewellyn told the other Wag-boys of June's part in his escape his story was met with exclamations that would have pleased her to hear, but the Scrap Iron Kid broke in to say, menacingly:

"Look here, George, don't aim to take no advantage of what she done for you when you was hurt, or I'll tip her off!"

"Aw, rats!" cried Llewellyn, furiously. "What do you take me for?" Then, staring coldly at the Kid, he said, "And it won't do her any good to have you hanging around, either."

June's action toward Llewellyn, and her mode of life, gained the admiration and respect of the Wag-boys, and although they avoided her carefully, they watched over her from a distance. Nor was it long before they found a means of serving her, although she did not hear of it for many months.

The Dummy came home one night to inform his partners that Sammy Sternberg, who owned the Miners' Rest, was boasting of his conquest of June, whereupon Sammy was notified by Llewellyn, acting as a committee of one, that his lies must cease. Sammy got a little drunk a few nights later and boasted again, with the result that the Scrap Iron Kid, who was playing blackjack, promptly floored him with a clout of his .45, and the Swede who was standing near by kicked the prostrate Sternberg in the most conspicuous part of his green-and-purple waistcoat, thereby loosening a rib.

It was not long before the sporting element of

the camp learned to treat June with the highest
courtesy, and, since she had been adopted in a
measure by the Wag-boys, she became known as
the Wag-lady.

Meanwhile June was prospering. The homeless
men who patronized her place began to intrust
their gold-sacks to her care; so she went to Harry
Hope, the P. C. agent, and bought a safe in which
to deposit her lodgers' valuables. Frequently
thereafter she sat guard all night over considerable
sums of money while the owners snored peacefully
in the big back room.

When winter closed down June began to see
more and more of Harry Hope. And she began to
like him, too; for he was the sort to win women's
hearts, being big and boyish and full of merriment.
He had spent several years in the Northland, and
its winds had blown from him many of the city-
born traits, leaving him unaffected, impulsive,
and hearty. While the frontier takes away some
evil qualities it also takes some good ones, and
Harry Hope was not by any means a saint. As
the nights grew longer he gained the habit of
dropping in to talk with June on his way up-town.
One evening he paused before leaving and asked:

"Can you take care of something for me,
June?"

"Of course," she answered.

He flung a leather wallet into her lap, laughing.
"You're the banker for the community; so lock
that up overnight, if you please."

"Oh-h!" she gasped. "There are thousands of dollars! I'd rather not."

"Come! you must! I didn't get it in time to put it in the company's safe, and if I carry it around somebody will frisk me."

"Where are you going?"

"Down to Sternberg's. I'm going to outguess his faro - dealer. This is my lucky night, you know."

Realizing full well the lawlessness of the camp, June felt a bit nervous as she laid the money away. In the course of the evening, however, she gradually lost her fears.

Some time after midnight, when the big front room of the bunk-house was empty, the outside door opened, admitting a billow of frost out of which emerged two men. They were strangers to June, and when she asked them if they wished beds they said "No." They backed up to the stove and began staring at their surroundings curiously.

It had never been June's practice to forbid any man the comfort of her coal-burner, even though he lacked the price for a bed, but, remembering the money in her safe, she sharply ordered these two out.

Neither man stirred. They blinked at her in a manner that sent little spasms of nervousness up her spine.

"I tell you it's too late—you can't stay!"

"That's too bad," said one of them. He

crossed toward the desk behind which she sat, at which she softly closed the heavy safe door. It gave out a metallic click, however, which caused the fellow's eyes to gleam.

"That safe ain't locked, eh?" he inquired.

"Yes, it is," she lied.

He smiled as if to put her at her ease, but it was an evil leer and set her heart to pounding violently. She was tempted to cry out and arouse her lodgers, but merely flung back the fellow's glance defiantly.

The stranger ran his eye over the place and then said, "I guess we'll set awhile." Drawing a chair up beside the door, he motioned to his partner to do the same. They tilted back at their ease, and June fancied they were listening intently. For a half-hour, an hour, they sat there, following her every movement, now and then exchanging a word in a tone too low for her to hear.

She was well-nigh hysterical with the strain of waiting, when she saw both men lower the front legs of their chairs and rise together. The next instant the door swung violently yet noiselessly inward and a masked man with a gun in his hand leaped out of the night. Another man was at his heels, and they covered her simultaneously. Then a most amazing thing occurred.

June's mysterious visitors pounced upon them from behind, there was a brief, breathless struggle, and the next instant all four swept out into the snow amid a tangle of arms and legs. Followed the sounds of a furious scuffle, of heavy blows, curses and groans, then a voice:

"Beat it now or we'll croak the two of you! And peddle the word that no rough stuff goes here. Do you get that?" There was the impact of a boot planted against flesh, and the next instant June's deliverers had re-entered and closed the door.

One of them was sucking a wound in the fleshy part of his hand where a falling revolver hammer had punched him, but he inquired in a thoroughly business-like tone, "Got a little hot water, June?"

June emerged weakly from behind her desk. "W-what does it all—mean?"

"Oh, it's all right. They won't trouble you no more."

"They came to—rob me, and you knew it—"

"Sure! Harry Hope got full and told about leaving eight thousand dollars with you; so we beat 'em to it."

"But why didn't you say so? You frightened me."

"We wasn't sure they'd try it, and we didn't like to work you up."

"Please—who are you?"

"Us? Why, we're Wag-boys! Llewellyn's our pal. I'm Charley Fitzhugh; they call me the Dummy. And this is Thomasville."

Thomasville nodded and mumbled greetings without removing his thumb from his mouth, whereupon June began to express her gratitude.

But thanks threw the Wag-boys into confusion,
it seemed, and they quickly bade her an embarrassed good night.

Now that they had removed the weight of
obligation that had rested upon them, the Wags
became more neighborly. Llewellyn and the
Scrap Iron Kid called to explain that the Dummy
and Thomasville had broken all rules of friendship by "hogging the spotlight" and to express
their own regret at having been absent during the
attempted hold-up.

June was eating her midnight lunch when they
came, and after they had left Llewellyn said:

"She didn't have any butter, Kid. Notice it?"

"Sure. Butter's peluk. Rothstein cornered
the supply, and he's holding it for a raise."

"Where does he keep it?"

"In that big tent back of his store, along with
his other stuff."

Now, the Wag-boys did nothing by halves.
About dusk the following day the Rothstein
watchman was accosted by a stranger who had
just muched in from the creek. The two gos-
siped for a moment. Then, as the stranger made
off, he slipped and fell, injuring himself so painfully that the watchman was forced to help him
down to Kelly's drug-store. Upon returning from
this labor of charity the watchman discovered, to
his amazement and horror, that during his absence
two men had entered the tent by means of a six-
foot slit in the rear wall. They had brought a

sled with them, moreover, and had made off with about five hundred dollars' worth of Rothstein's heart's blood, labeled "Cold Brook Creamery, Extra Fine."

The next morning when June returned to her cabin she found a case of butter.

A few days later the Dummy discovered a string of ptarmigan hanging beside the rear door of a restaurant, and, desiring to offer June some delicate little attention, he returned after dark and removed them. As ptarmigan were selling at five dollars a brace, he was careful to protect the girl; he sat on the back steps of the restaurant and picked the birds thoroughly, scattering the feathers with a careless hand.

Scarcely a day passed that June did not receive something from the Wags, but of course she never dreamed that her gifts had been stolen. As for her admirers, it was the highest mark of their esteem thus to lay at her feet the choicest fruits of their precarious labors, and, although they were common thieves—nay, worse than that— they stole rather from love of excitement than for hope of gain, and the more fantastic the adventure the more it tickled their distorted fancies.

They were most amusing, and June grew to like them immensely. She began to mother them in the way that pleases all women. She ruled them like a family of wayward children, she settled their disputes, and they submitted with subdued, though extravagant, joy. She asked Llewel-

lyn once about that wound in his arm, but he lied
fluently, and she believed him, for she was not the
kind to credit evil of her friends.

Once they had received encouragement, they
fairly monopolized her. She was never safe from
interruption, for the Wag-boys never slept. They
came to her cabin singly and collectively at all
hours of day or night, during her absence or during
her presence, and they never failed to leave something behind them.

Reddy was a good cook, but he loathed a stove
as he loathed a policeman, yet he donned an apron,
and at the cost of much profanity and sweat pro-
duced a chocolate cake that would have done
credit to a New England housewife. Further-
more, it bore June's name in a beautiful scroll
surrounded by a chocolate wreath, and she found it
on her bed when she came home one morning.

Chancing to express a liking for oysters in the
hearing of the Scrap Iron Kid, she mysteriously received a whole case of them when she knew very
well that there were none in camp. Of course she
did not dream that in securing them the Kid had
put his person in deadly peril.

On returning from her duties at another time
she found that during the night the interior walls
of her cabin had been painted, and, although she
did not want them painted and although the
smell gave her a violent headache, she pretended
to be overcome with delight. In order to beautify
her little nest Reddy had burgled a store and

stolen all the paint there was of the particular
shade that pleased his eye.

Now, the Wag-boys pretended to be care-free
and happy as time went on. In reality they were
gnawed by a secret trouble—it was June's growing fondness for Harry Hope. After careful observation they decided that the P. C. agent would
not do at all; he was too wild. He had undeni-
ably lost his head and was gambling heavily,
tempted perhaps by the lax morality of the camp
and the license of good times.

It was the Dummy who finally proposed a means
of safeguarding June's wandering affections.

"Somebody's got to split her away from this
Hope," he declared. "It's up to us, and Llewellyn's the only one in her class."

The Scrap Iron Kid's face assumed an ugly
yellow cast as he inquired, quietly, "D'you mean
George is to marry her?"

"Hardly!" exploded the Dummy. "Just toll
her away."

"Why shouldn't I marry her?" Llewellyn demanded.

"I can think of five reasons," the Kid retorted.
He tapped his chest with his finger. "Here's one,
and there's the other four." He pointed to the
other Wag-boys. "D'you think we'd let you
marry her? Huh! I'd sooner marry her myself."

Llewellyn ended the discussion by stamping out
of the cabin, cursing his partners with violence.

Business of the P. C. Company took Harry

THE WAG-LADY

Hope to Council City in February; so the Wags felt easier—but only for a time. They found that June was grieving for him, and were plunged into deep despair until Scrap Iron came home with the explanation that the lovers had quarreled before parting. It was a signal for a celebration during which Reddy cooked wildly for a week, making puddings and pies and pastries, most of which were smuggled into June's cabin. Thomasville journeyed out to a certain roadhouse run by a Frenchman, and returned with a case of eggs wrapped up in a woolen comforter. It required the combined perjury of the other Wags to prove an alibi for him, but June had an omelet every morning thereafter.

Then, just as they were weaning her away, as they thought, the blow fell. It came with a crushing force that left them dumb and panic-stricken. June took pneumonia! The Scrap Iron Kid brought the first news of her illness, and he blubbered like a baby, while Dummy, the woman-hater, cursed like a man bereft.

"How d'you know it's pneumonia?" queried Thomasville.

"The doc says so. Me 'n' George dropped in with some beefsteaks we copped from the butcher, and found her in bed, coughing like the devil. She couldn't get up—pains in her boosum. We run' for Doc Whiting and — fellers, it's true! George is there now." The Kid swallowed bravely, and two tears rolled down his cheeks.

THE WAG-LADY

The Wag-boys broke out of their cabin on the run, then strung out down the snow-banked street toward June's cabin, where they found Dr. Whiting, very grave, and Llewellyn with his face blanched and his lips tight drawn. They tiptoed in and stood against the wall in a silent, stricken row, twirling their caps and trying to ease the pain in their throats.

The Wag-lady was indeed very ill. Her yellow hair was tumbled over her pillow and she was in great pain, but she smiled at them and made a feeble jest—which broke in her throat, for she was young and all alone and very badly frightened. It was too much for the Scrap Iron Kid, who stumbled out into the freezing night and fought with his misery. He tried to pray, but from long inexperience he fancied he made bad work of it.

An hour later they assembled and laid plans to weather the storm.

"She's worried about her hotel," Llewellyn announced. "If that was off her mind she'd have a better chance."

"Let's manage it for her," the Dummy offered. "I'll watch it to-night."

"An' who'll watch you?" queried the Kid.

"D'you reckon I'd run out on a pal like June?" stormed the Dummy, whereat Scrap Iron assured him he was positive that he would not, for the very good reason that he and Reddy would take care that no opportunity offered.

"You run the joint like you say, an' we'll look-

out her game for her; then to-morrow night the
other three can do it. We'll take turn an' turn
about, an' them that's off shift will nurse her.
I've been thinkin' now—if only we knowed something about women folks—"

"I been married once or twice, if that's any
good," Thomasville ventured to confess; whereupon he was elected head nurse by virtue of his
experience, and accordingly they went to work.

Dr. Whiting had promised to secure a woman to
care for the sick girl, but women were scarce that
winter and he was only partly successful, so the
greater portion of the responsibility fell upon the
Wags. He also spoke of removing June to the
excuse for a hospital, but they would not hear to
this. And so the battle for her life began.

It was a battle, too, for she grew rapidly worse
and soon was delirious, babbling of strange things
which tore at the hearts of the Wag-boys. Day
after day, night after night, she lay racked and
tortured, fighting the brave fight of youth, and
through it all the six thieves tended her. They
were ever at her side, coming and going like the
wraiths of her distorted fancy, and while three of
them divided the day into watches the other three
ran the bunk-house, keeping strict account of every penny taken in. They O. K.'d one another's
books, and it would have fared badly indeed with
any one of them had he allowed the least dis-
crepancy to appear in his reckoning.

It was a strange scene, this, a sick and friendless girl mothered by a gang of crooks. When June's condition improved they rejoiced with a deep ferocity that was pitiful; when it grew worse they went about hushed and terror-stricken. Through it all she called incessantly for Harry Hope, and it was Llewellyn who finally volunteered to go to Council City and fetch him—an offer that showed the others he was game.

But before the weather had settled sufficiently to allow it, Hope came. He arrived one night in a blinding smother which whined down over the treeless wastes, driving men indoors before its fury. Hearing of June's illness, he had taken the trail within an hour, fighting his way for a hundred trackless miles through a blizzard that daunted even a Wag-boy, and he showed the marks of battle. His face was bitten deeply by the cold, his dogs were dying in the harness, and it was evident that he had not slept for many hours. He whimpered like a child when Llewellyn met him at June's door; then he heard her wearily babbling his name, as she had done these many, many days, and he went in, kneeling beside her with his frozen breath still caked upon his parka hood.

Llewellyn stood by and heard him tenderly calling to the wandering girl, saw the peace that came into her face as something told her he was near; then the Wag-boy who had once been a gentleman came forward and gave Hope his hand, and thanked him for his coming.

June began to mend after that, and it was not

long before Whiting said she might recover if she had proper food. She would, however, need nourishment—milk; but there was only one cow in camp, and other sick people, and not sufficient milk to go round. The Wag-boys lumped their bank-rolls and offered to buy the animal from its owner, but he refused. So they stole the cow and all her fodder.

Now it is no difficult matter to steal a cow, even in a mining-camp in the dead of winter, but it is not nearly so easy for a cow to remain stolen under such conditions, and the Wags were hard put to prevent discovery. It would have been far easier, they realized, to steal a two-story brick house or a printing-office, and then, too, not one of them knew how to secure the milk even after they had gained the cow's consent. They made various experiments, however, one of which resulted in Reddy's having the breath rammed out of him, and another causing Thomasville to adopt crutches for a day or so. But eventually June got her milk, a gallon of it daily. Every night or two the cow had to be moved, every day they gagged her to muffle her voice. Then, when discovery was imminent, they made terms of surrender, exacting twenty-five per cent. of the gross output as the consideration for her return.

They breathed much easier when the cow was off their hands.

Spring was in sight when June became strong enough to take up her duties, and she was sur-

prised to find her hotel running as usual, also a
flour-sack full of currency beneath her bed, together with a set of books showing her receipts. It
was signed by Llewellyn and witnessed by the other
Wags. There was no record of disbursements.

One day Whiting advised her to get out in the
air, and the Scrap Iron Kid volunteered to take
her for a dog ride.

"I didn't know you had a team," she said.

"Who? Me? Sure! I got as good a team as
ever you see," he declared, and when she accepted
his invitation he proceeded to get his dogs together
in a startling manner. He tied a soup-bone on a
string and walked the back streets; then, when
he beheld a likely-looking husky, he dragged the
bone behind him, enticing the animal by degrees
to the Wag-boys' cabin, where he promptly tied
it up. He repeated the performance seven times.
The matter of harness and sled was but a detail;
so June enjoyed a ride that put pink roses into her
cheeks and gave the Scrap Iron Kid a feeling of
pure, exalted joy such as he had never felt in all his
adventurous career.

The day she walked over to the Wag house un-
assisted was one of such wild rejoicing that she
was forced to tell them shyly of her own happiness,
a happiness so new that as yet she could scarcely
credit it. She was to be Mrs. Harry Hope, and
asked them to wish her joy.

Llewellyn made a speech that evoked the admiration of them all, even to the Kid, who was

miserably jealous, and June went home with her heart very warm and tender toward these six adventurers who had been so true to her.

It was to be expected that Hope would share in his sweetheart's extravagant gladness, for he loved her deeply, with all the force of his big, strong nature, yet he acted strangely as time went on. Now he was sad and worried, again he seemed tortured by a lurking disquietude of spirit. This alarmed the Wag-lady, and she set out to find the secret of his trouble.

The ice was breaking when he made a clean breast of it, and when he had finished June felt that her heart was breaking also. It was the commonplace story of a young man tempted beyond his strength. Hope's popularity had made him a host of friends, while his generosity had made "no" a difficult answer. He had plunged into excesses during the early winter; gambled wildly, not to win, but for the fun of it. He had lost company money, trusting to his ability to make it good from his own pocket when the time came. The time was coming, and his pockets were empty. Spring was here, the first boats would arrive any day, and with them would come the P. C. men to audit his accounts. It was possible to cover it up, to be sure, but he scorned to falsify his books.

"I should have stayed in Council City," he said, "but when I heard you were—sick—" He buried his brown face in his hands.

THE WAG-LADY

The girl's lips were white as she asked, "How much is it?"

"Nearly twenty thousand."

She shook her head hopelessly. "I haven't nearly that much, Harry, but perhaps they would let us pay off the balance as we are able."

"June!" he cried. "I wouldn't let you! I'll go to jail first! I—I suppose you won't want to marry me, now that you know?"

"I love you more than twenty thousand dollars' worth," she replied. "We'll face it out together."

"If only I had time I could pay it back and they'd never know, for I have property that will sell, once the season opens."

"Then you must take time."

"I can't. Sternberg will tell."

"What has Sternberg to do with it?"

"I lost the money in his place—his books will show. He suspects, even now, and he's talking about it. He doesn't like me, you know, since he heard of our engagement."

The days fled swiftly by; the hills thrust their scarred sides up through the melting snow; the open sea showed black beyond the rim of anchor ice. As nature awoke and blossomed, June faded and shrank until she was no more than the ghost of her former self. Then one day smoke was reported upon the horizon, and the town became a bedlam; for the door of the frozen North was creaking on its hinges, and just beyond lay the good, glad world of men and things.

June could stand it no longer; so she told her sorrow to Llewellyn, who had half guessed it, anyhow, and he in turn retold it to his fellow-Wags.

The Scrap Iron Kid was for killing Hope at once, and argued that it was by far the simplest way out of June's trouble, carrying with it also an agreeable element of retribution. Hope had hurt the Wag-lady, therefore the least atonement he could offer was his blood. But Dummy, the foxy old alibi man of the outfit, said:

"I've got a better scheme. Hope wants to do the right thing, and June 'll make him if she has a chance. The company will get its coin, she'll get her square guy, an' nobody 'll be hurt, provided he has time to swing himself. The ace in the hole is Sammy Sternberg; he's got the books. Now what's the answer?"

"Steal the books!" chorused the Wags; and Dummy smiled.

"Why, sure."

"You can't stick up no saloon full of roughnecks and sleepers," said Scrap Iron. "Sammy caches his books in the safe when he's off shift, and we can't blow the safe, 'cause the joint never closes."

But the Dummy only grinned, for this was the sort of job he liked, and then he proceeded to make known his plan.

Those were terrible hours for June. She prayed with all the earnestness of her earnest being that her lover might be spared; repeatedly she strained her tear-filled eyes to the southward. As for Hope, he had tasted the consequences of his guilt, and his face grew lined and haggard with the strain of waiting. He could have met the future with some show of resignation had it not been for the knowledge of his sweetheart's suffering; but as the hours passed and that thin black line of soot still hung upon the horizon, he thought he would go mad.

On the second day a steamer showed, hull down, having wormed her way through the floes, and Nome marched out upon the shore ice in a body.

June and Harry went with the others, hand in hand, and the man walked as if he were marching to the gallows. It was not the P. C. steamer, after all; it was the whaler *Jeanie*. The fleet was in the offing, however, so she reported, and would be in within another twenty-four hours, if the pack kept drifting.

Hope ground his teeth, and muttered: Poor little June! I wish it were over for your sake!" and she nodded wearily.

But as they neared the shore again they heard rumors of strange doings in their absence. There had been a daring daylight hold-up at the Miners' Rest. Six masked men had taken advantage of the exodus to enter and clean out the place at the point of the gun, and now Sammy Sternberg was poisoning the air with his complaints.

Details came flying faster as they trudged up into Front Street, and Doc Whiting paused to say:

"That's the nerviest thing yet, eh, Harry?"

"Was anybody hurt?"

"No damage done except to Sammy's feelings."

"They surely didn't get much money?"

"Oh, no! Their total clean-up wasn't a hundred dollars; but they lugged off Sammy's books."

June felt herself falling, and grasped weakly at her lover's arm, for she saw it all. "Come!" she said, and dragged him up to her own cabin, then on to the Wag-boys' door. They were all there, sprawled about and smoking.

"You did this!" she said, shakingly. "You did it for me!"

"Did what?" they asked in chorus, looking at her blankly.

"Oh, we know," said Harry Hope. "You've given me a chance—and I'll make good!" His own voice sounded strange in his ears.

There was an instant's awkward pause, and then the Scrap Iron Kid said, simply, "You'd better!" and the others nodded.

Llewellyn spoke up, saying, "Reddy is our regular chef; but I'd like to have you see me cook a goose." Then he drew from his inside pocket what seemed to be a leaf torn from a ledger, and, unfolding it, he struck a match, then lighted it.

"I suppose I ought to be a man and face the music," Hope managed to stutter, "but I'm going to cheat the ends of justice for June's sake. I'm much obliged to you."

162

THE WAG-LADY

When they had gone off, hand in hand, the Scrap
Iron Kid nodded approvingly to George, saying,
"That was sure some cookin' you did, pal."

And Llewellyn answered, "Yes, I cooked your
goose and mine, but she'll be happy, anyhow."

"MAN PROPOSES—"

"MAN PROPOSES—"

THE STORY OF A MAN WHO WANTED TO DIE

I

THERE were seventeen policies in all and they aggregated an even million dollars. It thrilled Butler Murray to note his own name neatly typed upon the outside of each. Those papers possessed a remarkable fascination for him, not only because they meant the settlement of his debt to Muriel, but because his life, instead of being the wholly useless thing he had come to regard it, was really, by virtue of those documents, a valuable asset upon which he could realize at once.

One million dollars was a great deal of money, even to Butler Murray, and yet it was so easy! Why, it was even easier to make that amount than it had been to spend it! Although the former process might not prove so amusing, it at least offered a degree of interest wholly lacking in the latter.

When DeVoe entered, Murray greeted him

warmly. "I'm glad I caught you, Henry. They told me you've been out West somewhere."

"Yes, I'm promoting, you know—mines!" DeVoe flung off his fur coat and settled into an easy-chair.

"Getting along all right?"

"No. My friends either know too little about mines or too much about me. I've a good proposition, though, and if I could ever get started, I'd clean up a million."

"It's not so hard to make a million dollars."

"How the deuce do you know? You've never had to try. By the way, why are you living here at the club? Where is Mrs. Murray?"

"She is at the farm with the children. We have —separated."

"*No!* Jove! I'm sorry. What does it mean —the road to Reno?"

"I hardly think she will divorce me, on account of the publicity; although she ought to."

"Woman scrape, I suppose."

"No, nothing like that. I've spent all her money."

DeVoe opened his eyes in amazement. "Oh, see here now, you couldn't spend it *all!* Why, she had even more than you!"

"It's all gone—hers and mine."

"Good *Lord!*"

"Yes. I was always extravagant, but I've been speculating lately. I thought I'd get a sensation either way the market went, but I was disappointed. I dare say I have exhausted my capabilities for excitement. It's a long story, and I won't bore you with it, but, to be exact, all I have left is the town house and the farm and the place in Virginia. There isn't enough income, however, to keep any one of them going."

"Well, well! You *have* been stepping along. Why, it's inconceivable!" DeVoe stirred uneasily in his chair. The calm indifference of this broad-shouldered, immaculate fellow amazed him. He could not tell whether it was genuine or assumed, and in either event he was sorry he had come, for he did not like to hear tales of misfortune. Butler Murray, the millionaire, was a good man to know, but—

"I sent for you because I need—"

"See here, Butler," the younger man broke in, abruptly, "you know I can't lend. I'm borrowing myself. In fact, I was going to make a touch on you."

"Oh, I don't want your money; I want your help. I think, perhaps, I'm entitled to it, eh?"

Henry flushed a trifle. "You're welcome to that at all times, of course, and if I had a bankroll, I'd split it with you, but I just can't seem to get started."

"Suppose you had twenty-five thousand dollars, cash; would that help?"

"Help! Great Heavens! I could swing this deal; it would put me on my feet."

"I'm ready to pay you that amount for a few weeks of your time."

"Take a year of it, two years. Take my life's blood. Twenty-five thousand! You needn't tell me any more; just name the job and I'll take my chances of being caught. But—I say, you just told me you were broke."

"I received about fifty thousand dollars from the sale of the yacht, and I invested the money. I want you to help me realize on that investment." Murray tossed the packet of papers he had been examining into DeVoe's lap.

After scrutinizing them an instant, the latter looked up with a crooked, startled stare.

"Are you joking? Why, these are your insurance policies!"

"Exactly! There are seventeen of them, and they foot up one million dollars—the limit in every company. They begin to expire in March, and I don't intend to renew them. In fact, I couldn't if I wanted to."

The two men regarded each other silently for a moment, then the younger paled.

"Are you—crazy?" he gasped.

"The doctors didn't think so, and that is the heaviest life insurance carried by any man in America, with a few exceptions. Do you think they would have passed me if I'd been wrong up here?" He tapped his forehead. "I intend that you shall receive twenty-five thousand dollars of that money; the rest will go to Muriel."

DeVoe continued to stare alternately at the policies and his friend; then cleared his throat nervously.

"Let's talk plainly."

"By all means. You will need to know the truth, but you are the only one outside of myself who will. For some time I have felt the certainty that I am going to die."

"Nonsense! You are an ox."

"The more I've thought about it the more certain I've become, until now there isn't the slightest doubt in my mind. I took my last dollar and bought that insurance. Do you understand? I'm considered rich, therefore they allowed me to take out a million dollars."

"Sui— God Almighty, man!" DeVoe's sagging jaw snapped shut with a click.

"Let me finish; then you can decide whether I'm sane or crazy, and whether you want that twenty-five thousand dollars enough to help me. To begin with, I'll grant you that I'm young— —only forty—healthy and strong. But I'm broke, Henry. I don't believe you realize what that means to a chap who has had two fortunes handed to him and has squandered both. I'm really twice forty years of age, perhaps three times, for I have lived faster than most men. I have been everywhere, I have seen everything, I have done everything—except manual labor, and of course I don't know how to do that—I have had every sensation. I'm sated and old, and sometimes I'm a bit tired. I have no enthusiasm left, and I'm bankrupt. To make matters worse I have a wife who knows the truth and two lovely children who do not. Those kids believe I'm a hero and the greatest man in all the universe; in their eyes I'm a sort of demigod, but in a few years they'll learn that I have been a waster and thrown away not only my own fortune, but the million that belonged to them. That will be tough for all of us. Muriel knows how deeply I've wronged her, but she is too much a thoroughbred to make it public. Nevertheless, she detests me, and I detest myself; she may decide to divorce me. At any rate, I have wrecked whatever home life I used to have, for I'll never be able to support her, even if I sell the three places. I'll be known as a failure; I'll be ridiculed by the world. On the other hand, if I should die before next March she would be rich again." Murray's eyes rested upon the package of policies. "Perhaps time would soften her memory of me. The youngsters would have what they're entitled to, and they would always think of me as a grand, good, handsome parent who was taken off in his prime." He smiled whimsically at this. "That is worth something to a fellow, isn't it? I don't want them to be disillusioned, Henry; I don't want to endure their pity and toleration. I don't want to be in their way and hear them say, 'Hush! Here comes poor old father!' Do you understand?"

"To a certain extent. Then you really intend—to kill yourself?" DeVoe glanced about the cozy room as if to assure himself that he was not dreaming.

"Decidedly not. That insurance wouldn't be payable if—it was suicide. I intend to die from natural causes—before the first of March."

"What do you want me to do?"

"Very little; keep me company, answer questions about my illness, perhaps; attend to a few things after I'm gone. You might even have to prove that I didn't take my own life. Do you agree?"

"Whew! That's a cold-blooded proposition. Are you really in earnest?"

"It took nearly my last dollar to buy that insurance. I will execute a promissory note to you for twenty-five thousand dollars, payable one year from date. Borrowed money, understand? The executors will see that it is paid. Is that satisfactory?"

"But you say you can't kill yourself and yet—Good Lord! How calmly we're discussing this thing! What makes you think you'll die of natural causes within the next three months?"

"I shall see that I do. Oh, I've thought it all out. I've studied poisons, but there is the danger of discovery when one uses them. They'll do to fall back upon if necessary, but there is a better way which is quite as certain, reasonably quick, and utterly above suspicion."

"What is it?" questioned DeVoe, interéstedly.

"Pneumonia! I had a touch of it once, and I know. They nearly lost me. It takes us big, robust fellows off with particular ease and expedition. You and I will take a hunting trip; it is winter; I will suffer some unexpected exposure; you'll do what you can to save me, but medical attention will come too late. It won't take two weeks altogether."

"If you're looking for pneumonia I know the place. When I left, ten days ago, men were dying like flies. You won't need to go hunting it; it will come hunting you."

"Out West somewhere, eh?"

"The Nevada desert. That's where I'm mining."

"Deserts are usually hot."

DeVoe shivered. "Not this one, at this season. It's a hell of a country, Butler; five thousand feet elevation, biting winds, blizzards, and all that. You just can't keep warm. But the danger is in the Poganip."

"The what?"

"The Poganip; what they call 'the Breath of Death' out there. It's a sort of frozen fog peculiar to that locality."

"Then you accept my offer?"

Again DeVoe hesitated. "Are you really going to do it? Well then, yes. If I don't take your money, I suppose you'll employ somebody else."

"Good! We'll leave to-morrow."

"MAN PROPOSES—"

"Can you get your affairs in shape by then?"

"I don't want them in shape. Don't you understand?"

"I see." After a moment the younger man continued, "It's all very well for us to plan this way—but I'm not sure we'll succeed in our enterprise."

"Why not, pray?"

"Well, I dare say I'm a good deal of a rotter—I must be to go into a thing like this—but I have a superstitious streak in me. Possibly it's reverence; at any rate I believe there is a Power outside of ourselves which appoints the hour of our coming and the hour of our going. I'm not so sure you can pull this off until that Power says so."

Murray laughed. "Nonsense! What is to prevent my shooting myself at this moment, if I want to?"

"Nothing, if you want to—but you don't want to. Why don't you want to? Because that Power hasn't named this as your time. I don't make myself very clear."

"I think I see what you're driving at, but you're wrong. We are masters of our own destinies; we make our lives as full or as empty as we choose. I have emptied mine of all it contained, and I don't consider that I am doing any one an injury in disposing of what belongs alone to me. Now we'll complete the details."

The speaker drew a blank note from his desk and filled it in.

"MAN PROPOSES—"

It was with a very natural feeling of interest that Butler Murray watched the desert unfold before his car window a few days later as his train made its way southward from the main line and into the Bad Lands of the Nevada gold-fields. There was snow everywhere; not enough for warmth, but enough to chill the landscape with a gray, forbidding aspect. It lay, loose-piled and shifting, behind naked rocks, or streamed over the knife-edge ridges, swirling and settling in the gullies like filmy winding-sheets. All the world up here was barren, burned out, and cold, like his own life; it was a fitting place in which to end an existence which had proven such a mockery and failure.

Goldfield was a conglomerate city in the hectic stage of its growth. Rough, uncouth, primitive, it lay cradled in the lap of inhospitable hills upon the denuded slopes of which derricks towered like gallows. The whole naked country spoke of death and desolation.

A bitter wind laden with driving particles of sleet met the travelers as they stepped off the train.

DeVoe's headquarters consisted of a typical mining-camp shack in the heart of the town, containing a bare little office and two sleeping-rooms, the hindermost of which gave egress to a yard banked in snow and flanked by other frame buildings.

Murray selected the coldest apartment and unpacked his belongings, the most precious of which was a folding morocco case containing three photographs—one of Muriel and one each of the boy and the girl.

Then followed a week of careful preparation. Together the two men made frequent excursions to various mining properties. Murray mingled with the heterogeneous crowd of brokers, promoters, gamblers, and mine-owners; he took options on claims and made elaborate plans to develop them; he was interviewed by reporters from the local papers; articles were printed telling of his proposed activities. When he had laid a secure foundation, he announced to DeVoe that the time had come.

It appeared that the latter had by no means exaggerated the dangers of this climate, for men were really dying in such numbers as to create almost a panic, the hospitals were overcrowded, and Murray had been repeatedly warned to take the strictest care of himself if he wished to preserve his health. The altitude combined with the cold and wet and the lack of accommodations was to blame, it seemed, and accounted for the high mortality rate. Doctors assured him that once a man was stricken with pneumonia in this climate there was little chance of saving him.

That evening he let the fire die out of the stove in his room, then went next door to a little Turkish-bath establishment, and proceeded to sweat for an hour. Instead of drying himself off he flung a greatcoat over his streaming shoulders, slipped into boots and trousers, then stepped across the snow-packed yard to his own quarters, where he found DeVoe bundled up to the chin and waiting. His brief passage across the open snow had chilled him, for the wind was cruel, but he blew out the light in his chamber, flung off his over-coat, then, standing in the open door, drank the frost-burdened air into his overheated lungs.

"God! You're half naked!" chattered the on-looker. "You'll freeze."

The moisture upon Murray's body dried slowly. He began to shake in every muscle, but he con-tinued his long, deep breaths—breaths that con-gealed his lungs. He became cramped and stiff. He suffered terribly. He felt constricting bands about his chest; darting, numbing pains ran through him. He could not tell how long he con-tinued thus, but eventually the sheer agony of it drove him back. He closed the door and crept into bed, the clammy cotton sheets of which were warm against his flesh. Through rattling teeth he bade good night to his friend, saying:

"D-don't mind—anything I do or—say during the night."

DeVoe lost no time in seeking his own warm room, where Murray heard him stamping and threshing his arms to revive his circulation.

There could be but one outcome to such a suicidal action, the frozen man reflected. Stronger fellows than he were dying daily from half such exposure. Why, already he could feel his lungs congesting. Although the agony was almost unendurable, he forced himself to lie still, then traced the course of his blood as it gradually crept through his veins. Eventually he fell asleep, tortured, but satisfied.

Henry found him slumbering peacefully late the next morning, and when he arose he felt better and stronger than he had for years.

"Jove! I'm hungry," he said as he dressed himself.

"I expected to find you mighty sick," his friend exclaimed, wonderingly. "I slept cold all night."

"It seems I didn't catch it that time. I must be stronger than I thought."

He ate a hearty breakfast, and, although he tramped the hills all day in the snow and cold, watching himself carefully for signs of approaching illness, he was disappointed to discover none whatever. At bedtime he repeated his performance of the night before, but with the same result. When he awoke on the second morning, however, he found the desert town wrapped in the dark folds of a fog that chilled his marrow and clung to his clothing in little beads. It was a strange phenomenon, for the air was bitterly cold and yet saturated with moisture; mountain and valley were hidden in an impalpable dust that was neither fog nor snow, but a freezing, uncomfortable combination of both.

DeVoe hugged the fire all day, saying to his

guest: "You'll have to do the trick alone, Butler; it's too deucedly unpleasant sitting there in the cold every night. I'll get sick."

"It's not very agreeable for me, either, and the least you can do is to keep me company. That's the agreement, you know."

After some argument DeVoe acceded, saying, "Oh, if you want me to hold your hand while you freeze I suppose I'll have to do it, although I can't see the use of it."

That night when Murray had regained his cheerless room after taking his Turkish bath he drank a goblet of raw whisky, then flung wide the door, and, standing upon the sill, half nude and gleaming with perspiration, inhaled the deadly Poganip. When the fiery liquor had driven the last drop of his hot blood to the surface he seized a bottle of alcohol and, upending it, drenched his body. If he had suffered previously, he now endured supreme agony. As the alcohol evaporated upon his naked skin it fairly froze the blood he had forced up from his heart's cavities. He groaned with the pain of it. Again he felt as if his body were coating with ice; his lungs contracted with that agonizing grip.

"This is too c-cold for me," DeVoe chattered, finally. "I'm going to beat it."

As Butler Murray cowered and shook in his bed an hour later he decided that his third and final effort had succeeded, for not only did he plainly feel the effects of that terrible ordeal, but by every law of nature and hygiene he was doomed. He had drunk the whisky to increase the peripheral circulation of his body to the highest point, then by the use of the alcohol had reduced his temperature to a frightful extent and driven his blood back, frozen and sluggish. That was inevitably suicidal, as the least knowledge of medicine would show; it could not be otherwise. He was very glad, too, for this suffering was more than he had bargained for.

He awoke in the morning feeling none the worse for his action. He did not even have a cold.

DeVoe's amazement at this miracle was mingled with annoyance which he showed by complaining: "See here, Butler, are you kidding? You might at least have a little consideration for my feelings; this suspense is awful."

"My dear fellow, I'm doing all I can." Murray filled his chest, then pressed it gingerly with his palm. There was not a trace of soreness; his muscles lacked even a twinge of rheumatism.

That day he had another window cut in the wall of his room, immediately over his bed, and, after exposing himself as usual upon retiring, left it open and slept in the draught. Finding that this had no effect, he undertook to sleep without covers, but the bitter weather would not permit, so he purchased drugs and, after returning from his Turkish bath, swallowed a sleeping - potion. When he could no longer keep his eyes open he lay down nude and dripping where the frigid wind sucked over him. Some time, somehow, before morning he must have covered himself, for he awoke between the sheets as usual. With the exception of a thick feeling in his head, however, which quickly wore off, he possessed no ill effects.

Day after day, night after night, he exposed himself with a deliberate methodical recklessness that seemed fatal; time after time his good constitution threw off the assault. DeVoe declared querulously that his friend looked even better than when they had arrived, and the scales showed he had put on five pounds of weight. The affair assumed an ironical, grisly sort of humor which amused Murray. But it was maddening to DeVoe.

One howling, stormy afternoon the former bundled his accessory into warm clothes and took him for a long walk. Leaving the town behind them, they plowed up through the snow to the summit of a near-by mountain where the gale raged past in all its violence. Henry was cursing the cold and grumbling at his idiocy in coming along, and, when he had regained his breath, growled:

"Understand, Butler, this ends it for me. I never agreed to kill *myself*. Hereafter you can make your Alpine trips alone. I've had a cold now for a week."

Murray laughed good-naturedly. "Remember, if I fail I can't pay you."

"For Heaven's sake, then, get it over with! I need that money and—I have nerves."

"MAN PROPOSES—"

The former speaker opened his coat and DeVoe saw that he had left the house with no protection whatever beneath it, except trousers and foot-gear. His body was wet from the climb, but he exposed it openly to the storm until he was blue with cold, while the younger man stamped about, threshing his arms and lamenting his own dis-comfort.

That night Murray repeated his Turkish bath, swallowed his usual narcotic, and lay down upon his draughty couch to be awakened some time after midnight by a cry of "Fire." He noted dully that a vivid glare was flickering through his open windows, and saw that the roofs adjoining were silhouetted against a redly glowing sky; he heard a great clamor of shouting voices, gun-shots, bells, running feet, so arose and dressed him-self. Instead of donning his regular clothing, how-ever, he drew on a pair of trousers, thrust his bare feet into rubber boots, then buttoned a rubber coat over his naked shoulders.

When he undertook to rouse DeVoe, Henry re-fused to get up, murmuring sourly beneath his blankets:

"It's too cold and I've just fallen asleep—been tossing around for hours."

"Very well. If it should spread in this direction I'll come back and help get the things out."

The blizzard of the previous day had increased in violence, and as Murray stepped out into it the cold sank through his thin garb and cut him to the bone. His rain-coat was almost no protection, the rubber boots upon his bare feet froze quickly, but he smiled with a grim, distorted sense of satisfaction as he decided that here perhaps was his long-awaited opportunity.

A winter fire in a desert mining-camp is a serious calamity. Water is scarce at all times, and at this particular season Goldfield was even drier than usual. Volunteers had already joined the insufficient fire department, but the blaze was gaining headway in spite of all. The wind played devilish pranks, serving not only to fan the conflagration, but to deaden human hands and reduce human bodies to helpless, clumsy things.

Butler Murray plunged into the fight with an abandon that won admiration even in this chaos. He had no fear, he courted danger, he led where others shrank from following. In and out of the flames he went, now blistered by the heat, now numbed by the wintry gale. His body became drenched with sweat, only to be caked in ice from the spray a moment later. Icicles clung to his brows, his boots filled with water. It was he who laid the dynamite, it was he who set it off and razed the buildings in the path of the conflagration, checking the swift march of destruction. Although he labored like a giant, taking insane risks at every opportunity, his life seemed charmed, and dawn found him uninjured, although staggering from weakness. Women brought him hot coffee and sandwiches, then when the fire was under control he returned to his quarters, half naked, as he had set out. It had been one long battle against the blind god luck and he had emerged unscathed. And yet he had not lost, for no human body could withstand a strain like this; his previous exposures had been as nothing compared with what he had undergone these many hours. If this did not bring pneumonia nothing could.

As he lurched up the frozen street men cheered him and something warm awoke in his heart, but when he stumbled into DeVoe's room he found that young man still in bed, his cheeks flushed and feverish. Henry was coughing and groaning; he complained of pains in his head and chest.

An hour later a doctor pronounced it pneumonia, and when the patient grew rapidly worse he was moved to the wretched excuse for a hospital. Murray snatched a few hours' sleep that night as he sat by his friend's bedside and the next day found him as fit as ever. But in spite of every attention DeVoe's fever mounted, his lungs began to fill, and on the second night he died.

The suddenness of this tragedy stunned Butler Murray and its mockery enraged him. He had promised DeVoe, toward the last, to take his body East, and now decided it was just as well to do so, for he had proven, to his own satisfaction at least, that he could not catch pneumonia, no matter how hard he tried. A few hours later, therefore, he was on the overland train bound for New York.

He had wasted a month of valuable time, but as
to relinquishing his purpose, the idea never occurred to him.

II

THE physical comfort of his club was most agreeable after his recent ordeal, but he enjoyed it only
a few days, then began to look about for a suitable
place in which to end his grim comedy. He
selected the spot with little delay—a sharp turn
in a hillside road that wound down from the
heights near Spuyten Duyvil—he had often passed
it in summer and knew the danger well. If his
automobile went over the edge, now that the
roads were icy, who could say it was not acci-
dental?

He did not advise Muriel of his return, fearing
to trust himself either to write or to telephone, but
spent much time in front of the morocco case with
its three photographs, longing desperately to see
her and the children.

When he felt that an auspicious time had arrived, he 'phoned his friend, Dr. Herkimer, and
invited himself to dinner. Herkimer was delighted, and a few evenings later the clubman
motored out toward Yonkers, where he was made
welcome and spent an agreeable evening.

"Where's your chauffeur?" the doctor inquired
as his guest drew on his fur coat and driving-
gloves, preparatory to leaving.

"MAN PROPOSES—"

"I let him go to-night. I thought I'd enjoy running the machine, for a change."

"The roads are bad; be careful you don't skid on the hills. I nearly went over to-day."

Murray promised to heed the warning, and a few moments later was gliding toward the city.

The beauty of this cold, sharp night was inspiriting; the moon was brilliant; the air was charged with life and vigor. It gave him a thrill to realize that he was sweeping to probable death; that nothing now could intervene to thwart him, and while, of course, there was the unpleasant possibility that a plunge over the declivity might do no more than maim him, he had studied the place carefully and intended to reduce that chance to a minimum by driving his car down the hill with sufficient velocity to hurl it far out over the edge. There were railroad tracks beneath; anything short of instant death would be miraculous.

As he came out upon the heights at last it occurred to him that he was behaving very well for a man about to die. His hand was steady, his heart was not greatly quickened, he was absolutely sane and healthy and full of the desire to live. A short distance from the crest he stopped his machine, then sat motionless for a few moments drinking in the beauty of the night and taking his farewell of Muriel. When he had arrived at peace with himself he fixed his wife's image in his mind, then, thrusting down the accelerator, let in the clutch. There was a jar, a jerk, a spasmodic shudder of the machinery; the motor went dead.

This unexpected interruption affected Murray oddly, until he realized that after stopping the car he had neglected to shift his gears to neutral. With an imprecation at his stupidity he clambered out and cranked the motor. When it failed to start he primed his carbureter and cranked again. It was an expensive, foreign-built machine, and one turn should have served to set it going, but, strangely enough, there was no explosion. For fifteen minutes he did everything his limited knowledge permitted, but the car remained stationary upon the crest of the hill, a stubborn, lifeless mass of metal.

Evidently that jerk had wrought havoc with some delicate adjustment, he reasoned, perhaps the wiring, but it was too dark to diagnose just where the trouble lay. It was cold, also, and his numb fingers refused to be of much assistance. He gave over his efforts finally, and stared about with a troubled look in his eyes. This was childish, utterly idiotic. He wanted to laugh, but instead he cursed, then cranked the motor viciously until the sweat stood out upon his forehead.

An hour later he was towed into town behind a rescue-car summoned by telephone from the nearest garage. As he left his machine to board a Subway train, the mechanic announced:

"Maybe it was a good thing you broke down

before you hit that hill, boss. There was a bad accident at the turn, to-day; the police are going to close the street till spring."

Murray was not superstitious, but, recalling his many failures at Goldfield, he decided he would make no further attempt to do away with himself by means of his motor-car. Now that this particular road was closed to traffic, he knew of no other place so favorable to his project, and, inasmuch as the time was growing short, to be only partially successful in his attempt would mean utter ruin. With no little regret, therefore, he made up his mind to fall back upon poison, which at least was certain, even though possessed of obvious drawbacks.

His experience with DeVoe had rendered him a bit cynical regarding the value of friendship, hence it was with no fear of a checkmate that he telephoned to Dr. Herkimer and made an appointment for that afternoon. When the doctor arrived at the club, Murray laid the matter before him in a concise, cold-blooded manner, and was relieved to hear him voice exactly the words DeVoe had used.

"What do you want me to do?"

"I want you to call here for me to-morrow morning. You will find me dead in my bed. I want you to examine me and call it heart failure or whatever you think best. Your word will be sufficient; there will be no suspicion, no further examination, at least, until the poison I intend to use will have had time to disappear or change its form."

"And why should I do this?" The doctor looked his friend over oddly.

"Here is one reason which I hope is sufficient." Murray held out a promissory note for the same amount as the one he had executed for DeVoe.

Herkimer took it, then, as he read the figures, his face paled. Crushing it in his palm, he rose, and in a voice harsh with fury unloosed a stream of profanity that surprised his hearer.

"You contemptible, short-bred loafer!" he concluded. "What do you take me for? What makes you think I'd do such a rotten thing as that?"

Murray smiled. "You'll *have* to, old man. It isn't pleasant, of course, but you won't allow Muriel and the children to lose that money. I like your spirit, but I shall kill myself just the same, and it's up to you to see that they are not ruined."

Again Herkimer became incoherent.

"Oh, swear as much as you please, I'm going to do it, nevertheless. I've made a wretched failure of everything else, but I intend to right one of my wrongs while there is time."

"Right! Wrong!" bellowed the physician. "Damn it, man! You're asking me to help you steal a million dollars. Does that occur to you?"

"The end justifies the means in this case. You're not rich. That twenty-five thousand—"

"MAN PROPOSES—"

Herkimer flung the paper at the speaker.

"Well, if you won't take my money, you'll have to help me, out of friendship. At nine o'clock to-morrow morning I shall be dead. Knowing the truth and all it means, you'll *have* to come. You—*can't—stay—away*."

"Oh, is that so?" the doctor mocked, furiously. "I'll show you whether I can or not." He jerked his watch from his pocket and consulted it. "There's a train for Boston in twenty minutes and I'm going to take it. I couldn't get back here in time even if I wanted to. Now, kill yourself and be damned to you." He seized his hat and rushed out of the room, slamming the door behind him.

A moment later Murray heard a taxi-cab whir noisily away from the club-house door.

Manifestly, there were more difficulties in the way of this enterprise than he had counted upon. Without the co-operation of some reliable physician the clubman dared not do away with himself in New York; coroners are curious, medical attention is too prompt, he was too well known, the very existence of that tremendous amount of life insurance would lead to investigation. He decided to go hunting, and he knew just the right place to go, too, he thought.

Several years before he had joined a gunning club which owned a vast expanse of rice-fields and marsh lands in North Carolina, and, knowing the place thoroughly, he concluded that it offered perfect facilities for such an action as he contemplated. Accordingly, he packed his guns, wired for a guide, and boarded a train for the South that very night. In his pocket he carried a vial containing twenty-five grains of powdered cocaine.

The club launch met him at Boonville, the nearest station, and during the twenty-mile trip down the Sound he learned all he wished to know. The shooting was well-nigh over; there were no other members at the club-house; he would have the place all to himself.

For several days he hunted diligently, taking pains to write numerous letters to his friends, and among others to Muriel. It was his first letter since their parting, and the strain of holding his pen within formal bounds was almost too much for him. It was a pity she would never understand his motives in doing this thing, he reflected. It was a pity he had never understood his own feelings before it was too late. Manlike, he had thrown away the only precious thing of his life while searching for counterfeit joys, and, manlike, he regretted his folly now that he had lost her.

That evening he informed his guide that he intended to hunt by himself on the following morning, and in answer to the old negro's warning assured him that he knew the channels well and was amply able to handle a canoe.

He rose early, forced himself to eat a substantial breakfast, for the sake of appearances, then set out in his Peterboro. The morning was

chilly and he had purposely donned a heavy
sweater, shell vest, leather coat, and hip-boots.
He paddled down the river for a mile or more,
then let his craft drift with the current. Far
away on one horizon was a dark, low-lying fringe of
pines marking the mainland; two miles to seaward sounded the slow rumble of the restless
Atlantic; on every hand were acres upon acres,
miles upon miles of waving marsh-grass inter-
laced with creeks and channels; nowhere was
there a sign of human life.

He took the little bottle from his pocket, reached
over the side and filled it with water. He replaced
the cork and shook the vial until the white pow-
der it contained was thoroughly dissolved. There
were twenty-five grains of it, eight fatal doses, and
he had seen that it was fresh. This time there
could be no question of failure, he reasoned. Nor
was there much chance of discovery, for after
that drug had remained in his body for a few
hours it would be exceedingly difficult of identifica-
tion, even at the hands of an expert toxicologist.
But there were no experts in this country, no
doctors at all, in fact, this side of Boonville, twenty
miles away.

He marveled at his coolness as he flung the cork
into the stream and raised the bottle to his lips.
His pulse was even, his mind was untroubled.
He drank the contents, filled the bottle and let it
sink; then rose to his feet, and, bearing his weight
upon the gunwale of his canoe, swamped it.

"MAN PROPOSES—"

Burdened as he was with shells and hunting-gear he sank, but the cold water sent him fighting and gasping to the surface again. The blind instinct of self-preservation mastered him and, being a powerful swimmer, he struck out. He had planned too well, however. His boots filled, his clothing became wet and he went down for a second time. Then commenced a senseless, terrible struggle, the more terrible because the man fought against his own determination. He rose slowly to the surface, but the shore was far away, the canoe, bottom up, was out of reach. He gasped wildly for breath as his face emerged, but instead of air he inhaled water into his lungs. He choked, horrible convulsions seized him, his limbs threshed, his ears roared, his chest was bursting. He rose and sank, rose and sank, enduring the agony of suffocation, all the time fighting with a strong man's desperation. After a time he seemed to hear shouting; something tugged and hauled at him; he discovered he could breathe again. His senses wavered, left him, returned; he saw faces bending above him. A moment later he heard his name spoken, then found himself awash in the bottom of a gamekeeper's batteau.

As in a dream he heard his rescuers explain that they had been out in search of poachers and had rounded the bend below in time to behold him struggling for his life. They were hurrying him back to the club-house now as fast as arms

and oars could propel them, and after he had
gained sufficient strength he sat up.

He strove to answer their excited questions, but
could not speak. A strange paralysis numbed his
vocal cords; he could not swallow; his tongue
was thick and unmanageable. This silence alarmed
the wardens, but Murray knew it to be nothing
more than a local anæsthesia due to the contact
of the cocaine. He became conscious of feeling
very wretched.

They helped him up to the club-house, and on
the way he caught glimpses of horrified black
faces. He saw the superintendent preparing to
send to Boonville for a doctor, but, knowing that
the launch had already left, calculated the time it
would take for a canoe to make the trip, and was
vaguely amused to realize that all this excitement
was useless. He experienced a feeling of triumph
at the knowledge that he had succeeded in spite
of all.

A short time later he was in bed, packed in
warm blankets and hot-water bags, but through
it all he maintained that distressing dumbness.
Despite the artificial heat his hands and feet
tingled, as if asleep, then became entirely numb,
and he reasoned that the cocaine had begun to
affect his circulation. He noted how the chill
crept upward slowly, showing that the drug was
working. On the mantel opposite he saw Muriel
smiling at him from the morocco case and realized
that she was very beautiful. After a time her

outlines became less distinct, which told him that
his optic nerve was becoming affected. Next
the contents of the room grew hazy. That was
quite as it should be.

He was much interested to note his heart
action, which by now had become very erratic.
Every pulsation that ran through him sounded
as plainly in his ears as a drum-beat. He noticed
that they were regular for a time, then gradually increased in speed until his heart raced
like a runaway motor, then ceased suddenly, began
again slowly, faintly, grew slower and fainter, until
with every flutter he thought, "This is the end!"

When this phenomenon had been repeated time
after time the sick man endeavored to assist the
poison's effect. At each feeble recovery of his
heart he held his breath and strained with all his
might, striving by every force of will to stop the
systolic action.

As he had often heard that men live again their
evil deeds in the hour of dissolution, and while he
had perhaps more than the average number of
sins upon his soul, he determined to die thinking
only of pleasant things, if possible. He recalled
his wedding-day, and pictured Muriel as she had
appeared that morning. How sweet and gentle
she had been, what a wonderful time it had
proved for him. They had sailed for the Mediter-
ranean on the following morning, landing at
Naples, where they had spent a week. From
there they had gone to Rome for three dreamlike

months and then to Nice and to Cairo, all the time in a lovers' paradise. From Egypt they had turned back to Morocco. Yes, Morocco, and how she had loved it there. Thence they had journeyed—where? To Spain, of course. Murray realized that his mind was working more slowly, which meant that the circulation to his brain was becoming sluggish. In a few moments he would be unable to think at all, it would be over— Muriel would be rich again. She was still young; she might marry some good man. From Spain they had gone by rail to—Paris? No, the Riviera— It was very difficult to think. In Germany, he remembered, they had taken an old castle for the— From Germany they had gone —gone. Yes. Muriel was—gone!

Murray awoke to find a trained nurse at his bedside. He was still in his room at the club, and after a time reasoned that the cocaine must be working very slowly. At the first words the nurse laid a hand upon his lips, saying:

"Don't speak, please. You have been very ill." Stepping to the door, she called some one, whereupon a man came quickly. Murray recognized him instantly as the famous Dr. Stormfield. They had met here three years previous and shot from the same blind.

"Hello, Murray!" the doctor began. "I'm glad you came around finally. You've given us the devil of a fight."

"MAN PROPOSES—"

"How long—have I been ill?" whispered the sick man.

"Two days; unconscious all the time. Lucky for you that I ran down for a little shooting and happened to be on the launch from Boonville the morning you upset. We picked up your messenger on his way to town, and I got here just in time. Now don't talk. You're not out of danger by any means." That evening the physician explained further: "You must have suffered a terrible shock in that cold water. I never saw a case quite like it. Your heart puzzled me; it behaved in the most extraordinary manner."

"You say I'm not out of danger?"

"Far from it. Your heart is nearly done for, and the slightest exertion might set you off. If you got up, if you raised yourself off the bed, you might—go out like that." Stormfield snapped his fingers.

"I suppose my wife has been notified?"

"Yes." The doctor looked at his patient curiously. "Would you like to have her come—"

"No, no!" A frightened look leaped into Murray's eyes. "That's not necessary, you know." After a time he said: "Leave me, please. I'm tired."

When the doctor had closed the door he lifted himself to his elbow, swung his feet out upon the floor and stood up; then, faint as he was, he began to stoop and raise himself, flexing his arms, meanwhile, as if performing a calisthenic exercise.

"MAN PROPOSES—"

He was possessed by the one idea, that he must succeed while there was still time.

The nurse found him face downward upon his bed and sounded a quick alarm. All that night Stormfield sat beside him, his eyes grave, his brow furrowed anxiously. At intervals a woman came to the door, then at a sign from the watcher disappeared noiselessly. Thereafter Murray was never left alone.

A day or two later he complained of this over-attention, saying that the nurse's constant presence annoyed him, but Stormfield paid no attention. After a time the physician startled him by inquiring, abruptly:

"See here, Murray, what did you take?"

"I don't understand."

"Yes, you do."

"Why— What makes you think I took anything?"

"Come, come! I'm a specialist; I have some intelligence."

There was a pause, then the sick man finally admitted, "I took twenty-five grains of cocaine."

"*Twenty-five grains!* God! It's incredible! . Eight grains is the largest dose on record. You're dreaming, or else the drug was stale."

"I was particular to see that it was fresh."

Stormfield paced the room, shaking his head and muttering. "I wouldn't dare report such a thing; I'd be called a faker, and yet—there are no hard-and-fast laws of medicine." He stopped and stared at his patient. "What the devil prompted you to do it—with such a wife?"

"That's just it," the latter cried, miserably. "Oh, you've done for her a great injury by saving me, Doctor. But I won't allow it. I—won't!"

"I see!" The doctor went to the door, where he motioned some one to enter.

A woman rose from her chair in the hall and came swiftly to the bedside. Her face showed the signs of a long and sleepless vigil, but her eyes were aflame with a hunger that held Butler Murray spellbound and amazed.

"*You!*" he said, weakly. "When did you come?"

"I have been here for days," she answered. "Did you think I could stay away?"

"My—Muriel." He held up his shaking arms, whereupon she knelt and took his tired head to her breast.

"I thought I was doing right," he confided, after he had told her everything, "but I see now that I was all wrong."

"God will name the day," she declared, simply, "and until He does no man can say 'I will.'"

"Are you quite sure you have acted wisely in showing me my folly? Remember we are poor. Even yet I might make you rich again, for there is time, and—I'm not worth this great sacrifice."

"Sacrifice? This is the day of our triumph, dear. When we had all those other riches we never knew contentment, love, or happiness. Now we can start again, with nothing but ourselves and our children. We won't have time to be unhappy. Are you willing to try with me?"

He stroked her soft hair lovingly and smiled up into her eyes. "DeVoe was right, there *is* a Power. I shall pray God every day to spare me, sweetheart, for now I want to live."

14

TOLD IN THE STORM

TOLD IN THE STORM

THE front room of the roadhouse was deserted save for the slumbering bartender,
back-tilted in a corner, his chin upon his chest,
and one other man who sat in the glare of a swing
lamp playing solitaire. It was, perhaps, three
hours after midnight. The last carouser had
turned in. There was no sound save the scream
of the black night and the cry of the salt wind.
At intervals only, when the storm lulled, there
came from the back room the sound of many men
asleep.

I stumbled out from the rear room, heavy-eyed,
half clad, and of a vicious temper, dressing in sour
silence beside the stove.

"Did they wake you up?" the card-player inquired.

"Yes."

"Me, too. I'd rather bunk in with a herd of
walrus in the mating season."

He was a long, slim man, with blue-black hair
and a gas-bleached face of startling pallor from
which glittered two wild and roving eyes that
flitted in and out of my visual line toward, to, and

past me with a baffling elusive glimmer like that of jet spangles. His hands were slender and bony and colorless, but while he talked they worked, each independently. They performed queer, wizard antics with the cards—one-handed cuts, rapid, fluttering shuffles and "frame-ups," after each pass leaving the pile of pasteboards as square-edged and even as before. While he observed me over his shoulder one hand wandered to some scattered poker-chips which clicked together beneath his touch into a solid-ivory column as if separately magnetized. He shuffled and dealt and cut the disks and made them do odd capers like the cards.

"I slept in a menagerie tent once," said he, "but these people have got it on the animals." He nodded toward the sleeping-quarters.

"The open life seems to make a Pan's pipe out of the human nose," said I, with disgust.

My indignation was intense and underlaid with a sullen fury at losing my rest. I seized the stranger and led him with me to the open door, saying, roughly, "Listen to that."

The room was large and low, dim-lighted and walled with tiers of canvas-bottomed "standees" three high. The floor was a litter of boots, the benches piled with garments. Every bed was full, and the place groaned with sounds of strangulation, asphyxiation, and other disagreeable demises. The bunks were peopled by tortured bodies, which seemed to cry of throttlings, garrotings, and sundry hideous punishments. My

nervous system, unable to stand it, had risen
a-quiver, then shrieked for mercy.

From the nearest sleeper came the most unhappy sounds. He snored at free-and-easy intervals with the voice of a whistling-buoy in a
ground swell—a handsome, resonant intake that
died away reluctantly, then changed to a loath-
some gurgle, as if he blew his breath through a
tube into a pot of thick liquid. Now and then
he smacked his lips and ground his teeth until the
gooseflesh arose on my neck.

"That's the fellow that drove me out," said my
new acquaintance as we went back to our seats
oeside the stove. "I had the berth below him.
I sleep light, anyhow, since I woke up one night
down on the Texas Panhandle and found a China-
man astraddle of my brisket with a butcher-
knife."

"That must have been nice," said I at random.
"What did you do?"

"I doubled up my legs and kicked him into the
camp-fire." The stranger was dealing the cards
again, this time into a fanlike, intricate solitaire
much affected by gamblers. "I tried the trick
again to-night, but I went wrong. I wanted to
stop the swan-song of the guy over my head, so I
lifted up my feet and put them where the canvas
sagged lowest. Then I stretched my legs like a
Jap juggler, but I fetched away my own bunk and
came down on the man below. I broke a snore
short off in him. He'll never get it out unless

he has it pulled. That was us you heard two hours ago."

I was too tired and sleepy to talk, for I had come down from the hills the previous afternoon to find the equinoxial raging, and as a result the roadhouse full from floor to ridge-pole with the motley crew that had sifted out from the interior. The coastwise craft were hugging the lee of the sandy islet, waiting for the blow to abate; telephone-wires were down, and Bering's waters had piled in from the south until they flooded the endless sloughs and tide flats behind Solomon City, destroyed the ferries, and cut us off both east and west, by land and by sea. It were better, I had thought, to wait on the coast for a day or so, watching for a chance to dodge to Nome, than to return to the mines, so I had lugged my war bag into Anderson's place and made formal demand for shelter.

The proprietor had apologized as he assigned me a bunk. "It's the best I've got," said he. "I've put you alongside of the stove, so if the boys snore too loud you can heave coal on 'em. Them big lumps is better than your boots."

I had tried both fuel and footgear fruitlessly, and when my outraged ears would not permit further slumber I had given up the attempt. Now, while the blue-haired man with insomnia dealt "Idiot's Delight" I sat vaguely fascinated by the play of his hands, half dozing under the drone of his voice.

TOLD IN THE STORM

The wind rioted without, whipping the sea spray across the sand-dunes until it rattled upon our walls like shot. Meanwhile my companion adventured aimlessly, his strange and vagrant fancies calling for no answer, his odd and morbid journeyings matching well with the whimpering night. His stories were without beginning, and they lacked any end. They commenced without reason, led through unfrequented paths, then closed for no cause. Through them ran no thread of relevancy. They were neither cogent nor cohesive. Their incidents took shape and tumbled forth irrelated and inconsequent. Wherefore I knew them for the truth, and found myself ere long wide-eyed and still, my brain as keen as ever nature made it.

The story of the dead Frenchman has seemed strained and gruesome to me since, but that night the storm made it real, and the stranger's unsmiling earnestness robbed it of offense. His words told me a tale of which he had no thought, and painted pictures quite apart from those he had in mind. His very frame of mind, his pagan superstition, his frank, irreverent philosophy, disclosed queer glimpses of this land where morals are of the fourth dimension, where life is a gamble and death a joke. Whether he really believed all he said or whether he made sport of me I do not know. It may be that the elfin voices of the storm roused in him an impulse to gratify his distorted sense of humor at my

expense—or at his own. He began somewhat as
follows:

"It's a good night for a dead man to walk."
Then, seeing the flicker in my eyes, he ran on:
"You don't think they can do it, eh? Well, I
didn't believe it neither, and I'm not sure I believe
it now, but I've seen queer things—queer things
—and I've only got one pair to draw to. Either
they happened as I saw them or I'm crazy." He
leaped at his story boldly.

"I'm pretty tired and hungry when I hit
Council City late one fall, for I'd upset my row-
boat, lost my outfit, and 'mushed' it one hundred
fifty miles. My whole digestive paraphernalia is
in a state of *innocuous desuetude*, if you know what
that is, because all I save from the wreck is a flour-
sack full of cigarette-papers and a package of
chocolate pills about the size of a match-head.
Each one of these pellets is warranted to contain
sufficient nourishment to last the Germany army
for one month. I read it on the label. They
may have had it in them; I don't know. I swallowed one every morning and then filled up on
reindeer moss till I felt like the leaping-pad in a
circus.

"Now, when I reach camp I find there ain't
any fresh grub to speak of. But I can't get away,
so I stick on until spring. See! In time we
begin to have scurvy something terrible. One
man out of every five cashes in. I'm living in a
cabin with a lot of Frenchmen and we bury seven

from this one shack—seven, that's all! It gets on my nerves finally. I don't like dead men. Now, the last two who fall sick is old man Manard and my pal, young Pete De Foe. Pete has a ten-dollar gold piece and Manard owns a dog. Inasmuch as they both knew that they can't weather it out till the break-up, Pete bets his ten dollars against the dog that he'll die before Manard. Well, this is something new in the sporting line, and we begin to string our bets pretty free. There ain't much excitement going on, so the boys visit the cabin every day, look over the entries, then go outside and make book. I open up a Paris mutuel. The old man is a seven-to-one favorite at the start because he had all the best of it on form, but the youngster puts up a grand race. For three weeks they seesaw back and forth. First one looks like a winner, then the other. It's as pretty running as I ever see. Then Pete lets out a wonderful burst of speed, 'zings' over the last quarter, noses out Manard at the wire, and brings home the money. He dies at 3 A.M. and wins by four hours. I cop eighty-four dollars, six pairs of suspenders, a keg of wire nails, and a frying-pan, which constitutes all the circulating medium of the camp. I'm the stakeholder for the late deceased also, so I find myself the administrator of Manard's dog and the ten dollars that Pete put up.

"Now, seeing that it had been a killing finish, we arrange for a double-barreled burial and a swell funeral. The ground is froze, of course, but we dig two holes through the gravel till we break a pick-point and decide to let it go at that. The 'Bare-headed' Kid is clergyman because he has a square-cut coat that buttons up the front to his chin. There ain't any Bible in camp, so he read some recipes out of a baking-powder cook-book, after which Deaf Mike tries to play 'Taps' on the cornet. But he's held the horn in his mit during the services, and, the temperature being forty degrees below freezo, when he wets his lips to play they stick to the mouthpiece and crab the hymn. As a whole, it is an enjoyable affair, however, and the best-conducted funeral of the winter. Everybody has a good time, though nothing rough.

"Now, I've been friendly to young Pete De Foe —him and I bunked together—and the next night he comes to me, saying that he can't rest. I see him as plain as I see you.

"'What's wrong?' says I. 'Are you cold?'

"'No. The ground is chilly, but it ain't that. Manard, the old hellion, won't let me sleep. He's doing a sand jig on my grave. He says I won that bet crooked and died ahead of time just to get his dog. He's sore on you, too.'

"'What's he sore on me for?' says I.

"'He says he's an old man, and he'd 'a' died first if you hadn't put in with me to double-cross him. He's laying for you,' says Pete.

"Well, I'm pretty sick myself, with a four months' diet of pea soup and oatmeal, and when

TOLD IN THE STORM

I wake up I think it's a dream. But the next night Pete is back again, complaining worse than ever. It seems the ghost of old man Manard is still buck-and-winging on Pete's coffin, and he begs me to come down and call the old reprobate off so that he can get some rest. He comes back the third night, the fourth, and the fifth, and by and by Manard himself comes up to the cabin and begins to abuse me. He says he wants his dog back, but naturally I can't give it to him. It gets so that I can't sleep at all. Finally, when Pete ain't sitting on my bunk Manard is calling me names and gritting his teeth at me. I begin to fall off in weight like a jockey in a sweat bath. It gets so I have to sit up all night in a chair and make the fellers prod me in the stomach with a stick whenever I doze off. I tell you, stranger, it was worse than horrible. I don't know how I made it through till spring.

"Well, in the early summer I get a letter from the steamboat agent at Nome saying Manard's people out in the States have slipped him some coin, with instructions to send the old man out so they can give him decent burial. He offers me one-fifty to bring him down to the coast. Now, this decent-burial talk makes me sore, for I staged the obsequies myself, and they were in perfect form. It was one of the tastiest funerals I ever mixed with. However, I'm broke, so I agree to deliver what is left of Manard at the mouth of the river, and the agent says he'll have a first-class coffin shipped down to the trader at Chinik, our landing. When I deliver Manard, ready for shipment, I get my hundred and fifty.

"I give you my word I ain't tickled pink with this undertaking. I'm not strong on body-snatching, and I have a hunch that the shade of old Manard is still hanging around somewhere. However, a bird in the hand is the noblest work of God, and I need that roll, so I make ready. It takes me half a day to get drunk enough to want to do the job, and when I get drunk enough to want to do it I'm so drunk I can't. Then I have to sober up and begin all over again. The minute I get sober enough to do the trick I realize I ain't drunk enough to stand the strain. I jockey that way for quite a spell till I finally strike an average, being considerable scared and reckless to the same extent.

"I remembered that we planted the old man in the left-hand grave, but when I get to the graveyard I can't recollect whether I stood at the foot or at the head of the hole during the services— a pint of that mining-camp hootch would box the compass for any man—so I think I'll make sure.

"I have brought along three tools—a pick, a shovel, and a bottle of rye. The ground is froze, so I use all of them. Naturally I can't afford to get the wrong Frenchman, so I pry up the lid of the first box I uncover and take a good rubber. Well, sir, it is a shock! Instead of rags and bones

like I'm expecting, there is old Manard in statuary
quo, so to speak. Froze? Maybe so. Anyhow,
he grins at me! That's what I said! He grins
at me, and I take it on the lam. Understand, I
have no intentions of running away—in fact, I
don't know I'm doing it until I fetch up back in
the saloon. It seems I just balanced my body on
my legs and they did all the work.

"Well, I'm pretty well rattled, so I blot up another pint of pain-killer, and finally the bartender
goes back with me and helps load Manard into
my Peterboro. I'm pretty wet by this time. We
get the box into the canoe all right, but it's too
big to fit under the seat, so we place the foot of it
on the bottom of the boat and rest the other end
on a paddle laid across the gunnels. This sort
of gives Manard the appearance of lounging back
on an incline. You see, when I ripped up the
boards to take a look I broke off a piece at a knot-
hole, and that allows him a chance to look out
with one eye. He seems to approve of the position, however, so I get in at the stern, facing
him, and ask if he's ready. He gives me the nod,
and I shove off. Just for company I take my
grave-digging tools along—that is, all but the
pick and the shovel. It was pretty near full
when I started, but I lose the cork and drink it
up for safety.

"I don't remember much about the first part
of the trip except that I get awful lonesome.
By and by I begin to sing:

"'Oh, the French are in the bay!' said the Shaun Van Vocht.
'The French are in the bay,' said the Shaun Van Vocht.
'The French are in the bay. They'll be here without delay.
'But their colors will decay,' said the Shaun Van Vocht."

"I've got a mean singing-voice when I'm sober, but when I'm kippered it's positively insulting. It makes my passenger sore, and he shows it. Now, I'm not saying that Manard wasn't as dead as a dried herring. He was past and gone, and he'd made his exit all right. He'd moved out, and his lease had expired. But I saw that box move. It shifted from side to side. I quit singing. My song-fountain ran dry. Says I to myself: 'I just neglected to lash you down, Mr. Manard; you didn't really turn over. It was the motion of the boat.' Then, just to make sure, I break forth into 'Johnny Crapaud,' keeping my eye on the right lens of the old man where it showed through the broken board. This time there ain't a doubt of it. He lurches, box and all, clean out of plumb and nearly capsizes me. His one lamp blazes. Yes, sir, blazes! I tries to get out of range of it, but it follers me like a search-light. I creeps forward to cover it up with my coat, but the old frog-eater leans to starboard so far that I have to balance on the port gunnel to keep from going over. We begin to spin in the current. Manard sees he has me buffaloed, and it pleases him. He wags his head at me and grins like he did when he came to me in my sleep.

"Well, sir, that eye enthralls me. It destroys

my chain of thought. I feel the chills stealing into my marrow, and that one hundred and fifty dollars looks mighty small and insignificant. By and by I begin to figure it out this way: says I, 'I've outrun him once to-day, and if I can get ashore I'll try it again.' But when I turn the canoe toward shore Manard heels over till we take water.

"'Lie still, you blame fool!' says I. 'If you feel that way about it I'll stay with the ship, of course.' I can see the corner of his mouth curl up at that, and he slides back into position. Then I know that he'll let me stick as long as I don't try to pull out and leave him flat. You really can't blame a corpse much under the circumstances. However, I can't swim, so I try to square myself. I make conversation of a polite and friendly nature, and the old boy settles back to enjoy himself.

"Well, this one-sided talkfest gets tiresome after a while. I run out of topics, so I tell him funny stories. Sometimes he likes them, and sometimes he 'most jumps out of the box. Sore? Say, when I pull a wheeze that he don't like he makes it known quick, and I sit clutching the gunnels, with my hair on end while he rocks the boat like a demon.

"When I get to the mouth of the river it's night. I find a stiff breeze blowing and the bay covered with whitecaps, so I try to convince Manard that we'd better camp. But I no more than suggest it till I have to bail for dear life. Seeing that he's dead set to keep going, I kiss myself good-by and paddle out across the bay. How we ever made it I don't know, but along about midnight we blow into Chinik, with me singing songs to my passenger and cracking 'Joe Millers' that came over in seventy-six. I'm still pretty drunk.

"'The trader tells me that the coffin hasn't come from Nome yet. But the steamer is due before morning, so I ask him to cache Manard somewhere and wake me up when the boat comes. Then I go to the hay. I'm tuckered out. It seems that the coaster comes in a few hours later, but the trader is dealing a stud game and tells the purser to dump his freight on the beach. They do as ordered, then pull out. About daylight the wind shifts, the tide rises and begins to wash the merchandise away. Two 'rough-necks' get busy saving their outfit, when what comes bobbing past on the waves but a handsome zink-lined casket—the one from Nome.

"'Hey, Bill, cop that box; it 'll make a swell bath-tub,' says one. So the other pulls up his rubber boots, wades out, and brings it in. The trader, hearing that his goods are in danger, adjourns the game long enough to see about it. He hurries down to the beach, looks over his stuff, then inquires:

"'Where's my coffin?'

"'You 'ain't got no more coffin than a rabbit,' says one of the miners.

"'Oh, yes, I have. That's it right there.'

"'I guess not. That's my coffin. I copped it on the high seas—flotsam and jetsam,' says the 'rough-neck.' 'What's more, I'm going to use it for a cupboard or a cozy corner. If you want it bad pay me fifty dollars salvage and it's yours.' Naturally the trader belched.

"'All right. If you don't want it I'll use it myself,' says the miner. 'It's the first one I ever had, and I like it fine. There's no telling when I'll get another.'

"'Said time ain't but a minute,' observes the trader, 'unless you gimme that freight.'

"There is some further dispute till the miner, being a quick-tempered party, reaches for his Gat. After the smoke clears away it is found that he has made an error of judgment, that the store-keeper is gifted as a prophet, and that the 'rough-neck' is ready for his coffin.

"Now, inasmuch as this had been a purely personal affair and the boys was anxious to re-open the stud game, they exonerated the trader from all blame complete, and he, being ever anxious to maintain a reputation for fair dealing and just to show that there ain't no animus behind his action, gives the coffin to the man who had claimed it. What's more, he helps to lay him out with his own hands. Naturally this is considered conduct handsome enough for any country. In an hour the man is buried and the poker game is open again. The trader apologizes to the boys for the delay, saying:

"'The box is mine, all right, and I'm sorry this play come up, but the late lamented was so set on having that piece of bric-à-brac that it seemed a shame not to give it to him.'"

At this point the narrator fell silent, much to my surprise, for throughout this weird recital I had sat spellbound, forgetful of the hour, the storm outside, and the snoring men in the bunk-room. When he had gone thus far he began with a bewildering change of topic.

"Did you ever hear how Dawson Sam cut the ears off a bank dealer?"

"Hold on!" said I. "What's the rest of this story? What became of Manard?"

"Oh, he's there yet, for all I know," said the stranger as he shuffled the cards. "His folks wouldn't send no more money, the steamboat agent at Nome had done his share, and the trader at Chinik said he wasn't responsible."

"And you? Didn't you get your one hundred and fifty dollars?"

"No. You see, it was a C. O. D. shipment. I wake up along about noon, put my head under the pump, and then look up the trader. He is still playing stud.

"'Where's my casket?' says I. 'I've got my dead man, but I don't collect on him till he's crated and f. o. b.' The trader has an ace in the hole and two kings in sight, so he says over his shoulder:

"'I'm sorry, old man, but while you was asleep a tenderfoot jumped your coffin.' Now, this Dawson Sam has a crooked bank dealer named—"

"I think I'll go back to bed," said I.

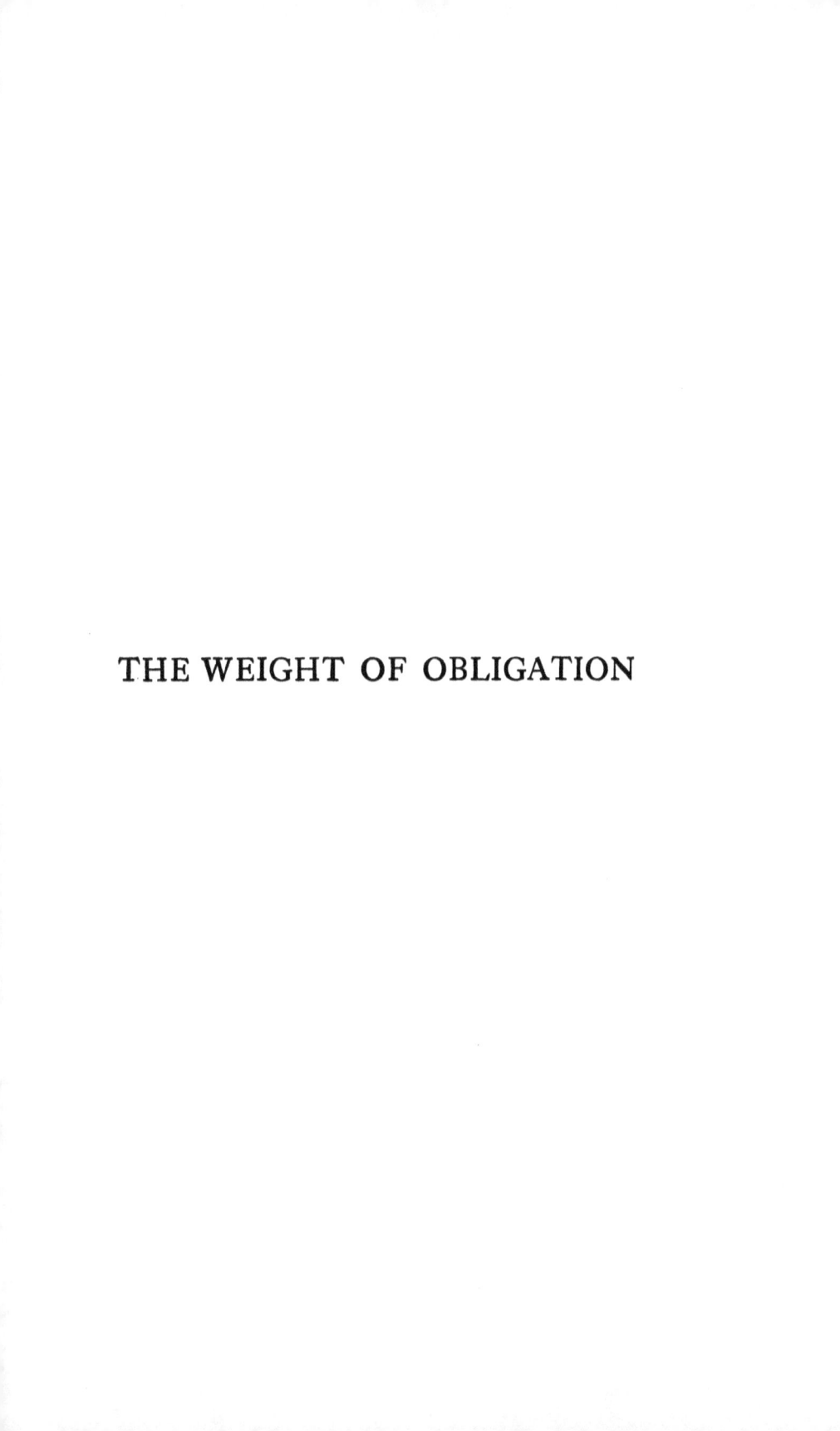

THE WEIGHT OF OBLIGATION

THE WEIGHT OF OBLIGATION

THIS is the story of a burden, the tale of a load
that irked a strong man's shoulders. To
those who do not know the North it may seem
strange, but to those who understand the humors
of men in solitude, and the extravagant vagaries
that steal in upon their minds, as fog drifts with
the night, it will not appear unusual. There are
spirits in the wilderness, eerie forces which play
pranks; some droll or whimsical, others grim.

Johnny Cantwell and Mortimer Grant were
partners, trail-mates, brothers in soul if not in
blood. The ebb and flood of frontier life had
brought them together, its hardships had united
them until they were as one. They were something of a mystery to each other, neither having
surrendered all his confidence, and because of this
they retained their mutual attraction. Had they
known each other fully, had they thoroughly
sounded each other's depths, they would have lost
interest, just like husbands and wives who give
themselves too freely and reserve nothing.

They had met by accident, but they remained
together by desire, and so satisfactory was the

union that not even the jealousy of women had come between them. There had been women, of course, just as there had been adventures of other sorts, but the love of the partners was larger and finer than anything else they had experienced. It was so true and fine and unselfish, in fact, that either would have smilingly relinquished the woman of his desires had the other wished to possess her. They were young, strong men, and the world was full of sweethearts, but where was there a partnership like theirs, they asked themselves.

The spirit of adventure bubbled merrily within them, too, and it led them into curious byways. It was this which sent them northward from the States in the dead of winter, on the heels of the Stony River strike; it was this which induced them to land at Katmai instead of Illiamna, whither their land journey should have commenced.

"There are two routes over the coast range," the captain of the *Dora* told them, "and only two. Illiamna Pass is low and easy, but the distance is longer than by way of Katmai. I can land you at either place."

"Katmai is pretty tough, isn't it?" Grant inquired.

"We've understood it's the worst pass in Alaska." Cantwell's eyes were eager.

"It's a heller! Nobody travels it except natives, and they don't like it. Now, Illiamna—"

THE WEIGHT OF OBLIGATION

"We'll try Katmai. Eh, Mort?"

"Sure! They don't come hard enough for us, Cap. We'll see if it's as bad as it's painted."

So, one gray January morning they were landed on a frozen beach, their outfit was flung ashore through the surf, the life-boat pulled away, and the *Dora* disappeared after a farewell toot of her whistle. Their last glimpse of her showed the captain waving good-by and the purser flapping a red table-cloth at them from the after-deck.

"Cheerful place, this," Grant remarked, as he noted the desolate surroundings of dune and hillside.

The beach itself was black and raw where the surf washed it, but elsewhere all was white, save for the thickets of alder and willow which protruded nakedly. The bay was little more than a hollow scooped out of the Alaskan range; along the foot-hills behind there was a belt of spruce and cottonwood and birch. It was a lonely and apparently unpeopled wilderness in which they had been set down.

"Seems good to be back in the North again, doesn't it?" said Cantwell, cheerily. "I'm tired of the booze, and the street-cars, and the dames, and all that civilized stuff. I'd rather be broke in Alaska—with you—than a banker's son, back home."

Soon a globular Russian half-breed, the Katmai trader, appeared among the dunes, and with him were some native villagers. That night the partners slept in a snug log cabin, the roof of which was chained down with old ships' cables. Petellin, the fat little trader, explained that roofs in Katmai had a way of sailing off to seaward when the wind blew. He listened to their plan of crossing the divide and nodded.

It could be done, of course, he agreed, but they were foolish to try it, when the Illiamna route was open. Still, now that they were here, he would find dogs for them, and a guide. The village hunters were out after meat, however, and until they returned the white men would need to wait in patience.

There followed several days of idleness, during which Cantwell and Grant amused themselves around the village, teasing the squaws, playing games with the boys, and flirting harmlessly with the girls, one of whom, in particular, was not unattractive. She was perhaps three-quarters Aleut, the other quarter being plain coquette, and, having been educated at the town of Kodiak, she knew the ways and the wiles of the white man.

Cantwell approached her, and she met his extravagant advances more than half-way. They were getting along nicely together when Grant, in a spirit of fun, entered the game and won her fickle smiles for himself. He joked his partner unmercifully, and Johnny accepted defeat gracefully, never giving the matter a second thought.

When the hunters returned, dogs were bought, a guide was hired, and, a week after landing, the friends were camped at timber-line awaiting a favorable moment for their dash across the range. Above them white hillsides rose in irregular leaps to the gash in the saw-toothed barrier which formed the pass; below them a short valley led down to Katmai and the sea. The day was bright, the air clear, nevertheless after the guide had stared up at the peaks for a time he shook his head, then re-entered the tent and lay down. The mountains were "smoking"; from their tops streamed a gossamer veil which the travelers knew to be drifting snow-clouds carried by the wind. It meant delay, but they were patient.

They were up and going on the following morning, however, with the Indian in the lead. There was no trail; the hills were steep; in places they were forced to unload the sled and hoist their outfit by means of ropes, and as they mounted higher the snow deepened. It lay like loose sand, only lighter; it shoved ahead of the sled in a feathery mass; the dogs wallowed in it and were unable to pull, hence the greater part of the work devolved upon the men. Once above the foot-hills and into the range proper, the going became more level, but the snow remained knee-deep.

The Indian broke trail stolidly; the partners strained at the sled, which hung back like a leaden thing. By afternoon the dogs had become disheartened and refused to heed the whip. There was neither fuel nor running water, and therefore the party did not pause for luncheon. The men were sweating profusely from their exertions and had long since become parched with thirst, but the dry snow was like chalk and scoured their throats.

Cantwell was the first to show the effects of his unusual exertions, for not only had he assumed a lion's share of the work, but the last few months of easy living had softened his muscles, and in consequence his vitality was quickly spent. His undergarments were drenched; he was fearfully dry inside; a terrible thirst seemed to penetrate his whole body; he was forced to rest frequently.

Grant eyed him with some concern, finally inquiring, "Feel bad, Johnny?"

Cantwell nodded. Their fatigue made both men economical of language.

"What's the matter?"

"Thirsty!" The former could barely speak.

"There won't be any water till we get across. You'll have to stand it."

They resumed their duties; the Indian "swish-swished" ahead, as if wading through a sea of swan's-down; the dogs followed listlessly; the partners leaned against the stubborn load.

A faint breath finally came out of the north, causing Grant and the guide to study the sky anxiously. Cantwell was too weary to heed the increasing cold. The snow on the slopes above began to move; here and there, on exposed ridges, it rose in clouds and puffs; the clean-cut outlines of the hills became obscured as by a fog; the languid wind bit cruelly.

THE WEIGHT OF OBLIGATION

After a time Johnny fell back upon the sled and exclaimed: "I'm—all in, Mort. Don't seem to have the—guts." He was pale, his eyes were tortured. He scooped a mitten full of snow and raised it to his lips, then spat it out, still dry.

"Here! Brace up!" In a panic of apprehension at this collapse Grant shook him; he had never known Johnny to fail like this. "Take a drink of booze; it'll do you good." He drew a bottle of brandy from one of the dunnage bags and Cantwell seized it avidly. It was wet; it would quench his thirst, he thought. Before Mort could check him he had drunk a third of the contents.

The effect was almost instantaneous, for Cantwell's stomach was empty and his tissues seemed to absorb the liquor like a dry sponge; his fatigue fell away, he became suddenly strong and vigorous again. But before he had gone a hundred yards the reaction followed. First his mind grew thick, then his limbs became unmanageable and his muscles flabby. He was drunk. Yet it was a strange and dangerous intoxication, against which he struggled desperately. He fought it for perhaps a quarter of a mile before it mastered him; then he gave up.

Both men knew that stimulants are never taken on the trail, but they had never stopped to reason why, and even now they did not attribute Johnny's breakdown to the brandy. After a while he stumbled and fell, then, the cool snow being grateful to his face, he sprawled there motionless until Mort dragged him to the sled. He stared at his partner in perplexity and laughed foolishly. The wind was increasing, darkness was near, they had not yet reached the Bering slope.

Something in the drunken man's face frightened Grant and, extracting a ship's biscuit from the grub-box, he said, hurriedly: "Here, Johnny. Get something under your belt, quick."

Cantwell obediently munched the hard cracker, but there was no moisture on his tongue; his throat was paralyzed; the crumbs crowded themselves from the corners of his lips. He tried with limber fingers to stuff them down, or to assist the muscular action of swallowing, but finally expelled them in a cloud. Mort drew the parka hood over his partner's head, for the wind cut like a scythe and the dogs were turning tail to it, digging holes in the snow for protection. The air about them was like yeast; the light was fading.

The Indian snow-shoed his way back, advising a quick camp until the storm abated, but to this suggestion Grant refused to listen, knowing only too well the peril of such a course. Nor did he dare take Johnny on the sled, since the fellow was half asleep already, but instead whipped up the dogs and urged his companion to follow as best he could.

When Cantwell fell, for a second time, he returned, dragged him forward, and tied his wrists firmly, yet loosely, to the load.

232

THE WEIGHT OF OBLIGATION

The storm was pouring over them now, like water out of a spout; it seared and blinded them; its touch was like that of a flame. Nevertheless they struggled on into the smother, making what headway they could. The Indian led, pulling at the end of a rope; Grant strained at the sled and hoarsely encouraged the dogs; Cantwell stumbled and lurched in the rear like an unwilling prisoner. When he fell his companion lifted him, then beat him, cursed him, tried in every way to rouse him from his lethargy.

After an interminable time they found they were descending and this gave them heart to plunge ahead more rapidly. The dogs began to trot as the sled overran them; they rushed blindly into gullies, fetching up at the bottom in a tangle, and Johnny followed in a nerveless, stupefied condition. He was dragged like a sack of flour, for his legs were limp and he lacked muscular control, but every dash, every fall, every quick descent drove the sluggish blood through his veins and cleared his brain momentarily. Such moments were fleeting, however; much of the time his mind was a blank, and it was only by a mechanical effort that he fought off unconsciousness.

He had vague memories of many beatings at Mort's hands, of the slippery clean-swept ice of a stream over which he limply skidded, of being carried into a tent where a candle flickered and a stove roared. Grant was holding something hot to his lips, and then—

THE WEIGHT OF OBLIGATION

It was morning. He was weak and sick; he felt as if he had awakened from a hideous dream. "I played out, didn't I?" he queried, wonderingly.

"You sure did," Grant laughed. "It was a tight squeak, old boy. I never thought I'd get you through."

"Played out! I—can't understand it." Cantwell prided himself on his strength and stamina, therefore the truth was unbelievable. He and Mort had long been partners, they had given and taken much at each other's hands, but this was something altogether different. Grant had saved his life, at risk of his own; the older man's endurance had been the greater and he had used it to good advantage. It embarrassed Johnny tremendously to realize that he had proven unequal to his share of the work, for he had never before experienced such an obligation. He apologized repeatedly during the few days he lay sick, and meanwhile Mort waited upon him like a mother.

Cantwell was relieved when at last they had abandoned camp, changed guides at the next village, and were on their way along the coast, for somehow he felt very sensitive about his collapse. He was, in fact, extremely ashamed of himself.

Once he had fully recovered he had no further trouble, but soon rounded into fit condition and showed no effects of his ordeal. Day after day he and Mort traveled through the solitudes, their isolation broken only by occasional glimpses of native villages, where they rested briefly and renewed their supply of dog-feed.

But although the younger man was now as well and strong as ever, he was uncomfortably conscious that his trail-mate regarded him as the weaker of the two and shielded him in many ways. Grant performed most of the unpleasant tasks, and occasionally cautioned Johnny about overdoing. This protective attitude at first amused, then offended Cantwell; it galled him until he was upon the point of voicing his resentment, but reflected that he had no right to object, for, judging by past performances, he had proved his inferiority. This uncomfortable realization forever arose to prevent open rebellion, but he asserted himself secretly by robbing Grant of his self-appointed tasks. He rose first in the mornings, he did the cooking, he lengthened his turns ahead of the dogs, he mended harness after the day's hike had ended. Of course the older man objected, and for a time they had a good-natured rivalry as to who should work and who should rest—only it was not quite so good-natured on Cantwell's part as he made it appear.

Mort broke out in friendly irritation one day: "Don't try to do everything, Johnny. Remember I'm no cripple."

"Humph! You proved that. I guess it's up to me to do your work."

THE WEIGHT OF OBLIGATION

"Oh, forget that day on the pass, can't you?"

Johnny grunted a second time, and from his tone it was evident that he would never forget, unpleasant though the memory remained. Sensing his sullen resentment, the other tried to rally him, but made a bad job of it. The humor of men in the open is not delicate; their wit and their words become coarsened in direct proportion as they revert to the primitive; it is one effect of the solitudes.

Grant spoke extravagantly, mockingly, of his own superiority in a way which ordinarily would have brought a smile to Cantwell's lips, but the latter did not smile. He taunted Johnny humorously on his lack of physical prowess, his lack of good looks and manly qualities—something which had never failed to result in a friendly exchange of badinage; he even teased him about his defeat with the Katmai girl.

Cantwell did respond finally, but afterward he found himself wondering if Mort could have been in earnest. He dismissed the thought with some impatience. But men on the trail have too much time for their thoughts; there is nothing in the monotonous routine of the day's work to distract them, so the partner who had played out dwelt more and more upon his debt and upon his friend's easy assumption of pre-eminence. The weight of obligation began to chafe him, lightly at first, but with ever-increasing discomfort. He began to think that Grant honestly considered himself the

236

better man, merely because chance had played into his hands.

It was silly, even childish, to dwell on the subject, he reflected, and yet he could not banish it from his mind. It was always before him, in one form or another. He felt the strength in his lean muscles, and sneered at the thought that Mort should be deceived. If it came to a physical test he felt sure he could break his slighter partner with his bare hands, and as for endurance—well, he was hungry for a chance to demonstrate it.

They talked little; men seldom converse in the wastes, for there is something about the silence of the wilderness which discourages speech. And no land is so grimly silent, so hushed and soundless, as the frozen North. For days they marched through desolation, without glimpse of human habitation, without sight of track or trail, without sound of a human voice to break the monotony. There was no game in the country, with the exception of an occasional bird or rabbit, nothing but the white hills, the fringe of alder-tops along the watercourses, and the thickets of gnarled, unhealthy spruce in the smothered valleys.

Their destination was a mysterious stream at the headwaters of the unmapped Kuskokwim, where rumor said there was gold, and whither they feared other men were hastening from the mining country far to the north.

Now it is a penalty of the White Country that men shall think of women. The open life brings health and vigor, strength and animal vitality, and these clamor for play. The cold of the still, clear days is no more biting than the fierce memories and appetites which charge through the brain at night. Passions intensify with imprisonment, recollections come to life, longings grow vivid and wild. Thoughts change to realities, the past creeps close, and dream figures are filled with blood and fire. One remembers pleasures and excesses, women's smiles, women's kisses, the invitation of outstretched arms. Wasted opportunities mock at one.

Cantwell began to brood upon the Katmai girl, for she was the last; her eyes were haunting and distance had worked its usual enchantment. He reflected that Mort had shouldered him aside and won her favor, then boasted of it. Johnny awoke one night with a dream of her, and lay quivering.

"Hell! She was only a squaw," he said, half aloud. "If I'd really tried—"

Grant lay beside him, snoring, the heat of their bodies intermingled. The waking man tried to compose himself, but his partner's stertorous breathing irritated him beyond measure; for a long time he remained motionless, staring into the gray blur of the tent-top. He had played out. He owed his life to the man who had cheated him of the Katmai girl, and that man knew it. He had become a weak, helpless thing, dependent upon another's strength, and that other now accepted his superiority as a matter of course. The obligation was insufferable, and—it was unjust. The North had played him a devilish trick, it had betrayed him, it had bound him to his benefactor with chains of gratitude which were irksome. Had they been real chains they could have galled him no more than at this moment.

As time passed the men spoke less frequently to each other. Grant joshed his mate roughly, once or twice, masking beneath an assumption of jocularity his own vague irritation at the change that had come over them. It was as if he had probed at an open wound with clumsy fingers.

Cantwell had by this time assumed most of those petty camp tasks which provoke tired trailers, those humdrum duties which are so trying to exhausted nerves, and of course they wore upon him as they wear upon every man. But, once he had taken them over, he began to resent Grant's easy relinquishment; it rankled him to realize how willingly the other allowed him to do the cooking, the dish-washing, the fire-building, the bed-making. Little monotonies of this kind form the hardest part of winter travel, they are the rocks upon which friendships founder and partnerships are wrecked. Out on the trail, nature equalizes the work to a great extent, and no man can shirk unduly, but in camp, inside the cramped confines of a tent pitched on boughs laid over the snow, it is very different. There one must busy himself while the other rests and keeps his legs out of the way if possible. One man sits on the bedding at the rear of the shelter, and shivers, while the other squats over a tantalizing fire of green wood, blistering his face and parboiling his limbs inside his sweaty clothing. Dishes must be passed, food divided, and it is poor food, poorly prepared at best. Sometimes men criticize and voice longings for better grub and better cooking. Remarks of this kind have been known to result in tragedies, bitter words and flaming curses—then, perhaps, wild actions, memories of which the later years can never erase.

It is but one prank of the wilderness, one grim manifestation of its silent forces.

Had Grant been unable to do his part Cantwell would have willingly accepted the added burden, but Mort was able, he was nimble and "handy," he was the better cook of the two; in fact, he was the better man in every way—or so he believed. Cantwell sneered at the last thought, and the memory of his debt was like bitter medicine.

His resentment—in reality nothing more than a phase of insanity begot of isolation and silence— could not help but communicate itself to his companion, and there resulted a mutual antagonism, which grew into a dislike, then festered into something more, something strange, reasonless, yet terribly vivid and amazingly potent for evil. Neither man ever mentioned it—their tongues were clenched between their teeth and they held themselves in check with harsh hands—but it was constantly in their minds, nevertheless. No man who has not suffered the manifold irritations of such an intimate association can appreciate the gnawing canker of animosity like this. It was dangerous because there was no relief from it: the two were bound together as by gyves; they shared each other's every action and every plan; they trod in each other's tracks, slept in the same bed, ate from the same plate. They were like prisoners ironed to the same staple.

Each fought the obsession in his own way, but it is hard to fight the impalpable, hence their sick fancies grew in spite of themselves. Their minds needed food to prey upon, but found none. Each began to criticize the other silently, to sneer at his weaknesses, to meditate derisively upon his peculiarities. After a time they no longer resisted the advance of these poisonous thoughts, but welcomed it.

On more than one occasion the embers of their wrath were upon the point of bursting into flame, but each realized that the first ill-considered word would serve to slip the leash from those demons that were straining to go free, and so managed to restrain himself.

The crisis came one crisp morning when a dog-team whirled around a bend in the river and a white man hailed them. He was the mail-carrier, on his way out from Nome, and he brought news of the "inside."

"Where are you boys bound for?" he inquired

when greetings were over and gossip of the trail
had passed.

"We're going to the Stony River strike," Grant
told him.

"Stony River? Up the Kuskokwim?"

"Yes!"

The mail-man laughed. "Can you beat that?
'Ain't you heard about Stony River?"

"No!"

"Why, it's a fake—no such place."

There was a silence; the partners avoided each
other's eyes.

"MacDonald, the fellow that started it, is on
his way to Dawson. There's a gang after him,
too, and if he's caught it 'll go hard with him.
He wrote the letters—to himself—and spread the
news just to raise a grub-stake. He cleaned up
big before they got onto him. He peddled his
tips for real money."

"Yes!" Grant spoke quietly. "Johnny bought
one. That's what brought us from Seattle. We
went out on the last boat and figured we'd come
in from this side before the break-up. So—fake!
By God!"

"Gee! You fellers bit good." The mail-
carrier shook his head. "Well! You'd better
keep going now; you'll get to Nome before the
season opens. Better take dog-fish from Bethel—
it's four bits a pound on the Yukon. Sorry I
didn't hit your camp last night; we'd 'a' had a
visit. Tell the gang that you saw me." He

THE WEIGHT OF OBLIGATION

shook hands ceremoniously, yelled at his panting
dogs, and went swiftly on his way, waving a mitten
on high as he vanished around the next bend.

The partners watched him go, then Grant
turned to Johnny, and repeated: "Fake! By
God! MacDonald stung you."

Cantwell's face went as white as the snow behind
him, his eyes blazed. "Why did you tell him I
bit?" he demanded, harshly.

"Hunh! *Didn't* you bite? Two thousand
miles afoot; three months of hell; for nothing.
That's biting some."

"*Well!*" The speaker's face was convulsed,
and Grant's flamed with an answering anger.
They glared at each other for a moment. "Don't
blame me. You fell for it, too."

"I—" Mort checked his rushing words.

"Yes, *you!* Now, what are you going to do
about it? Welch?"

"I'm going through to Nome." The sight of
his partner's rage had set Mort to shaking with a
furious desire to fly at his throat, but, fortunately,
he retained a spark of sanity.

"Then shut up, and quit chewing the rag.
You—talk too damned much."

Mort's eyes were bloodshot; they fell upon the
carbine under the sled lashings, and lingered
there, then wavered. He opened his lips, re-
considered, spoke softly to the team, then lifted
the heavy dog-whip and smote the malamutes
with all his strength.

THE WEIGHT OF OBLIGATION

The men resumed their journey without further
words, but each was cursing inwardly.

"So! I talk too much," Grant thought. The
accusation struck in his mind and he determined
to speak no more.

"He blames me," Cantwell reflected, bitterly.
"I'm in wrong again and he couldn't keep his
mouth shut. A hell of a partner, he is!"

All day they plodded on, neither trusting himself to speak. They ate their evening meal like
mutes; they avoided each other's eyes. Even
the guide noticed the change and looked on
curiously.

There were two robes and these the partners
shared nightly, but their hatred had grown so
during the past few hours that the thought of
lying side by side, limb to limb, was distasteful.
Yet neither dared suggest a division of the bedding, for that would have brought further words
and resulted in the crash which they longed for,
but feared. They stripped off their furs, and lay
down beside each other with the same repugnance
they would have felt had there been a serpent in
the couch.

This unending malevolent silence became terrible. The strain of it increased, for each man now
had something definite to cherish in the words and
the looks that had passed. They divided the
camp work with scrupulous nicety, each man
waited upon himself and asked no favors. The
knowledge of his debt forever chafed Cantwell;

THE WEIGHT OF OBLIGATION

Grant resented his companion's lack of gratitude.

Of course they spoke occasionally—it was beyond human endurance to remain entirely dumb—but they conversed in monosyllables, about trivial things, and their voices were throaty, as if the effort choked them. Meanwhile they continued to glow inwardly at a white heat.

Cantwell no longer felt the desire to merely match his strength against Grant's; the estrangement had become too wide for that; a physical victory would have been flat and tasteless; he craved some deeper satisfaction. He began to think of the ax—just how or when or why he never knew. It was a thin-bladed, polished thing of frosty steel, and the more he thought of it the stronger grew his impulse to rid himself once for all of that presence which exasperated him. It would be very easy, he reasoned; a sudden blow, with the weight of his shoulders behind it—he fancied he could feel the bit sink into Grant's flesh, cleaving bone and cartilages in its course— a slanting downward stroke, aimed at the neck where it joined the body, and he would be forever satisfied. It would be ridiculously simple. He practised in the gloom of evening as he felled spruce-trees for fire-wood; he guarded the ax religiously; it became a living thing which urged him on to violence. He saw it standing by the tent-fly when he closed his eyes to sleep; he dreamed of it; he sought it out with his eyes when he first awoke. He slid it loosely under the sled lashings every morning, thinking that its use could not long be delayed.

As for Grant, the carbine dwelt forever in his mind, and his fingers itched for it. He secretly slipped a cartridge into the chamber, and when an occasional ptarmigan offered itself for a target he saw the white spot on the breast of Johnny's reindeer parka, dancing ahead of the Lyman bead.

The solitude had done its work; the North had played its grim comedy to the final curtain, making sport of men's affections and turning love to rankling hate. But into the mind of each man crept a certain craftiness. Each longed to strike, but feared to face the consequences. It was lonesome, here among the white hills and the deathly silences, yet they reflected that it would be still more lonesome if they were left to keep step with nothing more substantial than a memory. They determined, therefore, to wait until civilization was nearer, meanwhile rehearsing the moment they knew was inevitable. Over and over in their thoughts each of them enacted the scene, ending it always with the picture of a prostrate man in a patch of trampled snow which grew crimson as the other gloated.

They paused at Bethel Mission long enough to load with dried salmon, then made the ninety-mile portage over lake and tundra to the Yukon. There they got their first touch of the "inside" world. They camped in a barabara where white men had slept a few nights before, and heard their own language spoken by native tongues. The time was growing short now, and they purposely dismissed their guide, knowing that the trail was plain from there on. When they hitched up, on the next morning, Cantwell placed the ax, bit down, between the tarpaulin and the sled rail, leaving the helve projecting where his hand could reach it. Grant thrust the barrel of the rifle beneath a lashing, with the butt close by the handle-bars, and it was loaded.

A mile from the village they were overtaken by an Indian and his squaw, traveling light behind hungry dogs. The natives attached themselves to the white men and hung stubbornly to their heels, taking advantage of their tracks. When night came they camped alongside, in the hope of food. They announced that they were bound for St. Michaels, and in spite of every effort to shake them off they remained close behind the partners until that point was reached.

At St. Michaels there were white men, practically the first Johnny and Mort had encountered since landing at Katmai, and for a day at least they were sane. But there were still three hundred miles to be traveled, three hundred miles of solitude and haunting thoughts. Just as they were about to start, Cantwell came upon Grant and the A. C. agent, and heard his name pronounced, also the word "Katmai." He noted that Mort fell silent at his approach, and instantly his anger blazed afresh. He decided that the latter had been telling the story of their experience on the pass and boasting of his service. So much the better, he thought, in a blind rage; that which he planned doing would appear all the more like an accident, for who would dream that a man could kill the person to whom he owed his life?

That night he waited for a chance.

They were camped in a dismal hut on a wind-swept shore; they were alone. But Grant was waiting also, it seemed. They lay down beside each other, ostensibly to sleep; their limbs touched; the warmth from their bodies inter-mingled, but they did not close their eyes.

They were up and away early, with Nome drawing rapidly nearer. They had skirted an ocean, foot by foot; Bering Sea lay behind them, now, and its northern shore swung westward to their goal. For two months they had lived in silent animosity, feeding on bitter food while their elbows rubbed.

Noon found them floundering through one of those unheralded storms which make coast travel so hazardous. The morning had turned off gray, the sky was of a leaden hue which blended perfectly with the snow underfoot, there was no horizon, it was impossible to see more than a few yards in any direction. The trail soon became obliterated and their eyes began to play tricks. For all they could distinguish, they might have been suspended in space; they seemed to be treading the measures of an endless dance in the center of a whirling cloud. Of course it was cold, for the wind off the open sea was damp, but they were not men to turn back.

They soon discovered that their difficulty lay not in facing the storm, but in holding to the trail. That narrow, two-foot causeway, packed by a winter's travel and frozen into a ribbon of ice by a winter's frosts, afforded their only avenue of progress, for the moment they left it the sled plowed into the loose snow, well-nigh disappearing and bringing the dogs to a standstill. It was the duty of the driver, in such case, to wallow forward, right the load if necessary, and lift it back into place. These mishaps were forever occurring, for it was impossible to distinguish the trail beneath its soft covering. However, if the driver's task was hard it was no more trying than that of the man ahead, who was compelled to feel out and explore the ridge of hardened snow and ice with his feet, after the fashion of a man walking a plank in the dark. Frequently he lunged into the drifts with one foot, or both; his glazed mukluk soles slid about, causing him to bestride the invisible hog-back, or again his legs crossed awkwardly, throwing him off his balance. At times he wandered away from the path entirely and had to search it out again. These exertions were very wearing and they were dangerous, also, for joints are easily dislocated, muscles twisted, and tendons strained.

THE WEIGHT OF OBLIGATION

Hour after hour the march continued, unrelieved by any change, unbroken by any speck or spot of color. The nerves of their eyes, wearied by constant near-sighted peering at the snow, began to jump so that vision became untrustworthy. Both travelers appreciated the necessity of clinging to the trail, for, once they lost it, they knew they might wander about indefinitely until they chanced to regain it or found their way to the shore, while always to seaward was the menace of open water, of air-holes, or cracks which might gape beneath their feet like jaws. Immersion in this temperature, no matter how brief, meant death.

The monotony of progress through this unreal, leaden world became almost unbearable. The repeated strainings and twistings they suffered in walking the slippery ridge reduced the men to weariness; their legs grew clumsy and their feet uncertain. Had they found a camping-place they would have stopped, but they dared not forsake the thin thread that linked them with safety to go and look for one, not knowing where the shore lay. In storms of this kind men have lain in their sleeping-bags for days within a stone's-throw of a road-house or village. Bodies have been found within a hundred yards of shelter after blizzards have abated.

Cantwell and Grant had no choice, therefore, except to bore into the welter of drifting flakes.

It was late in the afternoon when the latter met with an accident. Johnny, who had taken a spell at the rear, heard him cry out, saw him stagger, struggle to hold his footing, then sink into the snow. The dogs paused instantly, lay down, and began to strip the ice pellets from between their toes.

Cantwell spoke harshly, leaning upon the handle-bars: "Well! What's the idea?"

It was the longest sentence of the day.

"I've—hurt myself." Mort's voice was thin and strange; he raised himself to a sitting posture, and reached beneath his parka, then lay back weakly. He writhed, his face was twisted with pain. He continued to lie there, doubled into a knot of suffering. A groan was wrenched from between his teeth.

"Hurt? How?" Johnny inquired, dully.

It seemed very ridiculous to see that strong man kicking around in the snow.

"I've ripped something loose—here." Mort's palms were pressed in upon his groin, his fingers were clutching something. "Ruptured—I guess." He tried again to rise, but sank back. His cap had fallen off and his forehead glistened with sweat.

Cantwell went forward and lifted him. It was the first time in many days that their hands had touched, and the sensation affected him strangely. He struggled to repress a devilish mirth at the thought that Grant had played out—it amounted to that and nothing less; the trail had delivered him into his enemy's hands, his hour had struck.

THE WEIGHT OF OBLIGATION

Johnny determined to square the debt now, once for all, and wipe his own mind clean of that poison which corroded it. His muscles were strong, his brain clear, he had never felt his strength so irresistible as at this moment, while Mort, for all his boasted superiority, was nothing but a nerveless thing hanging limp against his breast. Providence had arranged it all. The younger man was impelled to give raucous voice to his glee, and yet— his helpless burden exerted an odd effect upon him.

He deposited his foe upon the sled and stared at the face he had not met for many days. He saw how white it was, how wet and cold, how weak and dazed, then as he looked he cursed inwardly, for the triumph of his moment was spoiled.

The ax was there, its polished bit showed like a piece of ice, its helve protruded handily, but there was no need of it now; his fingers were all the weapons Johnny needed; they were more than sufficient, in fact, for Mort was like a child.

Cantwell was a strong man, and, although the North had coarsened him, yet underneath the surface was a chivalrous regard for all things weak, and this the trail-madness had not affected. He had longed for this instant, but now that it had come he felt no enjoyment, since he could not harm a sick man and waged no war on cripples. Perhaps, when Mort had rested, they could settle their quarrel; this was as good a place as any.

THE WEIGHT OF OBLIGATION

The storm hid them, they would leave no traces, there could be no interruption.

But Mort did not rest. He could not walk; movement brought excruciating pain.

Finally Cantwell heard himself saying: "Better wrap up and lie still for a while. I'll get the dogs underway." His words amazed him dully. They were not at all what he had intended to say.

The injured man demurred, but the other insisted gruffly, then brought him his mittens and cap, slapping the snow out of them before rousing the team to motion. The load was very heavy now, the dogs had no footprints to guide them, and it required all of Cantwell's efforts to prevent capsizing. Night approached swiftly, the whirling snow particles continued to flow past upon the wind, shrouding the earth in an impenetrable pall.

The journey soon became a terrible ordeal, a slow, halting progress that led nowhere and was accomplished at the cost of tremendous exertion. Time after time Johnny broke trail, then returned and urged the huskies forward to the end of his tracks. When he lost the path he sought it out, laboriously hoisted the sledge back into place, and coaxed his four-footed helpers to renewed effort. He was drenched with perspiration, his inner garments were steaming, his outer ones were frozen into a coat of armor; when he paused he chilled rapidly. His vision was untrustworthy, also, and he felt snow-blindness coming on. Grant begged him more than once to unroll the bedding and

prepare to sleep out the storm; he even urged
Johnny to leave him and make a dash for his own
safety, but at this the younger man cursed and
told him to hold his tongue.

Night found the lone driver slipping, plunging,
lurching ahead of the dogs, or shoving at the
handle-bars and shouting at the dogs. Finally,
during a pause for rest he heard a sound which
roused him. Out of the gloom to the right came
the faint, complaining howl of a malamute; it was
answered by his own dogs, and the next moment
they had caught a scent which swerved them
shoreward and led them scrambling through the
drifts. Two hundred yards, and a steep bank
loomed above, up and over which they rushed,
with Cantwell yelling encouragement; then a
light showed, and they were in the lee of a low-
roofed hut.

A sick native, huddled over a Yukon stove,
made them welcome to his mean abode, explaining
that his wife and son had gone to Unalaklik for
supplies.

Johnny carried his partner to the one unoccupied
bunk and stripped his clothes from him. With
his own hands he rubbed the warmth back into
Mortimer's limbs, then swiftly prepared hot food,
and, holding him in the hollow of his aching arm,
fed him, a little at a time. He was like to drop
from exhaustion, but he made no complaint.
With one folded robe he made the hard boards
comfortable, then spread the other as a covering.

For himself he sat beside the fire and fought his weariness. When he dozed off and the cold awakened him, he renewed the fire; he heated beef-tea, and, rousing Mort, fed it to him with a teaspoon. All night long, at intervals, he tended the sick man, and Grant's eyes followed him with an expression that brought a fierce pain to Cantwell's throat.

"You're mighty good—after the rotten way I acted," the former whispered once.

And Johnny's big hand trembled so that he spilled the broth.

His voice was low and tender as he inquired, "Are you resting easier now?"

The other nodded.

"Maybe you're not hurt badly, after—all. God! That would be awful—" Cantwell choked, turned away, and, raising his arms against the log wall, buried his face in them.

The morning broke clear; Grant was sleeping. As Johnny stiffly mounted the creek bank with a bucket of water he heard a jingle of sleigh-bells and saw a sled with two white men swing in toward the cabin.

"Hello!" he called, then heard his own name pronounced.

"Johnny Cantwell, by all that's holy!"

The next moment he was shaking hands vigorously with two old friends from Nome.

"Martin and me are bound for Saint Mikes,"

one of them explained. "Where the deuce did you come from, Johnny?"

"The 'outside.' Started for Stony River, but—"

"Stony River!" The new-comers began to laugh loudly and Cantwell joined them. It was the first time he had laughed for weeks. He realized the fact with a start, then recollected also his sleeping partner, and said:

"'Sh-h! Mort's inside, asleep!"

During the night everything had changed for Johnny Cantwell; his mental attitude, his hatred, his whole reasonless insanity. Everything was different now, even his debt was canceled, the weight of obligation was removed, and his diseased fancies were completely cured.

"Yes! Stony River," he repeated, grinning broadly. "I bit!"

Martin burst forth, gleefully: "They caught MacDonald at Holy Cross and ran him out on a limb. He'll never start another stampede. Old man Baker gun-branded him."

"What's the matter with Mort?" inquired the second traveler.

"He's resting up. Yesterday, during the storm he—" Johnny was upon the point of saying "played out," but changed it to "had an accident. We thought it was serious, but a few days' rest 'll bring him around all right. He saved me at Katmai, coming in. I petered out and threw up my tail, but he got me through. Come inside and tell him the news."

"Sure thing."

"Well, well!" Martin said. "So you and Mort are still partners, eh?"

"*Still* partners?" Johnny took up the pail of water. "Well, rather! We'll always be partners." His voice was young and full and hearty as he continued: "Why, Mort's the best damned fellow in the world. I'd lay down my life for him."

THE STAMPEDE

THE STAMPEDE

FROM their vantage on the dump, the red gravel of which ran like a raw scar down the mountainside, the men looked out across the gulch, above the western range of hills to the yellow setting sun. Far below them the creek was dotted with other tiny pay dumps of the same red gravel over which men crawled, antlike, or upon which they labored at windlass. Thin wisps of smoke rose from the cabin roofs, bespeaking the supper hour.

They had done a hard day's work, these two, and wearily descended to their shack, which hugged the hillside beneath.

Ten hours with pick and shovel in a drift where the charcoal-gas flickers a candle-flame will reduce one's artistic keenness, and together they slouched along the path, heedless alike of view or color.

As Crowley built the fire Buck scoured himself in the wet snow beside the door, emerging from his ablutions as cook. The former stretched upon the bunk with growing luxury. "Gee whiz! I'm tuckered out. Twelve hours in that air is too much for anybody."

"Sure," growled the other. "Bet I sleep good to-night, all right, all right. What's the use, anyhow?" he continued, disgustedly. "I'm sore on the whole works. If the Yukon was open I'd chuck it all."

"What! Go back to the States? Give up?"

"Well, yes, if you want to call it that, though I think I've shown I ain't a quitter. Lord! I've rustled steady for two years, and what have I got? Nothing—except my interest in this pauperized hill claim."

"If two years of hard luck gives you cold feet, you ain't worthy of the dignity of 'prospector.' This here is the only honorable calling there is. There's no competition and cuttin' throats in our business, nor we don't rob the widders and orphans. A prospector is defined as a semi-human being with a low forehead but a high sense of honor, a stummick that shies at salads, but a heart that's full of grit. They don't never lay down, and the very beauty of the business is that you never know when you're due. Some day a guy comes along: 'I hit her over yonder, bo,' says he, whereupon you insert yourself into a pack-strap, pound the trail, and the next you know you're a millionaire or two."

"Bah! No more stampedes for me. I've killed myself too often—there's nothing in 'em. I'm sick of it, I tell you, and I'm going out to God's country. No more wild scrambles and hardships for Buck."

THE STAMPEDE

A step sounded on the chips without, and a slender, sallow man entered.

"Hello, Maynard!" they chorused, and welcomed him to a seat.

"What are you doing out here?"

"D'you bring any chewing with you?"

Evidently he labored under excitement, for his face was flushed and his eyes danced nervously. He panted from his climb, ignoring their questions.

"There's been a big strike—over on the Tanana —four bits to the pan."

Forgetting fatigue, Crowley scrambled out of his bunk while the cook left his steaming skillet.

"When?"

"How d'you know?"

"It's this way. I met a fellow as I came out from town—he'd just come over—one of the discoverers. He showed me the gold. It's coarse; one nugget weighed three hundred dollars and there's only six men in the party. They went up the Tanana last fall, prospecting, and only just struck it. Three of 'em are down with scurvy, so this one came over the mountains for fresh grub. It 'll be the biggest stampede this camp ever saw." Maynard became incoherent.

"How long ago did you meet him?" Crowley inquired, excitedly.

"About an hour. I came on the run, because he'll get into camp by eleven, and midnight will see five hundred men on the trail. Look at this— he gave me a map." The speaker gloatingly pro-

263

duced a scrap of writing-paper and continued, "Boys, you've got five hours' start of them."

"We can't go; we haven't got any dogs," said Buck. "Those people from town would catch us in twenty miles."

"You don't want dogs," Maynard answered. "It's too soft. You'll have to make a quick run with packs or the spring break-up will catch you. I wish I could go. It's big, I tell you. Lord! How I wish I could go!"

They were huddled together, their eyes feverish, their fingers tracing the pencil-markings. A smell of burning food filled the room, but there is no obsession more absolute than the gold-lust.

"Get the packs together while me and Buck eats a bite. We'll take the fox-robe and the Navajo. Glad I've got a new pair of mukluks, 'cause we need light footgear; but what will you wear, boy? Them hip-boots is too heavy—you'd never make it."

"Here," said Maynard, "try these." He slipped off his light gossamer sporting-boots, and Buck succeeded in stamping his feet into them.

"Little tight, but they'll go."

They snatched bites of food, meanwhile collecting their paraphernalia, Maynard helping as he could.

Each selected a change of socks and mittens. Then the grub was divided evenly—tea, flour, bacon, baking-powder, salt, sugar. There was nothing else, for spring on the Yukon finds only the heel of the grub-stake. Each rolled his portion in his blanket and lashed it with light rope. Then an end of the bundle was thrust into the waist of a pair of overalls and the garment closely cinched to it. The legs were brought forward and fastened, forming two loops, through which they slipped their arms, balancing the packs, or shifting a knot here and there. A light ax, a coffee-pot, frying-pan, and pail were tied on the outside, and they stood ready for the run. They stored carefully wrapped bundles of matches in pockets, packs, and in the lining of their caps. The preparations had not taken twenty minutes.

"Too bad we 'ain't got some cooked grub, like chocolate or dog-biscuits," said Crowley, "but seeing as we've got five hours' start over everybody we won't have to kill ourselves."

Maynard spoke hesitatingly. "Say, I told Sully about it as I came along."

"What!" Crowley interrupted him sharply.

"Yes! I told him to get ready, and I promised to give him the location an hour after you left. You see, he did me a good turn once and I had to get back at him somehow. He and Knute are getting fixed now. Why, what's up?"

He caught a queer, quick glance between his partners and noted a hardness settle into the lined face of the elder.

"Nothing much," Buck took up. "I guess you didn't know about the trouble, eh? Crowley knocked him down day before yesterday and

THE STAMPEDE

Sully swears he'll kill him on sight. It came up over that fraction on Buster Creek."

"Well, well," said Maynard, "that's bad, isn't it? I promised, though, so I'll have to tell him."

"Sure! That's all right," Crowley agreed, quietly, though his lip curled, showing the strong, close-shut, ivory teeth. His nostrils dilated, also, giving his face a passing wolfish hint. "There's neither white man nor Swede that can gain an hour on us, and if he should happen to—he wouldn't pass."

Be it known that many great placer fortunes have been won by those who stepped in the warm tracks of the discoverers, while rarely does the goddess smile on the tardy; in consequence, no frenzy approaches that of the gold stampede.

Passing Sully's place, they found him and his partner ready and waiting, their packs on the saw-buck. Crowley glared at his enemy in silence while the other sneered wickedly back, and Big Knute laughed in his yellow beard.

Buck's heart sank. Could he outlast these two? He was a boy; they were reckless giants with thews and legs of iron. Knute was a gaunt-framed Viking; Sully a violent, florid man with the quarters of an ox. Through the quixotism of Maynard this trip bade fair to combine the killing grind of a long, fierce stampede with the bitter struggle of man and man, and too well he knew the temper of his red-headed partner to doubt that before the last stake was driven either he or Sully would be down. From the glare in their eyes at passing it came over him that either he or Knute would recross the mountains partnerless. The trail was too narrow for these other men. He shrank from the toil and agony he felt was coming to him through this; then, with it, there came the burning gold-hunger; the lust that drives starving, broken wrecks onward unremittingly, over misty hills, across the beds of lava and the forbidden tundra; on, into the new diggings.

It neared eight o'clock, and, although darkness was far distant, the chill that follows the sun fell sharply.

As they swung out on to the river their fatigue had dropped away and they moved with the steady, loose gait of the hardened "musher." Buck looked at his watch. They had been gone an hour.

"The race is on!" said he.

Though unhurried, their progress was likewise unhindered, and the miles slipped backward as the darkness thickened, hour by hour. Straight up the fifty-mile stream to its source, over the great backbone and into the unmapped country their course led. If they hurried they would have first choice of the good claims close about the discovery; if they lagged Sully and his ox-eyed partner would overtake them, and beyond that it was unpleasant to conjecture.

"We'll hit water pretty soon!" Crowley's voice broke hours of silence, for they were sparing of language. They neither whistled nor sang nor spoke, for Man is a potential body from which his store of energy wastes through tiny unheeded ways.

True to prophecy, in the darkness of midnight they walked out upon a thin skin of newly frozen ice.

"Look out for the overflow! She froze since dark," Crowley cautioned. "We're liable to go through."

On all sides it cracked alarmingly, while they felt it sag beneath their feet. It is bad in the dark to ride the ice of an overflow, for one may crash through ankle-deep to the solid body beneath or plunge to his armpits.

They skated over the yielding surface toward safety till, without warning, Crowley smashed in half-way to his hips. He fell forward bodily, and the ice let him through till he rolled in the water. Buck skimmed over more lightly, and, when they had reached the solid footing, helped him wring out his garments. Straightway the cloth whitened under the frost and crackled when they resumed their march, but there was no time for fires, and by vigorous action he could keep the cold from striking in.

They had threaded up into the region where spring was further advanced, and within half an hour encountered another overflow. Climbing the steep bank, they wallowed through thickets waist-deep in snow. Beneath the crust, which cut knifelike, it was wet and soggy, so they emerged saturated. Then debouching on to the glare ice the boy had a nasty fall, for he slipped, and his loose-hung pack flung him suddenly. Nothing is more wicked than a pack on smooth ice. The surface had frozen glass-smooth, and constant difficulty beset their progress. Their slick-soled footgear refused to grip it, so that often they fell, always awkwardly, occasionally crushing through into the icy water beneath.

Without warning Buck found that he was very tired. He also found that his pack had grown soggy and quadrupled in weight, tugging sullenly at his aching shoulders.

As daylight showed they slipped harness and, hurriedly gathering twigs, boiled a pot of tea. They took time to prepare nothing else, yet even though the kettle sang speedily, as they drank from around the bend below came voices. Crowley straightened with a curse and, snatching his pack, fled up the stream, followed by his companion. They ran till Buck's knees failed him. Thereupon the former removed a portion of the youngster's burden, adding it to his own, and they hurried on for hours, till they fell exhausted upon a dry moss hummock. Here they exchanged footgear, as Buck now found his feet were paining him acutely, owing to the tightness of his rubber boots. They proved too small for Crowley as well, and in a few hours his feet were likewise ruined.

Noon found them limping among the bald hills

of the river's source. Here timber was sparse
and the snows, too, had thinned; so to avoid the
convolutions of the stream they cut across points,
floundering among "niggerheads"—quaint, wobbly hummocks of grass—being thrown repeatedly
by their packs which had developed a malicious
deviltry. This footing was infinitely worse than
the reeking ice, but it saved time, so they took it.

Now, under their stiff mackinaws they perspired
freely as the sun mounted, until their heavy garments chafed them beneath arms and legs.
Moreover, mosquitoes, which in this latitude
breed within arm's-length of snow-drifts, con-
tinually whined in a vicious cloud before their
features.

Human nerves will weather great strains, but
wearing, maddening, unending trivialities will
break them down, and so, although their journey
in miles had been inconsiderable, the dragging
packs, the driving panic, the lack of food and firm
footing, had trebled it.

Scaling the moss-capped saddle, they labored
painfully, a hundred yards at a time. Back of
them the valley unrolled, its stream winding away
like a gleaming ribbon, stretching, through dark
banks of fir, down to the Yukon. After incredible
effort they reached the crest and gazed dully out
to the southward over a limitless jangle of peaks,
on, on, to a blue-veiled valley leagues and leagues
across. Many square miles lay under them in the
black of unbroken forests. It was their first

glimpse of the Tanana. Far beyond, from a groveling group of foot-hills, a solitary, giant peak soared grandly, standing aloof, serene, terrible in its proportions. Even in their fatigue they exclaimed aloud:

"It's Mount McKinley!"

"Yep! Tallest wart on the face of the continent. There's the creek we go down—see!" Crowley indicated a watercourse which meandered away through cañons and broad reaches. "We foller it to yonder cross valley; then east to there."

To Buck's mind, his gesture included a tinted realm as far-reaching as a state.

Stretched upon the bare schist, commanding the back stretch, they munched slices of raw bacon.

Directly, out toward the mountain's foot two figures crawled.

"There they come!" and Crowley led, stumbling, sliding, into the strange valley.

As this was the south and early side of the range, they found the hills more barren of snow. Water seeped into the gulches till the creek ice was worn and rotted.

"This 'll be fierce," the Irishman remarked. "If she breaks on us we'll be hung up in the hills and starve before the creeks lower enough to get home."

Small streams freeze solidly to the bottom and the spring waters wear downward from the surface. Thus they found the creek awash, and, following farther, it became necessary to wade in many places. They came to a box cañon where the winter snow had packed, forming a dam, and, as there was no way of avoiding it without retreating a mile and climbing the ragged bluff, they floundered through, their packs aloft, the slushy water armpit-deep.

"We'd ought 'a' took the ridges," Buck chattered. Language slips forth phonetically with fatigue.

"No! Feller's apt to get lost. Drop into the wrong creek—come out fifty mile away."

"I bet the others do, anyhow," Buck held, stubbornly. "It's lots easier going."

"Wish Sully would, but he's too wise. No such luck for me." A long pause. "I reckon I'll have to kill him before he gets back!" Again they relapsed into miles of silence.

Crowley's fancy fed on vengeance, hatred livening his work-worn faculties. He nursed carefully the memory of their quarrel, for it helped him travel and took his mind from the agony of movement and this aching sleep-hunger.

The feet of both men felt like fearful, shapeless masses; their packs leaned backward sullenly, chafing raw shoulder sores; and always the ravenous mosquitoes stung and stung, and whined and whined.

At an exclamation the leader turned. Miles back, silhouetted far above on the comb of the ridge, they descried two tiny figures.

THE STAMPEDE

"That's what we'd ought 'a' done. They'll beat us in."

"No, they won't. They'll have to camp to-night or get lost, while we can keep goin'. We can't go wrong down here; can't do no more than drownd."

Buck groaned at the thought of the night hours. He couldn't stand it, that was all! Enough is enough of anything and he had gone the limit. Just one more mile and he would quit; yet he did not.

All through that endless phantom night they floundered, incased in freezing garments, numb and heavy with sleep, but morning found them at the banks of the main stream.

"You look like hell," said Buck, laughing weakly. His mirth relaxed his nerves suddenly, till he giggled and hiccoughed hysterically. Nor could he stop for many minutes, the while Crowley stared at him apathetically from a lined and shrunken countenance, his features standing out skeleton-like. The younger man evidenced the strain even more severely, for his flesh was tender, and he had traveled the last hours on pure nerve. His jaws were locked and corded, however, while his drooping eyes shone unquenchably.

Eventually they rounded a bluff on to a cabin nestling at the mouth of a dark valley. Near it men were working with a windlass, so, stumbling to them, they spoke huskily.

"Sorry we 'ain't got room inside," the stranger

273

replied, "but three of the boys is down with scurvy, and we're all cramped up. Plenty more folks coming, I s'pose, eh?"

The two had sunk on to the wet ground and did not answer. Buck fell with his pack still on, utterly lost, and the miner was forced to drag the bundle from his shoulders. As he rolled him up he was sleeping heavily.

Crowley awakened while the sun was still golden; his joints aching excruciatingly. They had slept four hours. He boiled tea on the miners' stove and fried a pan of salt pork, but was too tired to prepare anything else, so they drank the warm bacon-grease clear with their tea.

As Buck strove to arise, his limbs gave way weakly, so that he fell, and it took him many moments to recover their use.

"Where's the best chance, pardner?" they inquired of the men on the dump.

"Well, there ain't none very close by. We've got things pretty well covered."

"How's that? There's only six of you; you can't hold but six claims, besides discovery."

"Oh yes, we can! We've got powers of attorney; got 'em last fall in St. Michael; got 'em recorded, too."

Crowley's sunken eyes blazed.

"Them's no good. We don't recko'nize 'em in this district. One claim is enough for any man if it's good, and too much if it's bad."

"What district you alludin' at?" questioned the

other, ironically. "You're in the Skookum District now. It takes six men to organize. Well! We organized. We made laws. We elected a recorder. I'm it. If you don't like our rules, yonder is the divide. We've got the U. S. government back of us. See!"

Crowley's language became purely local, but the other continued unruffled.

"We knew you-all was coming, so we sort of loaded up. If there's any ground hereabouts that we ain't got blanketed, it's purely an oversight. There's plenty left farther out, though," and he swept them a mocking gesture. "Help yourselves and pass up for more. I'll record 'em."

"What's the fee?"

"Ten dollars apiece."

Crowley swore more savagely.

"You done a fine job of hoggin', didn't you? It's two and a half everywhere else."

But the recorder of the Skookum District laughed carelessly and resumed his windlass. "Sorry you ain't pleased. Maybe you'll learn to like it."

As they turned away he continued: "I don't mind giving you a hunch, though. Tackle that big creek about five miles down yonder. She prospected good last fall, but you'll have to go clean to her head, 'cause we've got everything below."

Eight hours later, by the guiding glare of the Northern Lights, the two stumbled back into camp, utterly broken.

THE STAMPEDE

They had followed the stream for miles and miles to find it staked by the powers of attorney of the six. Coming to the gulch's head, to be sure, they found vacant ground, but refused to claim such unpromising territory. Then the endless homeward march through the darkness! Out of thickets and through drifts they burst, while fatigue settled on them like some horrid vampire from the darkness. Every step being no longer involuntary became a separate labor, requiring mental concentration. They were half dead in slumber as they walked, but their stubborn courage and smoldering rage at the men who had caused this drove them on. They suffered silently, because it takes effort to groan, and they hoarded every atom of endurance.

Many, many times Buck repeated a poem, timing his steps to its rhythm, rendering it over and over till it wore a rut through his brain, his eyes fixed dully upon the glaring fires above the hilltops. For years a faintness came over him with the memory of these lines:

Then dark they lie, and stark they lie, rookery, dune, and
    floe,
And the Northern Lights came down o' nights to dance with
    the houseless snow.

Reaching the cabin, they found an army of men sleeping heavily upon the wet moss. Among them was the great form of Knute, but nowhere did they spy Sully.

THE STAMPEDE

With much effort they tore off the constricting boots and, using them for pillows, sank into a painful lethargy.

Awakened early by the others, they took their stiffly frozen footgear beneath the blankets to thaw against their warm bodies, but their feet were swelled to double size and every joint had ossified rheumatically. Eventually they hobbled about, preparing the first square meal since the start—two days and three nights.

Still they saw no Sully, though Crowley's eyes darted careful inquiry among the horde of stampeders which moved about the cabin. Later, he seemed bent on some hidden design, so they crawled out of sight of the camp, then, commencing at the upper stake of Discovery, he stepped off the claims from post to post.

It is customary to blaze the boundaries of locations on tree trunks, but from topographical irregularities it is difficult to properly gauge these distances, hence, many rich fractions have been run over by the heedless, to fall to him who chained the ground.

Upon pacing the third one, he showed excitement.

"You walk this one again—mebbe I made a mistake."

Buck returned, crashing through the brush.

"I make it seventeen hundred."

The claim above figured likewise, and they trembled with elation as they blazed their lines.

Returning to camp, they found the recorder in the cabin with the scurvy patients. Unfolding the location notices, his face went black as he read, while he snarled, angrily:

"'Fraction between Three and Four' and 'Fraction between Four and Five,' eh? You're crazy."

"I reckon not," said Crowley, lifting his lips at the corners characteristically.

"There ain't any fraction there," the other averred, loudly. "We own them claims. I told you we had everything covered."

"You record them fractions!"

"I won't do it! I'll see you in—"

Crowley reached forth suddenly and strangled him as he sat. He buried his thumbs in his throat, forcing him roughly back against a bunk. Farther and farther he crushed him till the man lay pinioned and writhing on his back. Then he knelt on him, shaking and worrying like a great terrier.

At the first commotion the cripples scrambled out of bed, shouting lustily through their livid gums, their bloated features mottled and sickly with fright. One lifted himself toward the Winchester, and it fell from his hands full cocked when Buck hurled him into a corner, where he lay screaming in agony.

Drawn by the uproar, the stampeders outside rushed toward the shack to be met in the door by the young man.

THE STAMPEDE

"Keep back!"

"What's up!"

"Fight!"

"Let me in!"

A man bolted forward, but was met with such a driving blow in the face that he went thrashing to the slush. Another was hurled back, and then they heard Crowley's voice, rough and throaty, as he abused the recorder. Strained to the snapping-point, his restraint had shattered to bits and now passion ran through him, wild and unbridled.

From his words they grasped the situation, and their sympathies changed. They crowded the door and gazed curiously through the window to see him jam the recorder shapelessly into a chair, place pen and ink in his hand, and force him to execute two receipts. It is not a popular practice, this blanketing, as the temper of the watchers showed.

"Serves 'em right, the hogs," some one said, and he voiced the universal sentiment.

That night, as they ravened over their meager meal, Knute came to them, hesitatingly. He was greatly worried and apprehension wrinkled his wooden face.

"Saay! W'at you t'ink 'bout Sully?"

"I don't know. Why?"

"By yingo, ay t'ink he's lose!"

"Lost! How's that?"

In his dialect, broken by anxiety, he told how Sully and he had quarreled on the big divide.

THE STAMPEDE

Maddened by failure to gain on Crowley, the former had insisted on following the mountain crests in the hope of quicker travel. The Swede had yielded reluctantly till, frightened by the network of radiating gulches which spread out beneath their feet in a bewildering sameness, he had refused to go farther. They had quarreled. In a fit of fury Sully had hurled his pack away, and Knute's last vision of him had been as he went raving and cursing onward like a madman, traveling fast in his fury. Knute had retreated, dropped into the valley, and eventually reached his goal.

There is no time for reliefs on a stampede. The gentler emotions are left in camp with the women. He who would risk life, torture, and privation for a stranger will trample pitilessly on friend and enemy blinded by the gold glitter or drunken with the chase of the rainbow.

For five days and nights the army lived on its feet, streaming up gullies where lay the hint of wealth or swarming over the somber bluffs; and hourly the madness grew, feeding on itself, till they fought like beasts. Fabulous values were begotten. Giant sales were bruited about. Flying rumors of gold at the cross-roots inflamed them to further frenzy.

A town site was laid out and a terrible scramble for lots ensued.

One man was buried in the plot he claimed, his disputant being adjudged the owner by virtue of his quicker draw. It was manslaughter, they knew, but no one spared the time to guard him, so he went free. Nor did he run away. One cannot, while the craze is on.

Five days of this, and then the stream broke. With it broke the delirium of the five hundred. The valleys roared and bawled from bluff to bluff, while the flats became seas of seething ice and rubbish. Thus, cut off from home, they found their grub was gone, for every one had clung till his food grew low. As the obsession left them their brotherhood returned—food was apportioned in community, and they spoke vaguely of the fate of Sully.

For still another half-fortnight they lay about the cabin while the streams raged, and then Crowley spoke to his partner. Rolling their blankets, they started, and, although many were tempted to go, none had the courage, preferring to starve on quarter rations till the waters lowered.

Ascending for miles where the torrent narrowed, they felled a tree across for a bridge and, ascending the ridges, took the direction of camp. In a new and broken country, not formed of continuous ranges, this is difficult. So to avoid frequent fordings they followed the high ground, going devious, confusing miles. The snows were largely gone, though the nights were cruel, and thus they traveled.

At last, when they had worked through to the Yukon spurs, one morning on a talus high above Buck spied the flapping forms of a flock of ravens.

They fluttered ceaselessly among the rocks, rising noisily, only to settle again.

These are the gleaming, baleful vultures of the North, and often they attain a considerable size and ferocity.

The men gazed at them with apathy. Was it worth while to spend the steps to see what drew them? By following their course they would pass far to the right.

"I hate the dam' things," said Crowley, crossly. "I seen 'em, oncet, hangin' to a caribou calf with a broken leg, tryin' to pick his eyes out. Let's see what it is."

He veered to the left, scrambling up among the boulders. The birds rose fretfully, perching near by, but the men saw nothing. As they rested momentarily the birds again swooped downward, reassured.

Then, partly hidden among the detritus, they spied that which made Crowley cry out in horror, while the sound of Buck's voice was like the choking of a woman. As they started, one of the ebony scavengers dipped fiercely, picking at a ragged object. A human arm slowly arose and blindly beat it off, but the raven's mate settled also, and, sinking its beak into the object, tore hungrily.

With a shout they stumbled forward, lacerated by the jagged slide rock, only to pause aghast and shaking.

Sully lay crouched against a boulder where he

had crawled for the sun heat. Rags of clothing hung upon his gaunt frame, through which the sharp bones strove to pierce; also at sight of his hands and feet they shuddered. With the former he had covered his eyes from the ravens, but his cheeks and head were bloody and shredded. He muttered constantly, like the thick whirring of machinery run down.

"Oh, my God!" Buck whispered.

Crowley had mastered himself and knelt beside the figure. He looked up and tears lay on his cheeks.

"Look at them hands and feet! That was done by fire and frost together. He must have fell in his own camp-fires after he went crazy."

The garments were burned off to elbow and knee, while the flesh was black and raw.

Tenderly they carried the gabbing creature down to the timber and laid him on a bed of boughs. His condition told the grim tale of his wanderings, crazed with hunger and hardship.

Heating water, they poured it into him, dressing his wounds with strips from their underclothes. Of stimulants they had none, but fed him the last pinch of flour, together with the final rasher of salt pork, although they knew that these things are not good for starving men. For many days they had traveled on less than quarter rations themselves.

"What will we do?"

"It ain't over twenty miles to the niggers'.

He'll die before we can get help back. D'ye reckon we can carry him?"

It was not sympathy which prompted Crowley, for he sympathized with his boyish companion, whose sufferings it hurt him sorely to augment. It was not pity; he pitied himself, and his own deplorable condition; nor did mercy enter into his processes, for the man had mercilessly planned to kill him, and he likewise had nursed a bitter hatred against him, which misfortune could only dim. It was not these things which moved him, but a vaguer, wilder quality; an elemental, unspoken, indefinable feeling of brotherhood throughout the length of the North, teaching subtly, yet absolutely and without appeal, that no man shall be left in his extremity to the cruel harshness of this forbidding land.

"Carry him?" Buck cried. "No! You're crazy! What's the use? He'll die, anyhow—and so'll we if we don't get grub soon." Buck was new to the country, and he was a boy.

"No, he won't. He lived hard and he'll die hard, for he's a hellion—he is. We've got to pack him in!"

"By God! I won't risk *my* life for a corpse—'specially one like him." The lad broke out in hysterical panic, for he had lived on the raggedest edge of his nerve these many days. Now his every muscle was dead and numbed with pain. Only his mind was clear, caused by the effort to force movement into his limbs. When he stopped

walking he fell into a half-slumber which was
acutely painful. When he arose to redrive his
weary body it became freakish, so that he fell or
collided with trees. He was bloody and bruised
and cut. Carry a dead man? It was madness,
and, besides, he felt an utter giving away at every
joint.

He was too tired to make his reasoning plain;
his tongue was thick, and Crowley's brain too
calloused to grasp argument, therefore he squatted
beside the muttering creature and wept impo-
tently. He was asleep, with tears in his stubbly
beard, when his partner finished the rude litter,
yet he took up his end of the burden, as Crowley
knew he would.

"You'll kill us both, damn ye!" he groaned.

"Probably so, but we can't leave him to them
things." The other nodded at the vampires
perched observantly in the surrounding firs.

Then began their great trial and temptation.
For hours on end the birds fluttered from tree to
tree, always in sight and hoarsely complaining till
the sick fancies of the men distorted them into
foul, gibing creatures of the Pit screaming with
devilish glee at their anguish. Blindly they staggered through the forest while the limbs reached
forth to block them, thrusting sharp needles into
their eyes or whipping back viciously. Vines
writhed up their legs, straining to delay their
march, and the dank moss curled ankle-deep,
slyly tripping their dragging, swollen feet. Na-

285

ture hindered them sullenly, with all her heart-breaking implacability. They reeled constantly under their burden and grew to hate the ragged-barked trees that smote them so cruelly and so roughly tore their flesh. Ofttimes they fell, rolling the maniac limply from his couch, but they dragged him back and strained forward to the hideous racket of his mumblings, which grew louder as his delirium increased. They were forced to tie him to the poles, but could not stop his ghastly shriekings. At every pause the dismal ravens croaked and leered evilly from the shadows, till Buck shuddered and hid his face while Crowley gnashed his teeth. From time to time other birds joined them in anticipation of the feast, till they were ringed about, and the sight of this ever-growing, grisly, clamorous flock of watchers became awful to the men. They felt the horny talons searching their flesh and the hungry beaks tearing at their eyeballs.

A dog-sled and birch-bark practice covering both banks of the Yukon for two hundred miles yielded Doc Lewis sufficient revenue to grub - stake a Swede. Thus he slept warm, kept his feet dry, and was still a miner. He did not believe in hardship, and eschewed stampedes. Yet when he had seen the last able-bodied man vanish from camp on the Skookum run he grew restless. He scoffed at fake excitements to Jarvis, the faro-dealer, who also forbore the trail by virtue of his calling, but he got no satisfaction. A fortnight later he rolled his blankets and journeyed toilsomely up the river valley.

"Better late than never," he thought.

Arriving at the empty shack of the negroes, he camped, only to awaken during the night to the roar of the torrent at his door. Having seen other mountain streams in the break-up, he waited philosophically, hunting ptarmigan among the firs back of the cabin.

He had lost track of the days when, down the gulch, in the morning light, he descried a strange party approaching.

Two men bore between them a stretcher made from their shirts. They crawled with dreadful slowness, resting every hundred feet. Moreover, they stumbled and staggered aimlessly through the niggerheads. As they drew near he sighted their faces, from which the teeth grinned in a grimace of torture and through which the cheekbones seemed to penetrate.

He knew what the signs boded. For years he had ministered to these necessities, and no man had ever approached his success.

"It is the rape of the North they are doing," he sighed. "We ravage her stores, but she takes grim toll from all of us." He moved the hot water forward on the stove, cleared off the rude table, and laid out his instrument-case.

WHEN THE MAIL CAME IN

WHEN THE MAIL CAME IN

WE didn't like Montague Prosser at first—
he was too clean. He wore his virtue like
a bath-robe, flapping it in our faces. It was
Whitewater Kelly who undertook to mitigate him
one day, but, being as the nuisance stood an
even fathom high and had a double-action foot-
ball motion about him, Whitewater's endeavors
kind of broke through the ice and he languished
around in his bunk the next week while we sat
up nights and changed his bandages.

Yes, Monty was equally active at repartee or
rough-house, and he knocked Whitewater out
from under his cap, slick and clean, just the way
you snap a playing-card out from under a coin,
which phenomenon terminated our tendencies to
scoff and carp.

Personally, I didn't care. If a man wants to
wallow about in a disgusting daily debauch of
cleanliness, it is his privilege. If he squanders the
fleeting moments brushing teeth, cleaning finger-
nails, and such technicalities, it stands to reason
he won't have much time left to attend to his work
and at the same time cultivate the essentials of

life like smoking, drinking, and the proper valuation of a three-card draw. But, as I say, it's up to him, and outsiders who don't see merit in such a system shouldn't try to bust up his game unless they've got good foot-work and a knockout punch.

It wasn't so much these physical refinements that riled us as the rarefied atmosphere of his general mental and moral altitudes. To me there's eloquence and sentiment and romance and spiritual uplift in a real, full-grown, black-whiskered cuss-word. It's a great help in a mountainous country. Profanity is like steam in a locomotive—takes more to run you up-hill than on the level, and inasmuch as there's only a few men on the level, a violent vocabulary is a necessity and appeals to me like a certificate of good character and general capability.

There wasn't a thing doing with Prosser in the idiom line, however. His moral make-up was like his body, big and sound and white and manicured, and although his talk, alongside of ours, listened like it was skimmed and seminaried, still when we got to know him we found that his verbal structures had vital organs and hair on their chests just like anybody else's, and at the same time had the advantage of being fit to send through the mails.

He had left a widowed mother and come north on the main chance, like the rest of us, only he originated farther east. What made the particular ten-strike with us was the pride he took in that same mother. He gloried in her and talked about her in that hushed and nervous way a man speaks about a real mother or a regular sweetheart. We men-folks liked him all the better for it. I say we men, for he was a "shine" with the women—all nine of them. The camp was fifteen hundred strong that winter, over and above which was the aforesaid galaxy of nine, stranded on their way up-river to a Dawson dance-hall. The Yukon froze up and they had to winter with us. Of course there were the three married ladies, too, living with their husbands back on the Birch Ridge, but we never saw them and they didn't count. The others went to work at Eckert's theater.

Monty would have been right popular at Eckert's—he was a handsome lad—but he couldn't see those people with a field-glass. They simply scandalized him to death.

"I love to dance," said he, one night, as we looked on, "and the music sends thrills through me, but I won't do it."

"Why not?" I asked. "This is Alaska. Be democratic. You're not so awfully nice that a dance-hall girl will contaminate you."

"It's not democracy that I lack, nor contamination that I'm afraid of," he replied. "It's the principle back of it all. If we encourage these girls in the lives they lead, we're just as bad as they are."

"Look here, son, when I quit salt water I left

all that garbage and bilge-water talk about 'guilt' and 'responsibility' behind. The days are too short, the nights are too cold, and grub is too dear for me to spare time to theorize. I take people the way I take work and play—just as they come —and I'd advise you to do the same."

"No, sir; I won't associate with gamblers and crooks, so why should I hobnob with these women? They're worse than the men, for all the gamblers have lost is their honesty. Every time I see these girls I think of the little mother back home. It's awful. Suppose she saw me dancing with them?"

Well, that's a bad line of talk and I couldn't say much.

Of course, when the actresses found out how he felt they came back at him strong, but he wrapped himself up in his dignity and held himself aloof when he came to town, so he didn't seem to mind it.

It was one afternoon in January, cold and sharp, that Ollie Marceau's team went through the ice just below our camp. She was a great dog-puncher and had the best team in camp—seven fine malamoots—which she drove every day. When the animals smelled our place they ran away and dragged her into the open water below the hot springs. She was wet for ten minutes, and by the time she had got out and stumbled to our bunk-house she was all in. Another ten minutes with the "quick" at thirty below would have finished her, but we rushed her in by the fire and made her drink a glass of "hootch." Martin got her parka off somehow while I slashed the strings to her mukluks and had her little feet rubbed red as berries before she'd quit apologizing for the trouble she'd made. A fellow learns to watch toes pretty close in the winter.

"Lord! stop your talk," we said. "This is the first chance we have had to do anything for a lady in two years. It's a downright pleasure for us to take you in this way."

"Indeed!" she chattered. "Well, it isn't mutual—" And we all laughed.

We roused up a good fire and made her take off all the wet clothes she felt she could afford to, then wrung them out and hung them up to dry. We made her gulp down another whisky, too, after which I gave her some footgear and she slipped into one of Martin's Mackinaw shirts. We knew just how faint and shaky she felt, but she was dead game and joked with us about it.

I never realized what a cute trick she was till I saw her in that great, coarse, blue shirt with her feet in beaded moccasins, her yellow hair touseled, and the sparkle of adventure in her bright eyes. She stood out like a nugget by candle-light, backed, as she was, by the dingy bark walls of our cabin.

I suppose it was a bad instant for Prosser to appear. He certainly cued in wrong and found the sight shocking to his Plymouth Rock proprieties.

WHEN THE MAIL CAME IN

The raw liquor we had forced on her had gone
to her head a bit, as it will when you're fresh from
the cold and your stomach is empty, so her face
was flushed and had a pretty, reckless, daring look
to it. She had her feet high up on a chair, too—
not so very high, either—where they were thawing
out under the warmth of the oven, and we were
all laughing at her story of the mishap.

Monty stopped on recognizing who she was,
while the surprise in his face gave way to disap-
proval. We could see it as plain as if it was
blazoned there in printer's ink, and it sobered us.
The girl removèd her feet and stood up.

"Miss Marceau has just had an accident," I
began, but I saw his eyes were fastened on the
bottle on the table, and I saw also that he knew
what caused the fever in her cheeks.

"Too bad," he said, coldly. "If I can be of any
assistance you'll find me down at the shaft-house."
And out he walked.

I knew he didn't intend to be inhospitable;
that it was just his infernal notions of decency,
and that he refused to be a party to anything as
devilish as this looked—but it wasn't according
to the Alaska code, and it was like a slap in the
girl's face.

"I am quite dry," she said. "I'll be going now."

"You will not. You'll stay to supper and
drive home by moonlight," says we. "Why,
you'd freeze in a mile!" And we made her listen
to us.

WHEN THE MAIL CAME IN

During the meal Prosser never opened his mouth except to put something into it, but his manner was as full of language as an oration. He didn't thaw out the way a man should when he sees strangers wading into the grub he's paid a dollar a pound for, and when we'd finally sent the young woman off Martin turned on him.

'Young feller," said he—and his eyes were black—"I've rattled around for thirty years and seen many a good and many a bad man, but I never before seen such an intelligent dam' fool as you are."

"What do you mean?" said the boy.

"You've broke about the only law that this here country boasts of—the law of hospitality."

"He didn't mean it that way," I spoke up. "Did you, Monty?"

"Certainly not. I'd help anybody out of trouble—man or woman—but I refuse to mix with that kind of people socially."

"'That kind of people,'" yelled the old man. "And what's the matter with that kind of people? You come creeping out of the milk-and-water East, all pink and perfumed up, and when you get into a bacon-and-beans country where people sweat instead of perspiring you wrinkle your nose like a calf and whine about the kind of people you find. What do you know about people, anyhow? Did you ever want to steal?"

"Of course not," said Prosser, who kept his temper.

"Did you ever want to drink whisky so bad you couldn't stand it?"

"No."

"Did you ever want to kill a man?"

"No."

"Were you ever broke and friendless and hopeless?"

"Why, I can't say I ever was."

"And you've never been downright hungry, either, where you didn't know if you'd ever eat again, have you? Then what license have you got to blame people for the condition you find them in? How do you know what brought this girl where she is?"

"Oh, I pity any woman who is adrift on the world, if that's what you mean, but I won't make a pet out of her just because she is friendless. She must expect that when she chooses her life. Her kind are bad—bad all through. They must be."

"Not on your life. Decency runs deeper than the hives."

"Trouble with you," said I, "you've got a juvenile standard—things are all good or all bad in your eyes—and you can't like a person unless the one overbalances the other. When you are older you'll find that people are like gold-mines, with a thin streak of pay on bed-rock and lots of hard digging above."

"I didn't mean to be discourteous," our man continued, "but I'll never change my feelings about such things. Mind you, I'm not preaching, nor asking you to change your habits—all I want is a chance to live my own life clean."

The mail came in during March, five hundred pounds of it, and the camp went daffy.

Monty had the dogs harnessed ten minutes after we got the news, and we drove the four miles in seventeen minutes. I've known men with sweethearts outside, but I never knew one to act gladder than Monty did at the thought of hearing from his mother.

"You must come and see us when you make your pile," he told me, "or—what's better—we'll go East together next spring and surprise her. Won't that be great? We'll walk in on her in the summer twilight while she is working in her flower-garden. Can't you just see the green trees and smell the good old smells of home? The cat-birds will be calling and the grass will be clean and sweet. Why, I'm so tired of the cold and the snow and the white, white mountains that I can hardly stand it."

He ran on in that vein all the way to town, glad and hopeful and boyish—and I wondered why, with his earnestness and loyalty and broad shoulders, he had never loved any woman but his mother. When I was twenty-three my whole romantic system had been mangled and shredded from heart to gizzard. Still, some men get their age all in a lump; they're boys up till the last minute, then they get the Rip Van Winkle while you wait.

WHEN THE MAIL CAME IN

This morning was bitter, but the "sour doughs"
were lined up outside the store, waiting their turns
like a crowd of Parsifal first-nighters, so we fell
in with the rest, whipping our arms and stamping
our moccasins till the chill ate into our very bones.
It took hours to sort the letters, but not a man
whimpered. When you wait for vital news a
tension comes that chokes complaint. There
was no joking here, nor that elephantine persiflage
which marks rough men when they forgather in
the wilderness. They were the fellows who blazed
the trail, bearded, shaggy, and not pretty to look
at, for they all knew hardship and went out strong-
hearted into this silent land, jesting with danger
and singing in the solitudes. Here in the presence
of the Mail they laid aside their cloaks of care-
lessness and saw one another bared to the quick,
timid with hunger for the wives and little ones
behind.

There were a few like Prosser, in whom there was
still the glamour of the Northland and the mystery
of the unknown, but they were scattered, and in
their eyes the anxious light was growing also.

Five months is a wearying time, and silent suspense will sap the courage. If only one could
banish worry; but the long, unbearable nights
when the mind leaps and scurries out into the
voids of conjecture like sparks from a chimney—
well, it's then you roll in your bunk and your sigh
ain't from the snow-shoe pain.

A half-frozen man in an ice-clogged dory had

brought us our last news, one October day, just before the river stopped, and now, after five months, the curtain parted again.

I saw McGill, the lawyer, in the line ahead of me and noted the grayness of his cheeks, the nervous way his lips worked, and the futile, wandering, uselessness of his hands. Then I remembered. When his letter came the fall before it said the wife was very low, that the crisis was near, and that they would write again in a few days. He had lived this endless time with Fear stalking at his shoulder. He had lain down with it nightly and risen with it grinning at him in the slow, cold dawn. The boys had told me how well he fought it back week after week, but now, edging inch by inch toward the door behind which lay his message, it got the best of him.

I wrung his hand and tried to say something.

"I want to run away," he quavered. "But I'm afraid to."

When we got in at last we met men coming out, and in some faces we saw the marks of tragedy. Others smiled, and these put heart into us.

Old man Tomlinson had four little girls back in Idaho. He got two letters. One was a six-months-old tax-receipt, the other a laundry bill. That meant three months more of silence.

When my turn came and I saw the writing of the little woman something gripped me by the throat, while I saw my hands shake as if they belonged to somebody else. My news was good, though, and

I read it slowly—some parts twice—then at last when I looked up I found McGill near me. Unconsciously we had both sought a quiet corner, but he had sunk on to a box. Now, as I glanced at him I saw what made me shiver. The Fear was there again—naked and ugly—for he held one lonesome letter, and its inscription was in no woman's hand. He had crouched there by my side all this time, staring, staring, staring at it, afraid to read—afraid to open it. Some men smile in their agony, shifting their pitiful masks to the last, others curse, and no two will take their blows alike.

McGill was plucking feebly at the end of his envelope, tearing off tiny bits, dropping the fragments at his feet. Now and then he stopped, and when he did he shuddered.

"Buck up, old pal," I said.

Then, recognizing me, he thrust the missive into my hand.

"Tell me—for God's sake—tell me quick. I can't— No, no—wait! Not yet. Don't tell me. I'll know from your face. They said she couldn't live—"

But she had, and he watched me so fiercely that when the light came into my face he snatched the letter from me like a madman.

"Ah-h! Give it to me! Give it to me! I *knew* it! I told you they couldn't fool me. No, sir. I felt all the time she'd make it. Why, I knew it in my marrow!"

WHEN THE MAIL CAME IN

"What's the date?" I inquired.

"September thirtieth," he said. Then, as he realized how old it was, he began to worry again.

"Why didn't they write later? They must know I'll eat my heart out. Suppose she's had a relapse. That's it. They wrote too soon, and now they don't dare tell me. She—got worse—died—months ago, and they're afraid to let me know."

"Stop it," I said, and reasoned sanity back into him.

Monty had taken his mail and run off like a puppy to feast in quiet, so I went over to Eckert's and had a drink.

Sam winked at me as I came in. A man was reading from a letter.

"Go on. I'm interested," said the proprietor.

The fellow was getting full pretty fast and was down to the garrulous stage, but he began again:

"DEAR HUSBAND,—I am sorry to hear that you have been so unfortunate, but don't get discouraged. I know you will make a good miner if you stick to it long enough. Don't worry about me. I have rented the front room to a very nice man for fifteen dollars a week. The papers here are full of a gold strike in Siberia, just across Bering Sea from where you are. If you don't find something during the next two years, why not try it over there for a couple?"

"That's what I call a persevering woman," said Eckert, solemnly.

"She's a business woman, too," said the husband. "All I ever got for that room was seven-fifty a week."

WHEN THE MAIL CAME IN

It seems I'd missed Montague at the store, but when the crowd came out Ollie Marceau found him away in at the back, having gone there to be alone with his letters. She saw the utter abandon and grief in his pose, and the tears came to her eyes. Impulsively she went up and laid her hand on his bowed head. She had followed the frontier enough to know the signs.

"Oh, Mr. Prosser," she said, "I'm so sorry! Is it the little mother?"

"Yes," he answered, without moving.

"Not—not—" she hesitated.

"I don't know. The letters are up to the middle of December, and she was very sick."

Then, with the quick sentiment of her kind, the girl spoke to him, forgetting herself, her life, his prejudice, everything except the lonely little gray woman off there who had waited and longed just as such another had waited and longed for her, and, inasmuch as Ollie had suffered before as this boy suffered now, in her words there was a sweet sympathy and a perfect understanding.

It was very fine, I think, coming so from her, and when the first shock had passed over he felt that here, among all these rugged men, there was no one to give him the comfort he craved except this child of the dance-halls. Compassion and sympathy he could get from any of us, but he was a boy and this was his first grief, so he yearned for something more, something subtler, perhaps the delicate comprehension of a woman. At any

304

rate, he wouldn't let her leave him, and the tender-hearted lass poured out all the best her warm nature afforded.

In a few days he braced up, however, and stood his sorrow like the rest of us. It made him more of a man in many ways. For one thing, he never scoffed now at any of the nine women, which, taken as an indication, was good. In fact, I saw him several times with the Marceau girl, for he found her always ready and responsive, and came to confide in her rather than in Martin or me, which was quite natural. Martin spoke about it first.

"I hate to see 'em together so much," said he. "One of 'em is going to fall in love, sure, and it won't be reciprocated none. It would serve him right to get it hard, but if *she's* hit—it 'll be too dam' pitiful. You an' I will have to combine forces and beat him up, I reckon."

The days were growing long and warm, the hills were coming bare on the heights, while the snow packed wet at midday when we went into town to sled out grub for the clean-up. We found everybody else there for the same purpose, so the sap began to run through the camp. We were loading at the trading-post the next day when I heard the name of Ollie Marceau. It was a big-limbed fellow from Alder Creek talking, and, as he showed no liquor in his face, what he said sounded all the worse. I have heard as bad many a time without offense, for there is no code of loyalty concerning these girls, but Ollie had got

my sympathy, somehow, and I resented the remarks, particularly the laughter. · So did Prosser,
the Puritan. He looked up from his work, white
and dangerous.

"Don't talk that way about a girl," said he to
the stranger, and it made a sensation among the
crowd.

I never knew a man before with courage enough
to kick in public on such subjects. As it was, the
man said something so much worse that right
there the front busted out of the tiger-cage and
for a few brief moments we were given over to
chaos.

I had seen Whitewater walloped and I knew how
full of parlor tricks the kid was, but this time he
went insane. He knocked that man off the coun-
ter at the first pass and climbed him with his hob-
nails as he lay on the floor. A fight is a fight, and
a good thing for spectators and participants, for
it does more to keep down scurvy than anything
I know of, but the thud of those heavy boots into
that helpless flesh sickened me, and we rushed
Prosser out of there while he struggled like a
maniac. I never saw such a complete reversal of
form. Somewhere, away back yonder, that boy's
forefathers were pirates or cannibals or butchers.

When the fog had cleared out of his brain the
reaction was just as powerful. I took him out alone
while the others worked over the Alder Creek
party, and all at once my man fell apart like wet
sawdust.

WHEN THE MAIL CAME IN

"What made me do it—what made me do it?" he cried. "I'm crazy. Why, I tried to kill him! And yet what he said is true—that's the worst of it—it's true. Think of it, and I fought for her. What am I coming to?"

After the clean-up we came to camp, waiting for the river to break and the first boat to follow. It was then that the suspense began to tell on our partner. He read and reread his letters, but there was little hope in them, and now, with no work to do, he grew nervous. Added to everything else, our food ran short, and we lived on scraps of whatever was left over from our winter grub-stake. Just out of cussedness the break-up was ten days late, the ten longest days I ever put in, but eventually it came, and a week later also came the mail. We needed food and clothes, we needed whisky, we needed news of the great, distant world—but all we thought of was our mail.

The boy had decided to go home. We were sorry to see him leave, too, for he had the makings of a real man in him even if he shaved three times a week, but no sooner was the steamer tied than he came plunging into my tent like a moose, laughing and dancing in his first gladness. The mother was well again.

Later I went aboard to give him the last lonesome good wishes of the fellow who stays behind and fights along for another year. The big freighter, with her neat staterocms and long, glass-burdened tables, awoke a perfect panic in me to be going with him, to shake this cruel country and drift back to the home and the wife and the pies like mother made.

I found him on the top deck with the Marceau girl, who was saying good-by to him. There was a look about her I had never seen before, and all at once the understanding and the bitter irony of it struck me. This poor waif hadn't had enough to stand, so Love had come to her, just as Kink had predicted—a hopeless love which she would have to fight the way she fought the whole world. It made me bitter and cynical, but I admired her nerve—she was dressed for the sacrifice, trim and well-curried as a thousand-dollar pony. Back of her smile, though, I saw the waiting tears, and my heart bled. Spring is a fierce time for romance, anyhow.

There wasn't time to say much, so I squeezed Monty's hand like a cider-press.

"God bless you, lad! You must come back to us," I said, but he shook his head, and I heard the girl's breath catch. I continued, "Come on, Ollie; I'll help you ashore."

We stood on the bank there together and watched the last of him, tall and clear-cut against the white of the wheel-house, and it seemed to me when he had gone that something bright and vital and young had passed out of me, leaving in its stead discouragement and darkness and age.

"Would you mind walking with me up to my cabin?" Ollie asked.

WHEN THE MAIL CAME IN

"Of course not," I said, and we went down the long street, past the theater, the trading-post, and the saloons, till we came to the hill where her little nest was perched. Every one spoke and smiled to her and she answered in the same way, though I knew she was on parade and holding herself with firm hands. As we came near to the end and her pace quickened, however, and I guessed the panic that was on her to be alone where she could drop her mask and become a woman—a poor, weak, grief-stricken woman. But when we were inside at last her manner astounded me. She didn't throw herself on her couch nor go to pieces, as I had dreaded, but turned on me with burning eyes and her hands tight clenched, while her voice was throaty and hoarse. The words came tumbling out in confusion.

"I've let him go," she said. "Yes, and you helped me. Only for you I'd have broken down; but I want you to know I've done one good thing at last in my miserable life. I've held in. He never knew—he never knew. O God! what fools men are!"

"Yes," I said, "you did mighty well. He's a sensitive chap, and if you'd broken down he'd have felt awful bad."

"What!"

She grasped me by the coat lapels and shook me. Yes! That weak little woman shook me, while her face went perfectly livid.

"'He'd have felt badly,' eh? Man! Man! Didn't you *see!* Are you blind? Why, he asked me to go with him. He asked me to marry him. Think of it—that great, wonderful man asked me to be his wife—me—Olive Marceau, the dancer! Oh, oh! Isn't it funny? Why don't you laugh?"

I didn't laugh. I stood there, picking pieces of fur out of my cap and wondering if ever I should see another woman like this one. She paced about over the skin rugs, tearing at the throat of her dress as if it choked her. There were no tears in her eyes, but her whole frame shook and shuddered as if from great cold, deep set in her bones.

"Why didn't you go?" I asked, stupidly. "You love him, don't you?"

"You know why I didn't go," she cried, fiercely. "I couldn't. How could I go back and meet his mother? Some day she'd find me out and it would spoil his life. No, no! If only she hadn't recovered— No, I don't mean that, either. I'm not his kind, that's all. Ah, God! I let him go— I let him go, and he never knew!"

She was writhing now on her bed in a perfect frenzy, calling to him brokenly, stretching out her arms while great, dry, coughing sobs wrenched her.

"Little one," I said, unsteadily, and my throat ached so that I couldn't trust myself, "you're a brave—girl, and you're his kind or anybody's kind."

With that the rain came, and so I left her alone with her comforting misery. When I told Kink he sputtered like a pinwheel, and every evening thereafter we two went up to her house and sat with her. We could do this because she'd quit the theater the day the boat took Prosser away, and she wouldn't heed Eckert's offers to go back.

"I'm through with it for good," she told us, "though I don't know what else I'm good for. You see, I don't know anything useful, but I suppose I can learn."

"Now, if I wasn't married already—" I said.

"Humph!" snorted Kink. "I ain't so young as neither one of my pardners, miss, but I'm possessed of rare intellectual treasures."

She laughed at both of us.

When a week had passed after the first boat went down with Prosser, we began to look daily for the first up-river steamer, bringing word direct from the outside world. It came one midnight, and as we were getting dressed to go to the landing our tent was torn open and Montague tumbled in upon us.

"What brought you back?" we questioned when we'd finished mauling him.

It was June, and the nights were as light as day in this latitude, so we could see his face plainly.

"Why—er—" He hesitated for an instant, then threw back his head, squared his great young shoulders, and looked us in the eyes, while all his embarrassment fled. "I came back to marry Olive Marceau," said he. "I came to take her back home to the little mother."

He stared out wistfully at the distant southern mountains, effulgent and glorified by the midnight sun which lay so close behind their crests, and I winked at Martin.

"She's left—"

"What!" He whirled quickly.

"—the theater, and I don't suppose you can see her until to-morrow."

Disappointment darkened his face.

"Besides," Kink added, gloomily, "when you quit her like a dog I slicked myself up some, and I ain't anyways sure she'll care to see you now—only jest as a friend of mine. Notice I've cut my whiskers, don't you?"

We made Monty pay for that instant's hesitation, the last he ever had, and then I said:

"You walk up the river trail for a quarter of a mile and wait. If I can persuade her to come out at this hour I'll send her to you. No, you couldn't find her. She's moved since you left."

"I wouldn't gamble none on her meetin' you," Martin said, discouragingly, and combed out his new-mown beard with ostentation.

She was up the moment I knocked, and when I said that a man needed help I heard her murmur sympathetically as she dressed. When we came to our tent I stopped her.

"He's up yonder a piece," said I. "You run along while I fetch Kink and the medicine-kit. We'll overtake you."

"Is it anything serious?"

WHEN THE MAIL CAME IN

"Yes, it's apt to be unless you hurry. He seems to think he needs you pretty badly."

And so she went up the river trail to where he was waiting, her way golden with the beams of the sun whose rim peeped at her over the far-off hills. And there, in the free, still air, among the virgin spruce, with the clean, sweet moss beneath their feet, they met. The good sun smiled broadly at them now, and the grim Yukon hurried past, chuckling under its banks and swiggering among the roots, while the song it sang was of spring and of long, bright days that had no night.

21

McGILL

McGILL

THE ice was running when McGill arrived. Had he been two hours later he might have fared badly, for the ramparts above Ophir choke the river down into a narrow chute through which it hurries, snarling, and the shore ice was widening at the rate of a foot an hour. Early in the day the recorder from Alder Creek had tried to come ashore, but had broken through, losing his skiff and saving his life by the sheer good luck that favors fools and drunken men. It was October; the last mail had gone out a fortnight previous; the wiseacres were laying odds that the river would be closed in three days, so it was close running that McGill made—six hundred miles in an open whip-sawed dory.

They heard him calling, once he saw the lights, and, getting down to the water-level, they could make out his boat crunching along through the thin ice at the outer edge. He was trying to force his way inward to a point where the current would not move him, but the Yukon spun him like a top, and it looked as if he would go past. Fortunately, however, there happened to be a

man in the crowd who had learned tricks with a·
lariat back in Oklahoma; a line was put out, and
McGill came ashore with his bedding under one
arm and a sheet-iron stove under the other.
Stoves were scarce that winter, and McGill was
no tenderfoot.

They obtained their first good look at him when
he lined up with the crowd at Hopper's bar, ten
minutes later, by which time it was known who
he was. He had a great big frame, with a great
big face on top of it, and, judging from his reputation, he had a great big heart to match them both.
Some of the late-comers recalled a tale of how he
had lifted the gunwales out of a poling-boat that
was wedged in a timber-jam above White Horse,
and from the looks of his massive hands and
shoulders the tale seemed true. He was not
handsome—few strong men are—but he had level,
blue eyes, rather small and deep set, and a jaw
that made people think twice before angering him,
while his voice carried the rumbling bass note
one hears at the edge of a spring freshet when the
boulders are shifting.

"I missed the last boat from Circle," he explained, "so I took a chance with the skiff."

"Looks like you'd be the last arrival before the
trails open," offered Hopper. "I don't guess
there's nobody behind you?"

"I didn't pass anybody," said McGill, and it
was plain from his smile that he had made good
time.

McGILL

"Aim to winter here, Dan?"

"I do. Minook told me, four summers ago, that he'd found a prospect near here, and I've always figgered on putting some holes down. But it looks like I'm late."

"Oh, there's plenty of ground open. You've got as good a chance as the balance of us."

"Any grub in camp?"

"Nope. Ophir was struck too late in the fall."

McGill laughed. "I didn't think there would be; but that's nothing new."

"Didn't you bring none?"

"Nary a pound. There's women and children at the Circle, and there wasn't more than enough for them, so I pulled out."

"There's plenty below," Hopper assured him.

"How far?"

"We don't know yet. There's a boat-load of 'chekakos' bound for Dawson somewhere between here and Cochrane's Landing. They'll be froze in now, and tenderfeet always has grub. Soon's we get some more snow we'll do some freightin'."

Before he retired that night McGill had bought a town lot, and a week later there was a cabin on it, for he was a man who knew how to work. Then, during the interval between the close of navigation and the opening of winter travel he looked over the country and staked some claims. He did not locate at random, but used a discrimination based upon ten years' experience in

the arctics, and when cold weather set in he felt
satisfied with his work. Men with half his hold-
ings reckoned their fortunes at extravagant figures; transfers of unproved properties for handsome terms were common; millions were made
daily, on paper.

Soon after the winter had settled, two strangers
"mushed" in from down-river. For ten days they
had pulled their own sled through the first dry,
trackless snow of the season, and they were well
spent, but they brought news that the steamboat
was in winter quarters a hundred and fifty miles
below. They assured McGill, moreover, that
there was plenty of food aboard, so, a day later,
he set off on their back trail with his dog-team.
By now the melancholy autumn was gone, the air
was frozen clean of every taint, the frost made
men's blood gallop through their veins. It
changed McGill into a boy again. His lungs
ached from the throbbing power within them, his
loping stride was as smooth as that of a timber-
wolf, his loud, deep laughter caused the dogs to
yelp in answer.

When he finally burst out of the silence and
into the midst of the gold-seekers with tidings of
the new camp only a hundred and fifty miles away
they shook off their lethargy and awoke to a great
excitement. He told all he honestly knew about
Ophir, and with nimble fancies they added two
words of their own to every one of his. They
stopped work upon their winter quarters and made

ready to push on afoot—on hands and knees, if
necessary. Here was a man who had made a
fortune in one short autumn, for with the customary ignorance of tenderfeet they perceived no
distinction between a mining claim and a mine.
A gold-mine, they reasoned, was worth anything one wished to imagine, from a hundred
thousand to a million; thirty gold-mines were
worth thirty millions—figure it out for yourself.
The conservative ones cut the result in half and
were well satisfied with it. They were glad they
had come.

The steamboat captain offered McGill a bed in
his own cabin, for the log houses were not yet
completed, and that night at supper the miner
met the rest of the big family. Among them was a
girl. Once McGill had beheld her, he could see
none of the others; he became an automaton,
directing his words at random, but focusing his
soul upon her. He could not recall her name, for
her first glance had driven all memory out of his
head, and during the meal he feasted his hungry
eyes upon her, feeling a yearning such as he had
never before experienced. He did not pause to
argue what it foretold; it is doubtful if he would
have realized had he taken time to think, for he
had never known women well, and ten years in
the Yukon country had dimmed what youthful
recollections he possessed. When he went to bed
he was in a daze that did not vanish even when the
captain, after carefully locking the doors and clos-

ing the cabin shutters, crawled under the bunk
and brought forth a five-gallon keg of whisky,
which he fondled like a mother her babe.

"Wait till you taste it," crooned the old man.
"Nothing like it north of Vancouver. If I didn't
keep it hid I'd have a mutiny."

He removed a steaming kettle from the stove,
then, unearthing some sugar from the chart-case,
mixed a toddy, muttering: "Just wait, that's all.
You just wait!" With the pains of a chemist he
divided the beverage into two equal portions,
rolled the contents of his own glass under his
tongue with a look of beatitude on his wrinkled
features, then inquired, "What did I tell you?"

"It's great," McGill acknowledged. "First real
liquor I've tasted for months." Then he fell to
staring at the fire.

After a time he asked, "Who's the lady I was
talking to?"

"The one with the red sweater?"

"Yes."

"Miss Andrews. Her first name is Alice."

"Alice!" McGill spoke it softly. "I—I s'pose
she's married, of course?"

"No, *Miss* Andrews."

McGill started. "I thought she was the wife of
that nice-looking feller, Barclay."

The captain grunted, and then after a moment
added, "She's an actor of some kind."

McGill opened his eyes in genuine astonishment.
He opened his mouth also, but changed his mind

and fell to studying the flames once more. "She's plumb beautiful," he said at length.

"All actors is beautiful," the captain remarked, wisely.

McGill slept badly that night, which was unusual for him, but when he went to feed his dogs on the following morning he found Miss Andrews ahead of him.

"What splendid creatures!" she said, petting them.

"Do you like dogs?" he queried.

"I love them. You know, these are the first I have ever seen of this kind."

"Then you never rode behind a team?"

"No. I have only read about such things."

McGill summoned his courage and said, "Mebbe you'd like me to—give you a ride?"

"*Would* you? Oh, Mr. McGill!" She clapped her hands, and her eyes widened at the prospect.

He noted how the brisk air had brought the blood to her cheeks, but broke off the dangerous contemplation of her charms and fell to harnessing the team, his fingers stiff with embarrassment. He helped her into the basket-sled and then, at her request, tucked in the folds of her coat. It was a novel sensation and one he had never dreamed of having, for he would not have dared touch any woman without a command.

It was not much of a ride, for the trails were poor, but the girl seemed to enjoy it, and to McGill it was wonderful. He felt that he was making an awful spectacle of himself, however, and hoped no one had seen them leave; he was so big and so ungainly to be playing squire, and, above all, he was so old.

He could think of nothing to say on the excursion, but when she thanked him upon their return he was more than paid for his misery. As they drove up, Barclay was watching them from the high bank, and Miss Andrews waved a mitten at him. Later, when McGill had left for a moment, the young man began, sourly:

"Making a play for the old party, eh?"

"He isn't old," said Miss Andrews, carelessly.

"What's the idea?"

"I don't know that I have any idea. Why?"

"Humph! I'm interested—naturally."

"You needn't be. It's every one for himself up here, and you don't seem to be getting ahead very fast."

"I see. McGill's due to be a millionaire, and I'm down and out," Barclay sneered. "Well, we're neither of us children. If you can land him, more power to you."

"I wouldn't stand in your way," said Miss Andrews, coldly, "and I don't intend that you shall stand in mine."

"Is that the only way you look at it?" Barclay wore an ugly frown that seemed genuine. She met it with a mere shrug, causing him to exclaim, hotly, "If you don't care any more than that, I won't interfere." He turned and walked away.

McGILL

Those were wonderful days for McGill. Instead of hurrying back to his work he loitered. With a splendid disregard of convention he followed the girl about hourly and was too drunk with her smiles to hear the comment his actions evoked. He had moments of despair when he saw himself as a great, awkward bear, more aptly designed to frighten than to woo a woman, but these periods of depression gave way to the keenest delight at some word of encouragement from Alice Andrews. He did not fully realize that he had asked her to marry him until it was all over, but she seemed to understand so fully what was in his heart that she had drawn it from him before he really knew what he was saying. And then the joy of her acceptance! It stunned him. When he had finally torn himself away from her side he went out and stood bareheaded under the northern lights to let it sink in. There were no words in his vocabulary, no thoughts in his mind, capable of expressing the marvel of it. The gorgeous colors that leaped from horizon to zenith were no more glorious than the riot that flamed within his soul. She loved him, Dan McGill, and she was a white woman! When he thought how beautiful and young she was his heart overflowed with a gentle tenderness which rivaled that of any mother.

Still in a dream, he related the miracle to the steamboat captain, who took the announcement in silence. This old man had wintered inside the circle and knew something of the woman-hunger

325

that comes to strong men in solitude. He was observant, moreover, and had seen good girls made bad by the fires of the frontier, as well as bad women made good by marriage.

There being no priest nearer than Nulato, it was, perforce, a contract marriage. A lawyer in the party attended to the papers, and it pleased the woman to have Barclay sign as a witness. Then she and McGill set out for Ophir, a trip he never forgot. The sled was laden with things to make a bride comfortable, so they were forced to walk, but they might have been flying, for all he knew. Alice was very ignorant of northern ways, childishly so, and it afforded him the keenest delight to initiate her into the mysteries of trail life. And when night drew near and they made camp, what joy it was to hear her exclamations of wonder at his adeptness! She loved to see his ax sink to the eye in the frozen fir trunks and to join his shout when the tree fell crashing in a great upheaval of white. Then when their tiny tent, nestling in some sheltered grove, was glowing from the candle-light, and the red-hot stove had routed the cold, he would make her lie back on the fragrant springy couch of boughs while he smoked and did the dishes and told her shyly of the happiness that had come upon him. He waited upon her hand and foot; he stood between her and every peril of the wilds.

And while it was all delightfully bewildering to him, it was likewise very strange and exciting to his bride. The deathly silence of the bitter nights, illumined only by the awesome aurora borealis; the terrific immensity of the solitudes, with their white-burdened forests of fir that ran up and over the mountains and away to the ends of the world; the wild wolf-dogs that feared nothing except the voice of their master, and yet fawned upon him with a passion that approached ferocity — it all played upon the woman's fancy strangely. For the first time in her tempestuous career she was nearly happy. It was worth some sacrifice to possess the devotion of a man like McGill; it was worth even more to know that her years of uncertainty and strife were over. His gentleness annoyed her at times, but, on the other hand, she was grateful for the shyness that handicapped him as a lover. On the whole, however, it was a good bargain, and she was fairly well content.

As for McGill, he expanded, he effloresced, if such a nature as his could be said to bloom. He explored the hindermost recesses of his being, and brought forth his secrets for her to share. He told her all about himself, without the slightest reservation, and when he was done she knew him clear to his last, least thought. It was an unwise thing to do, but McGill was not a wise man, and the stories seemed to please her. Above all, she took an interest in his business affairs, which was gratifying. Time and again she questioned him shrewdly about his mining properties, which made him think that here was a woman who would prove a helpmate.

McGILL

Their arrival at Ophir was the occasion for a
rough, spontaneous welcome that further turned
her head. McGill was loved, and, once his towns-
men had recovered from their amazement, they did
their best to show his wife courtesies, which all
went to strengthen her belief in his importance
and to add to her complacence.

McGill was ashamed of his cabin at first, but she
surprised him with the business-like manner in
which she went about fixing it up. Before his
admiring eyes she transformed it by a few deft
touches into what seemed to him a paradise.
Heretofore he had witnessed women's handiwork
only from a distance, and had never possessed a
real home, so this was another wonder that it
took time to appreciate. Eventually he pulled
himself together and settled down to his affairs,
but in the midst of his tasks it would sometimes
come over him with a blinding rush that he was
married, that he had a wife who was no squaw,
but a white woman, more beautiful than any
dream-creature, and so young that he might have
been her father. The amazing strangeness of it
never left him.

But the adolescence of Ophir was short. It
quickly outgrew its age of fictitious values, and its
rapturous delusions vanished as hole after hole
was put to bed-rock and betrayed no pay. Entire
valleys that were formerly considered rich were
abandoned, and the driving snows erased the
signs of human effort. Men came in out of the

hills cursing the luck that had brought them there. The gold-bearing area narrowed to a proved creek or two where the ground was taken and where there were ten men for every job; the saloons began to fill with idlers who talked much, but spent nothing. One day the camp awakened to the fact that it was a failure. There is nothing more ghastly than a broken mining-town, for in place of the first feverish exhilaration there is naught but the wreck of hopes and the ruin of ambitions.

McGill's wife was not the last to appreciate the truth; she saw it coming even earlier than the rest. Once she had lost the first glamour and fully attuned herself to the new life she was sufficiently perceptive to realize her great mistake. But McGill did not notice the change and saw nothing to worry about in the town's affairs. He had been poor most of his life, and his rare periods of opulence had ended briefly, therefore this failure meant merely another trial. Ophir had given him his prize, greater than all the riches of its namesake, and who could be other than happy with a wife like his? His very optimism, combined with her own fierce disappointment, drove the woman nearly frantic. She felt abused, she reasoned that McGill had betrayed her, and at last owned to the hunger she had been striving vainly to stifle for months past. Now that there was nothing to gain, why blind herself to the truth? She hated McGill, and she loved another!

There had never been an instant when her heart had not called.

And then, to make matters worse, Barclay came. He had spent most of the long winter at the steamboat landing, being too angry to show himself in Ophir, but the woman-hunger had grown upon him, as upon all men in the North, and it finally drew him to her with a strength that would have snapped iron chains. Hearing, shortly after his arrival, that McGill was out on the creeks and never returned until dark, he went to the cabin. Alice opened the door at his knock, then fell back with a cry. He shut out the cold air behind him and stood looking at her until she gasped:

"Why have you come here?"

"Why? Because I couldn't stay away. You knew I'd have to come, didn't you?"

"McGill!" she whispered, and cast a frightened look over her shoulder.

"Does he know?"

She shook her head.

"I hear he's broke—like the rest." Barclay laughed mockingly, and she nodded. "Have you had enough?"

"Yes, yes! Oh yes!" she wailed, suddenly. "Take me away, Bob. Oh, take me away!"

She was in his arms with the words, her breast to his, her arms about his neck, her hot tears starting. She clutched him wildly, while he covered her face with kisses.

"Don't scold me," she sobbed. "Don't! I'm sorry, I'm sorry. You'll take me away, won't you?"

"Hush!" he commanded. "I can't take you away; there's no place to go to. That's the worst of this damned country. He'd follow—and he'd get us."

"You must, Bob! You *must!* I'll die here with him. I've stood it as long as I can—"

"Don't be a fool. You'll have to go through with it now until spring. Once the river is open—"

"No, no, no!" she cried, passionately.

"Do you want us to get killed?"

Mrs. McGill shivered as if some wintry blast had searched out her marrow, then freed herself from his embrace and said, slowly: "You're right, Bob. We must be very careful. I—I don't know what he might do."

That evening she met McGill with a smile, the first she had worn for some time, and she was particularly affectionate.

Instead of returning down-river, Barclay found lodgings and remained in Ophir. He was not the most industrious of men, and before long became a familiar figure around the few public places. McGill met him frequently, seeing which Barclay's fellow-passengers from below raised their eyebrows and muttered meaningless commonplaces; then, when the younger man took to spending more and more of his time at the miner's cabin, they ceased making any comment whatever. These are things that wise men avoid, and a loose tongue often leads to an early grave when fellows like McGill are about. Some of the old-timers who had wintered with the miner in the "upper country" shook their heads and acknowledged that young Barclay was a braver man than they gave him credit for being.

Of course McGill was the last to hear of it, for he was of the simple sort who have faith in God and women and such things, and he might have gone on indefinitely in ignorance but for Hopper, who did not care much for the Barclay person. The saloon-man, being himself uneducated and rough, like McGill, cherished certain illusions regarding virtue, and let drop a hint his friend could not help but heed. The husband paid for his drink, then went back to the rear of the room, where he sat for an hour or more. When he went home he was more gentle to his wife than ever. He brooded for a number of days, trying to down his suspicion, but the poison was sown, and he finally spoke to her.

"Barclay was here again this afternoon, wasn't he?"

She turned her face away to hide its pallor. "Yes. He dropped in."

"He was here yesterday, and the day before, too, wasn't he?"

"Well?"

"He'd ought to stay away; people are talking."

McGILL

She turned on him defiantly. "What of it? What do I care? I'm lonesome. I want company. Mr. Barclay and I were good friends."

"You're my wife now."

"Your wife? Ha! ha! Your wife!" She laughed hysterically.

"Yes. Don't you love me any more, Alice?"

She said nothing.

"I've noticed a change, lately, and—I can't blame you none, but if you loved me just a little, if I had even that much to start on, I wouldn't mind. I'd take you away somewhere and try to make you love me more."

"You'd take me away, would you?" the woman cried, gaining confidence from his lack of heat. "Away, where I'd be all alone with you? Don't you see I'm dying of lonesomeness now? That's what's the matter. I'm half mad with the monotony. I want to see people, and live, and be amused. I'm young, and pretty, and men like me. You're old, McGill. You're old, and I'm young."

Her husband withered beneath her words; his whole big frame sagged together as if the life had ebbed out of it; he felt weary and sick and burned out. His brain held but one thought—Alice did not love him, because he was old.

"Don't go on this way," he said, finally, to check her. "I suppose it's true, but I've felt like a daddy and a mother to you, along with the other feeling, and I hoped you wouldn't notice it.

I don't reckon any young man could care for you like that. You see, it's all the loves of my whole life wrapped up together, and I don't see, I don't see what we can do about it. We're married!" It was characteristic of him that he could devise no way out of the difficulty. A calamity had befallen them, and they must adjust themselves to it as best they could. In his eyes marriage was a holy thing, an institution of God, with which no human hands might trifle.

"No," he continued, "you're my wife, and so we've got to get along the best way we can. I know you couldn't do anything wrong—you ain't that kind." His eyes roved over the homely little nest and the evidences of their married intimacy. "No, you couldn't do that."

"Then you won't make it any harder for me than you can help?"

"No." He rose stiffly. "You're entitled to a fair show at anything you want. I don't like Barclay, but if you want him around, I won't object. Try to be as happy as you can, Alice; maybe it'll all come out right. Only—I wish you'd known it wasn't love before you married me." He put on his cap and went out into the cold.

During the ensuing week or two he devoted himself to his work, spending every daylight hour on his claim, in this way more than satisfying Barclay and the woman, who felt that a great menace had been removed. But Hopper determined that

his friend should know all and not part of the
truth, for good men are rare and weak women in
the way, so he put on his parka and walked out
to the place where McGill was working, and
there, under a bleak March sky, with the snow-
flurries wrapping their legs about, he told what he
had learned. Hopper was a little man, but he had
courage.

"I've heard it from half a dozen fellers," he
concluded, "and they'd ought to know, because
they come up on the same boat with them.
Anyhow, you can satisfy yourself easy enough."

McGill moistened his lips and, thanking his
informant, said, "Now you'd better hustle back
to camp; we're due for a storm."

It was still early afternoon when he walked
swiftly out of the gulch and into the straggling
little town. On his way down from the claim
the blizzard had broken, or so it seemed, for the
narrow valley had suddenly become filled with a
whirling smother through which he burst like a
ship through a fog. When he emerged upon the
flats he saw that it was no more than a squall and
the wind was abating again.

His moccasins made no sound as he came up to
his own house, and the first inkling of his presence
that the two inside received was when the door
opened and he stood before them. Something in
his bearing caused his wife to clutch at the table
for support, and Barclay to retreat with his back
to the opposite wall, his hand inside his coat.

McGILL

McGill never carried a weapon, having yet to feel the need of one. He spoke now in a harsh, cracked voice. "Take your hand off that gun, Barclay."

"What's the matter with you?" the younger man questioned.

Mrs. McGill's eyes were wide with terror, her frame racked by apprehension, when her husband turned upon her and asked:

"Is it true? Do you love—him?" He jerked his head in Barclay's direction. "Answer me!" he rumbled, savagely, as she hesitated.

Her lips moved, and she nodded without removing her gaze from him.

"How long have you loved him?"

When she still could not master herself, he softened his voice: "You needn't be scared, Alice. I couldn't hurt *you*."

"A long—time," she said, finally.

McGill leveled a look at the other man.

"That's right," Barclay agreed. "You might as well know."

"They tell me that you and her had—" McGill ground his teeth, and his little eyes blazed—"that she didn't have no right to marry without—telling me something about you."

The former answered through white lips: "Well? Everybody knew it except you, and you could have found out. I'd have married her sometime, myself, if you hadn't come along."

McGill's fingers opened slowly, at which the woman burst forth:

336

"Take your hand off that gun,
Barclay."

"No, no! Don't—do that. You can't blame him, Dan. I did it. Don't you understand? *I'm* the one. I loved him in 'Frisco, long before I saw you, and I've loved him ever since. Take it out on me, if you want to, but don't hurt him."

"I don't reckon I'd have minded it much if I'd known the truth at the start," said McGill. "Most women have made mistakes at one time or another, at least most of those I've known have. No, it ain't that, but you married me knowing that you loved him all the time."

"I tried to quit," cried the wife. "I tried to, but I couldn't."

"And what's the rottenest of all"—McGill's voice was ugly again—"you made him best man at the wedding, or just the same. He stood up with us. Didn't you, Barclay?"

The wife flung herself into the breach once more with a self-sacrifice that wrenched her husband's heart. "He didn't want to, but I made him. I thought you had money, and I was mad at him for letting me go, so I tried to hurt him. I wanted him to marry me, but he wouldn't, and I took you. When it was over and I saw the kind of man you are I tried to love you—honestly I did, but I couldn't. You're so— I—I couldn't do it, that's all." She broke into a torrent of tears, holding herself on her feet by an effort. Her wretched sobbing was the only sound in the cabin for a time, then Barclay inquired:

"Well, what are you going to do?"

McGill turned to his wife, ignoring Barclay.
"I guess I understand things pretty well now,
and I'm beginning to see your side. Of course I
never aimed to hurt *you*, Alice—I couldn't; but
I aimed to kill this man, and I will if he stays
here." Over his shoulder he flung out, quickly:
"Oh, the gun won't help you none. You've got
to go, Barclay."

"I'll go with him," cried Mrs. McGill, desperately. "If he goes, I'll go, too."

"That's exactly what you've got to do. You
can't stay here now, neither of you. If he ain't
able to take care of you, why, I will as long as I
live, but you've both got to go."

"It's the best course under the circumstances,"
Barclay agreed, with relief. "We'll take the
first boat—"

"You'll go to-day, now," said the husband,
grimly, "before I have time to think it over."

"But where?"

"To hell! That's where you're headed."

"We can't go afoot," the woman cried in a
panic.

"I've got dogs! And don't argue or I'll weaken.
I'm letting him go because you seem to need him,
Alice. Only remember one thing, both of you—
there ain't no town big enough to hold all three of
us. Now go, quick, before I change my mind,
for if the sun ever goes down on Barclay and me
together, so help me God! it won't rise on both
of us. There ain't no place in the world that's

big enough for him and me, no place in the world."

McGill stood on the river-bank and watched them vanish into the ghostly curtain that sifted slowly down from the heavens, and when they were finally lost to view he turned back to his empty cabin. Before entering he paused as usual to note the weather—it was a habit. He saw that the sky was strangely leaden and low, and in spite of the fact that the "quick" was falling rapidly, the air was lifeless and close. If McGill was any judge, that squall had been but a warning, and foretold more to follow. He sighed miserably at the thought of the night his wife would have to face.

He cooked his supper mechanically, then sat for hours staring at it. The wind rattling at his door finally roused him to the knowledge that his fire was out and the room chilly. Being unable longer to bear the silence and the mute evidences of her occupation that looked at him from every side, he slipped into his parka and went down to Hopper's place, where there were life and human voices at least.

The night was yelling with a million voices when he stepped out. The bitter wind snapped his fur garment as if to rend it to ribbons, the whirling particles of snow rasped his face like the dry grains from a sand-blast. Boreas had loosed his demons, and they were lashing the night into chaos. McGill felt a sudden tender concern for

the woman, a concern so great as almost to destroy
his bitterness, but he reflected that he had seen
to loading the sled himself, and among the other
paraphernalia had included a tent and a stove.
Unless Barclay was a fool, therefore, Alice was
perfectly safe. There was wood aplenty, and the
spruce forests offered shelter from the gale. The
thought awakened a memory of those night camps
he had made on that dreamlike wedding-journey
and brought forth a groan. How old and spiritless he had become; he could scarcely stand against
the wind!

Of course the story had gone broadcast, hours
before, for other eyes than his had watched the
man and woman take the outbound trail that
afternoon, so when he came stumbling into
Hopper's place a sudden silence fell. He went
directly to the bar and called for straight "hootch,"
to drive the cold from his bones, but, although
it warmed his flesh, his soul remained numb and
frozen. Inside him was a great aching emptiness
that even Hopper's kindly words could not reach.

"Looks like the worst night we've had this
year," said the proprietor. "Better have a drink
with me."

McGill's teeth rattled on the glass when he put
it to his lips. "She's gone!" he whispered, staring across the bar, "and I didn't kill him. I
couldn't—on her account."

Hopper nodded. "I'm awful sorry it came out
this way, Dan."

McGILL

McGill shivered and drew his head down between his gaunt shoulders. "Talk to me, will you?" he begged. "I'm hit hard."

His friend did as he was directed, but a few minutes later in the midst of his words the big man interrupted:

"There wasn't room for all of us here," he declared, fiercely. "I told her that, but she wanted him worse than her own life, so I had to give in."

They were still talking at midnight, after all but a few loiterers had gone home, when they heard a man's voice calling from outside. An instant later the front door burst open and a figure appeared; it was Cochrane, the trader from down-river.

"Here! Give me a hand!" he bellowed through his ice-burdened beard, then plunged back into the hurricane to reappear with a woman in his arms.

"I thought I'd never make it," he declared. "There's a man in the sled, too. Get some 'hootch' and send for a doctor, quick."

McGill uttered a cry, while the hand with which he gripped the bar went white at his pressure. "Where did you get them?" he questioned.

"Ten miles below," said Cochrane. "I was camped for the night when their dogs picked up my scent. They were half dead when they got to me, and he was in mighty bad shape, so I came through. I've been five hours on the road."

Two men brought in Barclay, at which McGill

flung out a long arm and cried in a loud voice, "Is that man dead?"

No one answered, so he strode forward, only to have the weakened traveler raise his head and say:

"No, I'm not dead, McGill. But we had to come back."

The wife was calling to her husband, wretchedly: "Don't do it, Dan. We couldn't help it. We'll go to-morrow. We'll go. Please don't! We'll go."

The onlookers, knowing something of the tragedy, drew back, watching McGill, who still stared into the face of the man who had robbed him of everything.

"Do you remember what I told you?" he questioned, inflexibly.

Barclay nodded, and the woman shrilled again: "Don't let him do it, men. *Don't!*"

"There ain't room for us here," went on McGill.

"Only to-night," supplicated his wife, the frost-bitten spots in her cheeks no more pallid than the rest of her countenance. "He *can't* go. Don't you see he isn't able? Wait, Dan; I'll go if you want me to"—she struggled forward. "I'll go, but he'll die if you send him out."

"It's always him, ain't it?" said the miner, slowly. "You seem to want him pretty bad, Alice. Well, you can have him. And you can stay, both of you." He drew his cap down over his grizzled hair and turned toward the door, but Hopper saw the light in his eye and intercepted him.

342

McGILL

"I'll go home with you, Dan," said he.

"I ain't going home."

"You mean—"

"There ain't room enough in Ophir for Barclay and me and the woman."

"My God, man, listen to that blizzard! It's suicide!"

But McGill only repeated, dully: "There ain't room, Hopper. There ain't room!" and with the gait of an old man shambled to the door. When he opened it the storm shrieked in glee and rushed in, wrapping him up to the middle in its embrace. He closed the door behind him, then went stumbling off into the night, and as he crept blindly forth upon the frozen bosom of the river the bellowing wind wiped out his footprints an arm's-length at his back.

THE BRAND

THE BRAND

THE valley was very still. No breath of wind
had stirred it for many days. It was
smothered so heavily in snow that the firs were
bent; even the bare birch limbs carried precarious
burdens, and when gravity relieved some sagging
branch the mass beneath welcomed the avalanche
so softly that the only sound was a whisper as the
bough returned to its position. The brooding
cold had cleared the air of sound as it had of
moisture. No birds piped, there was no murmur
of running water, no evidence of animal life except
an occasional wavering line etched into the white
by the feet of some tiny rodent.

The rolling hills were sparsely timbered, against
an empty north sky a jumble of saw-toothed
peaks were limned like carvings, and everywhere
was the same unending hush of winter. The
desolation was complete.

Yet there was life here, for spaced at regular
intervals across the gulch were mounds of white,
each forming the lips of a rectangular cavity re-

sembling an open grave. They were perfectly aligned and separated from each other by precisely thirty paces; surrounding each was a clearing out of which freshly cut stumps protruded bearing snow caps fashioned like the chapeau of a drum-major. There were six of these holes, and a seventh was in process of digging. Over the last one a crude windlass straddled and the heap of debris at its feet showed raw and dirty against the snow. Out of the aperture a thin vapor rose lazily, coating the drum and rope with rime; from the clearing a narrow trail wound to a cabin beside the creek-bank.

McGill came out into the morning and with him came his three giant malamutes, wolf-gray, shaggy, and silent like their master. He eyed the drooping, white-robed forest and the desolate ridges that shut him in, then said, in a voice harsh from disuse:

"Hello, people! Anything happened yet?"

He made it a practice to speak aloud whenever he thought of it, for the hush of an arctic winter plays pranks with a person's mind, and there is a certain effect of sanity in spoken words, senseless though they be.

After a moment he repeated his greeting: "Good morning, I said. Can't you answer?" Then his cheeks flamed above his heavy beard and he yelled, loudly, "*Good morning*, you ——! Can't you say anything?" He glared reproachfully at a giant spruce from the lower limbs of

which depended the quarters of several caribou.
"Tom, you ain't gone back on me? Say hello.
You and me are friends. Speak up!" After a
time he shook his head, murmuring: "It's no use.
I've got to make all the noise there is. If it
would only blow—or something. I'd like to hear
the wind."

He strode toward the prospect hole, the dogs
following sedately, their feet making no sound in
the snow. They, too, felt the weight of isolation
and never left his side. Arriving at the dump,
McGill stood motionless beside the windlass for a
long time, staring into nothingness with eyes that
were strained and miserable. When the cold bit
him he roused himself and addressed the steam-
filled opening dispiritedly:

"So, you didn't freeze up on me. That's good.
I'll get bed-rock to-day and show you up for a
dirty cheat. Pay! Bah! there ain't none!"

He descended a ladder at one end of the shaft,
gathered the charred logs, tied them into a bundle
with the end of the windlass rope, then, mounting
the ladder, hoisted them to the surface. Next,
hooking on the ungainly wooden bucket, he
lowered it, after which he descended for a second
time.

There began a long and monotonous series of
ascents and descents, for every bucket of gravel
meant two journeys the full depth of the pit.
It was a tedious and primitive process, involving a
tremendous waste of effort, but he was methodical,

and each time the tub rose it carried a burden sufficient to tax the strength of two men. He handled it easily, however, and by midday had removed the thawed ground and scraped a sample from close to frost. He laid a light fire, then took the heaping gold-pan under his arm and set off for his cabin, accompanied by the malamutes.

When he had prepared and eaten his lunch he seated himself before his panning-tub, a square box half filled with water melted from the creek ice, and began the process of testing his prospect.

Having worked down the gravel and sediment to a half-handful, he spread it with a movement of his wrists, leaving stranded at the tail of the black sand a few specks of yellow. These he eyed for a moment before washing them away.

"Too light—as usual," he said, aloud. The dogs stirred and raised their heads. "Always pretty near, but not quite. But it's here, somewhere, and I'll get it if I can last out this damned silence. That rim-rock didn't lie. And old Pitka didn't lie, either. Nobody lies except—women." He scowled at some remembrance, his whole face retreated behind a bristling mask of ferocity. He sat motionless over the tub of muddy water until the fire died out of the stove and the chill warned him that it was time to resume work.

For many weeks—how many McGill neither knew nor cared—he had pursued the routine of his search. He had penetrated this valley alone, unseen, in the late autumn, and every day since

then he had labored steadily, mechanically, almost
without physical sensation, for all feeling was
centered in his memory, which never gave him
time to consider his surroundings. Spring was
coming now—the sun was already peeping over the
southern hills in the middle of its daily journey—
and during this time there had been but two in-
terruptions which had roused him from his apathy.
One had occurred when, in quest of fresh meat, he
had discovered that he had neighbors ten miles to
the west. He had seen their camp from the
divide, then had turned and slunk away, cursing
them for intruding upon his privacy. The other
was when a herd of caribou had crossed. At that
time he had given brief rein to his desire to kill,
seeing ahead of his sights the face of the man who
had sent him into the wilderness. He could have
bagged half the herd, but checked himself in time,
realizing that it was not Barclay at whom he
leveled his rifle, but defenseless animals, the car-
casses of which were useless.

Barclay! The name maddened McGill. He
wondered dully why he continued to work so
steadily when Barclay had robbed him of the
need for gold. The answer to this, he supposed,
was easier than the answer to those other questions that forever troubled him—he had to do
something or die of his thoughts, and he knew
no other work than this. Even in his busiest
hours memories of Barclay and the woman ob-
truded themselves.

It was after dark when he had fired the hole a second time and returned to his cabin. He had not reached bed-rock and this fact irritated him—he was growing very irritable, it seemed. Lighting his pipe of rank "sheep-dip" tobacco when the supper-dishes were finally cleaned and the dogs fed, he once more prepared for the profitless process of panning. But he noticed that this sample of gravel was different to any he had yet found, being of a peculiar ashen color. He felt it with practised fingers and discovered it to be gritty and full of sediment.

"Feels good," he said, aloud, "but I'll bet it's barren."

He had panned so many samples that all eagerness, all curiosity as to the outcome, had long since disappeared, therefore his movements were purely perfunctory as he dissolved the clay lumps and washed the gravels down. He paused half-way through the operation to dry his hands and relight his pipe, then fell to thinking of Barclay and the woman once more, and remained so for a long time. When he resumed his task it was with glazed, unseeing eyes. He was about to dump the last dregs carelessly when something just slipping over the edge of the pan caught his eye and caused him to tilt the receptacle abruptly.

The breath whistling in his throat roused the dogs. McGill closed his eyes for an instant, then reached unsteadily for the candle. A movement of his wrist ran the water across the pan bottom and spread the black sand thinly. Instantly there leaped out against the black metal a heap of bright, clean, yellow particles which lay as if glued together.

"Coarse gold! Coarse gold!" he whispered, then cursed in the weak, meaningless manner of men under great excitement. Not trusting himself to hold the pan, he set it upon the table, but without removing his eyes from it. When his nerves had steadied he ran the prospect down, all the time muttering in his beard. He dried it over the fire, blew the iron sand free with his breath, then pushed the particles into a heap, striving to estimate their value.

"There's half an ounce," he said, finally. "Eight dollars a pan! God! that's big! Big! It's another Klondike." He rose and ran bareheaded out into the night, followed by the dogs, then stood staring at the smoke as it ascended vertically above his shaft, like a giant night-growing plant of some kind. He was tempted to descend the ladder and tear the crackling logs apart, but thought better of it. Swinging his eyes along the valley rim that stood out black against the aurora, he lifted his long arms. "It's mine, all mine! Understand?" He cried the words loudly, wildly, as if challenging the silence. "It's no good to me, but it's mine, and, by God, I'll keep it!"

McGill reached bed-rock the next evening and spent most of the night panning the pile of scrapings he had collected from the bottom of the pit. If the top of the streak had been rich, the lower concentration was amazing. Every seam in the shattered limestone, which stood on end like sluice riffles, contained little flattened pumpkin-seeds of gold; they lay embedded in the clay stringers like plums in a pudding or as if some lavish hand had inserted them there, as coins are slipped into the slot of a child's savings-bank. He could see them before the dirt was half washed, but took a supreme pleasure, nevertheless, in watching the yellow pile grow as the sediment disappeared. A baking-powder can was half filled when he had finished; it told him unmistakably the magnitude of his riches. He was a wealthy man, wealthier than he had ever dreamed of being there was more where this came from and the gulch lay unappropriated from end to end. Fortune had come in a day, and he would never want so long as he lived. His thoughts were wild and chaotic, for he was half mad from the silence.

But what use to make of his discovery he hardly knew, since he had slunk away from the world, ablaze with hatred for his fellow-men, intending to live alone for the rest of his days. His grudge was as bitter now as then, and he determined, therefore, to keep his find a secret. That would be a grim, if unsatisfactory, sort of revenge, he reflected. He would take what he wished, and let other men wear out their lives searching unsuccessfully. Those strangers to the westward, for instance, would toil and suffer through the long winter, then leave discouraged. There was money here for them and for hundreds—thousands—like them, but he decided to guard his secret and to let it die with him.

McGill pictured the result of this news if he gave it out; the stampede, the headlong rush that would bring men from every corner of the North. He saw this silent valley bared of its brooding forest and filled with people; he saw a log city in the flats down by the river; he heard the bass blasts of steamboats, the shrilling of saw-mills, the sound of music from dance-halls, the click of checks and roulette-balls, the noise of revelry—

"No! No! *No!*" He rose and shouted into the empty silence of his cabin. "I won't do it! I won't! I won't!"

But the voices called to him all through the night.

He rose early, for they would not let him rest, and during the darkness a terrible hunger had grown upon him. It was the hunger for compan-ionship, for speech. His secret was too great for imprisonment, it threatened to burst the con-fines of the valley by its own tremendous force; he knew he could never sleep with it, for it would smother him; vampire-like, it would suck the life from his veins and the reason from his brain.

When he had eaten he pocketed the baking-powder tin, slipped into his snow-shoes and, crossing the gulch, climbed the westward hills that hid his neighbors. The dogs went with him.

II

NEWS of the John Daniels strike reached Ophir in July, when a ragged, unkempt man arrived in a poling-boat. He was one of the party that had camped west of McGill, and he ate a raw potato with the ravenous appetite of an animal while waiting for his first meal at the Miner's Rest. Between mouthfuls he gave the word that set the town ablaze.

When he had bought a ton of grub at the A. C. store and weighed out payment in bright pumpkin-seed gold he went to Hopper's saloon and handed the proprietor a folded paper.

Hopper read it uncomprehendingly.

"This is a location notice, recorded in my name," the latter said, turning the document uncomprehendingly as if to see if it contained a message on the reverse side.

The stranger nodded. "Number Four Above, on John Daniels Creek. John staked for you, and told me to tell you to come. We've struck it rich."

Hopper's hand shook; he stared at the speaker in bewilderment. "John Daniels? I don't seem to remember him."

"He's a big slab-sided man with a deep voice and eyes like ice."

356

THE BRAND

The listener started. "Is he—skookum?"

"Stronger 'n any two men—"

"God! It's—McGill!"

"I thought so, but I never saw him only once—that was in Circle. He's changed now—got a beard. He said you done him a favor once. You're his friend, ain't you?"

"I am."

"What's the trouble with him?" There was a pause. "You can tell me. He put me and my five pardners in on his strike. I'm taking grub to him and the others."

"Oh, it was about a woman, of course. It always is. Everybody here knows the story. She was no good, except to look at. Feller named Barclay brought her into the country, but Dan didn't know it, so he up and marries her. She thought he had money, and when she found he was broke like the rest of us she and Barclay began cuttin' up again. It was rotten. I came near putting Barclay away, but figgered Dan wouldn't like nobody to do his work, so I told him. He went out to clean the slate, but found his wife was crazy about the skunk and always had been, so he sent 'em away together. He done it for her sake, but he warned 'em to stay off his trail, because no camp was big enough to hold all three of 'em. It was blizzardy, and what did the blame' fools do but get caught ten miles below here. Cochrane brought 'em back that night on his sled. McGill was here, right where you're

357

standing, when they were lugged in. When he seen Barclay he went after him again, figgerin', I suppose, that God was disgusted with his proposition and had sent the feller back to be finished."

"Good!" said the stranger. "And he got him, eh?"

"No! Barclay wasn't more 'n half dead, and the woman fell to beggin' for his life again. She appealed to all of us. McGill must have loved her more 'n we give him credit for, because when he saw that neither one of 'em was able to leave, he left instead. He walked right out of that door into the wickedest storm we had that season, and we never seen him again. Everybody thought he froze or the wolves got him. That was a year ago last winter."

"What become of the woman?"

"Oh, her and Barclay left for Dawson on the first boat. I guess they saw we didn't enjoy 'em here."

"And Barclay? Didn't nobody offer to bump him off?" The ragged stranger was incredulous.

"No, we just left him and the woman alone. Most of us was kind of sorry for her."

"Sorry? Why?"

"Well—" Hopper hesitated. "I don't think she exactly understood what she was doin'. You know the first winter up here is hard on tenderfeet, especially women. Most of 'em act mighty queer before they ca'm down. She'd have come to herself if McGill had given her time."

"Barclay wasn't more 'n half dead, and the woman fell
to beggin' for his life again."

THE BRAND

"Hm-m! It's too late now." Both men nodded. "When 'll you leave for John Daniels Creek?"

"When? *Now!* I've got enough of this camp, and I'll have these bar-fixtures packed in two hours."

McGill—or John Daniels, as he chose to call himself—saw his dream come true. The first stampeders came in August; gaunt fellows worn by sleepless days and nights during which they had fought the swift waters and the fear of pursuit. They were followed by a tiny river boat, then an A. C. packet, loaded heavy and carrying Hopper with his bar-fixtures and fifteen barrels of whisky. She had been aground a hundred times and had passed other stranded craft laden with men who cursed her as she gained the lead. A city of tents sprang up on the flats; it changed to one of cabins when the first snow flew. John Daniels Creek was overrun, at nights its tortuous course was lit by glowing fires, smoke hung above it constantly, it became pitted with prospect holes. Trails were broken to adjoining creeks where similar scenes were enacted. But of all who came, few saw, and almost none spoke to, John Daniels himself, for he never went to town and there was no welcome at his cabin. Of course his name was on every tongue, but he toiled underground by day and hid himself by night. Sometimes Hopper, on his way to or from Number

359

Four Above, would stop over and spend an evening with him, but not often.

Meanwhile great ash-gray pay dumps grew upon Discovery, and there were rumors of a fabulous bed-rock, inlaid with gold, but Daniels did all his own sampling, so there was no way of verifying the reports. When the spring sluicing was finished it was said that he had cleaned up half a million.

Daniels himself, huge, gaunt, gray-bearded, and silent, saw his gold loaded aboard the first steamer and accompanied it to the "outside"—this being his first trip to the States in ten years.

During his absence the new camp of Arcadia grew, for its fame had spread. It changed from a formless cluster of log shacks to a small city of sawed lumber and paint. One season had made the wilderness into a frontier town, the next made of it a metropolis. With the current that flowed thither from the distant camps came the scum of the north country. Following the first tide of venturesome, strong-limbed men came the weaklings, the maimed and crooked of body and soul, the parasites and idlers. Among these there were women of the customary kind and a number of men who lived upon their earnings. Barclay was one of them.

Arcadia was in the fullest riot of its growth when John Daniels returned, late in the autumn. He had expected to find a change, but he was unprepared for the startling transformation that greeted his eyes. It stirred him deeply, for the town was his, he had made it, his hands had given it life. He wondered if this could be his desolate camping-place of two seasons before. Where was the melancholy forest? the brooding silence? As he walked up the front street past the painted stores the vigorous life and optimism of the place electrified him; he heard laughter and music, the tinkle of pianos from the dance-halls, the sounds of revelry. The air was filled with clamor, it was pungent with smoke and with the manifold odors of a city. Everywhere was activity and haste.

Of course the news of his return spread swiftly, for he was a personage, but before the curious could mark him he had left for the creek that bore his name, where a hundred men were preparing to drift out Discovery pay-streak under his supervision. He remained there a month, during which the first gray snows turned white and brought that peculiar loneliness, that depression of spirit which marks the beginning of winter.

Then one day he decided to go to town. The impulse surprised him, for he had meant to shun the place, as always, but his summer in the world outside had worked a change and something within him hungered for companionship, the glare of lights, the sight of animated faces. Then, too, he was curious to examine this town of his at closer range.

It was worth seeing, he decided proudly, during his inspection; it was a splendid, healthy camp.

THE BRAND

He walked the front street, then prowled through
the regions behind. There were women in this
part of Arcadia, and these he regarded distrustfully, although he was more than once arrested
by a glimpse of some cozy home, and stood staring
until warned by the frowns of indignant house-
wives that his presence was suspicious. He remembered another cabin like these—his own. He
had never quite grown accustomed to its white
curtains and china dishes and similar delights, any
more than he had grown accustomed to the presence of that wonderful, mysterious creature who
had filled the place with light. It was all part
of another life, a bewildering dream too agreeable
to last.

In the course of his wanderings, however, he
came into a different district, one which offended
him sorely. Immediately behind the saloons he
found a considerable cluster of meaner shacks
which were inhabited by women and yet which
were not homes. These gaudily curtained houses
huddled close together, as if for moral support or
as if avoiding contact with their surroundings;
they crouched in the shelter of the gilded dance-
halls, seeking a sort of protection in one another's
disreputable company. From some of the windows haggard faces smiled at Daniels, and he heard
sounds of a merrymaking that were particularly
offensive at this hour. Until this moment he had
regarded Arcadia with fatherly pride, and had not
dreamed it was wicked, hence this discovery en-

raged him. He was not a sensitive man, having trod the frontier where vice is naked, but something about the rotten core of this new community sickened him. It reminded him of a child diseased.

And then, as if to point the comparison, he saw a child, a tiny, fat, round-faced person leading a puppy by a string.

Now, women were strange to John Daniels, since there had been but one in his life, and he had possessed her only briefly, but children were mysterious, incomprehensible creatures; phenomena which excited at once his awe and his amazement. They made him ill at ease; he had never touched one, with the possible exception of an Indian papoose, now and then, therefore his present meeting constituted an experience— almost an adventure. It was a white child, too, and it gazed at him with the disconcerting calmness of a full-grown person. Daniels was both embarrassed and shocked at its presence in this locality. He hesitated, then summoned his courage and said, timidly:

"Say, kid, ain't you lost?"

The child continued to stare at him in unaffected wonder, leaving him painfully conscious of his absurd size and forbidding appearance. He feared that once it had overcome its first amazement it would begin to cry and thus cover him with ignominy. But, happily for him, the puppy experienced none of its owner's doubts and uncertainties; it flattened its round stomach,

thumped its soft paws upon the sidewalk, then
approached the giant in a delirious series of wobbly
leaps, wiggling an eloquent, if awkward, declaration of friendship.

"Fine dog-team you're driving, sonny!" Daniels smiled, congratulating himself upon an admirable display of wit, only to realize with a start
that he had made a mistake. Some sixth sense
informed him that this was not a boy. It was a
humiliating error.

"Say, missie, you—you don't belong here.
You're plumb off your trail. That's a cinch!"
He cast a worried glance over his shoulder and
saw a hideous blanched face smile at him between
a pair of red curtains. He glared back at the
woman, and his cheeks grew hot. Meanwhile the
little girl continued her unwinking examination.

She wore a ridiculous fur parka, scarcely larger
than Daniels's cap, and tiny mukluks that made
her legs look shorter and fatter than they were.
Her mittens were the littlest things he had ever
seen and he was regarding them wonderingly when
she amazed him by approaching and laying one in
his hand.

Now, this frank and full declaration of friendship reduced Daniels to a helpless condition; he
had never been more troubled in his life. He was
vaguely frightened, and yet he thrilled in an unaccountable manner at the touch. He was half
minded to withdraw his hand from his glove and
retreat, leaving it in her possession, but thought

again of these evil surroundings, and of the responsibility that had devolved upon him with her surrender. In the midst of his dumbness the young lady burst into a bubbling and intimate recital of her adventures, which doubtless would have been perfectly intelligible to her mother, but which left the discoverer of John Daniels Creek floundering for a translation.

He concealed his disgraceful ignorance by an easy assumption of understanding. He nodded, he winked, he grinned. He eyed the infinitesimal hand that lay in his, then gingerly removed his own glove the better to safeguard its treasure, whereupon the small mitten promptly closed over one of his big knuckled fingers. Daniels gasped and held his digit as rigid as a pick-handle. Escape was no longer possible.

Having finished her recital the tot burst into a funny gurgle which plainly established a deep and undying intimacy between them, then, like all maidens who have pledged their affections, she made plain her readiness to accompany her protector to the end of the world.

But the puppy held back and delayed progress as effectively as a ship's anchor, so, fearing to exert too great a strain upon his extended finger, Daniels gave the animal bodily into her embrace. One short arm encircled the dog's neck, whereupon, as if by habit, it limply resigned itself to misery. The three went slowly out of that sin-ridden place, the man dazed and delighted, the child loquacious

and trustful, the puppy with lolling tongue and
legs protruding stiffly.

Daniels had mastered many dialects in his time,
from Chinook to Pidgin English, but to save himself he could make nothing out of this language.
Some words were plain, but they were lost in a
bubbling flow of strange, moist, lisping articula-
tions that left the general meaning obscure.

She answered all his questions eagerly, fully, and
he acknowledged:

"She knows what she's sayin', all right, but
I'm as rattled as a tenderfoot."

Nevertheless he derived a preposterous delight
from this experience, until he realized that they
were wandering aimlessly. Then thoughts of a
possible encounter with a distracted parent filled
him with such dismay that he appealed to the
first woman he met.

"Lady! If you know where this baby lives—"

"Certainly I know."

"Then take her home. Her mother 'll think I'm
a kidnapper." Daniels perspired at the thought.

The woman laughingly accepted the responsibility of a full explanation, but as she lifted the
child it turned up its face to Daniels, quite as a
matter of course. The rosebud lips awaited him,
yet he did not understand. He inquired, blankly:

"*Now* what does she want?"

"A kiss. Don't you, dearie?"

"God'lmighty!" breathed the man. Then he
lowered his bearded face.

THE BRAND

He was trembling when the strangers had gone; he felt those moist baby lips against his and the sensation almost overcame him. He didn't like the woman's appearance, but she seemed tender-hearted and—there was no better way of insuring the safety of his little charge than to give her over.

But that kiss! It remained upon his lips more fragrant, more holy than anything he had ever conceived. It left him conscious of his own uncleanliness and shortcomings.

Still in a daze, he looked down at his index finger, which remained rigid; it was blue with the cold, but he felt nothing except the clasp of a tiny woolen mit.

"*Well!*" he exploded. "I—don't *seem* to be dreaming. She liked me—she must of—or she wouldn't of kissed me. She sure did, and I—God! I'd trade Discovery for another one."

He felt no further interest in Arcadia; he thought only of the child and the amazing adventure that had come to him; he could think of nothing else during the afternoon. More than once he touched his lips timidly with his tongue and bared his hand to stare at his big finger.

When he had dined that evening he began a leisurely round of the saloons and gambling-halls, pausing in each to invite every one to drink, as befitted a man of wealth. He played, more or less, without knowing whether he won or lost, for his thoughts were directed in other and stranger channels.

THE BRAND

The Elite was the most pretentious place of amusement in Arcadia and it was running full blast when he strolled in, late that night. The show was over in the theater, but a dance was going on. Beyond the people at the gambling-tables he saw swiftly moving figures and heard the caller's shouts through the rhythmic beat of the orchestra.

He looked on with some interest until he could engage the attention of a bartender, then said:

"Call everybody up for a drink."

When the fellow eyed him distrustfully he explained:

"I'm John Daniels."

He was amused at the instant, almost ludicrous change of expression, and at the alacrity with which the crowd responded to his invitation. They stampeded, the games were deserted, the "sleepers" roused themselves, even the dancers came trooping forth with his name upon their lips. The music ended discordantly and the musicians followed them. The long bar was lined six deep by people who elbowed one another for a glimpse of the famous John Daniels. Those who succeeded beheld a huge, grim-featured man, bearded to the cheek-bones, who seemed deaf to their remarks and heedless of their stares. His hair was long and gray, his eyes were small and bright and hard; he looked like a Mormon elder.

It took time to serve such an assemblage, and during the delay Daniels stood motionless, vaguely resenting this curiosity. When the bartender said "All set!" he raised his glass and exclaimed, "Drink hearty!"

As the glass left his lips his eyes ran down the bar and along the bank of faces, clear to the end, where the dance-hall girls had squeezed themselves in. There they rested, and widened.

His hand fell heavily, crushing the glass beneath it, for facing him, clinging to the rail as if about to fall, stood his wife. Their eyes met fairly. Daniels saw in hers the first flaming light of recognition, then that expression of deathly terror that he remembered; he felt the floor sinking, saw the near-by figures whirling, heard the clamor die.

After his first start not a muscle of his face moved, but his eyes began slowly to search through the crowd as if for some one, and, seeing that, she understood. With a hand to her throat she groped her way blindly out of the crush, then made for the rear, but her knees forsook her and she paused, leaning against the wall. It never occurred to her that she might escape.

She knew without looking when he came toward her. He spoke in an emotionless tone, saying, "Come!" and she followed, half swooning —followed him up the stairs to the curtained boxes that ran round the gallery.

When they were alone, she faced him, managing to utter: "So! *You*—are John Daniels! They said you were dead."

369

She expected some violence—death, perhaps, but he only looked at her silently with an expression she could not read. She felt she must scream. She swayed, her eyes were filmed with terror.

"Well! Why don't you do it, McGill? Why don't you—?" she cried, hysterically.

"Where is Barclay?" he inquired.

"He's here—somewhere. We came three weeks ago— We—I didn't know—"

He saw that she was not the woman he had known: she was frail, broken; her fluttering hands were thin and bloodless; she had no spirit.

"So! He's got you working, eh? You're one of these—*rustlers!*"

"I had to do something. All I know is stage work."

"This ain't stage work!"

She nodded wearily. "He made me go the—limit."

"*Made* you! Did you get a divorce?"

"N-no!"

Daniels cursed so harshly that she flinched, although she had long since grown accustomed to profanity. Then he turned away, but, reading murder in his face, she seized him with fingers that were like claws.

"Wait! Don't do that!"

"You love him, don't you?"

"No, no! But—he's bad now, and—and probably drunk. He'll kill you, McGill. He's bad, I tell you—tough—don't you understand? He's bad, and he's made me bad, too, that's why I'm here. He's not worth it, McGill; neither am I!"

"You can't stay in Arcadia, neither of you. I got out of Ophir and let you alone, but this is my town; I can't leave it."

"We'll go," she cried, wringing her hands; "anyhow, I'll go, if you'll help me. But I'll need help— Oh, God! Yes, I'll need help! You don't know— You and he can settle things afterward."

"You want to leave him?"

"I've tried to break away, I've been trying ever since that first day in Ophir, but he won't let me. I kept trying—until I learned better; now I'm afraid. He's broken me, Dan, but you'll help me to leave him, won't you?"

After a time the husband answered, more to himself than to her: "I guess I'm even with *you*, anyhow. You've gone to hell, hand in hand with him. I won't interfere—not that way. I s'pose he beats you?"

She nodded, and saw his bearded face twitch. "Yes, and he'll make me like these other women— you understand? I've fought until I'm tired, worn out. I'm in a trap, McGill, and—I'm afraid—afraid for the little soul I have left."

"You sprung the trap," he told her, bitterly.

But his wife had seen a way to freedom and clutched at it with desperate persistence.

"Listen! I want to talk to you. Come with me for a minute."

"Come? Why?"

"Never mind. Oh, it's all right. You owe me something, for I still have your name. Do this for me, please! It's only a step."

He yielded to her imploring eyes and followed grudgingly down the back stairs and into the night, wondering the while at his own weakness. She led the way, bareheaded, heedless of the cold. They were in that ill-favored district he had penetrated earlier in the day, but if it had been offensive then it was doubly so now, with its muffled sounds of debauchery and wickedness. She paused finally, fumbling at the door of one miserable structure, whereupon he growled:

"You live here? You're worse than—"

"'Sh-h!" She laid a finger on her lips as she let him in and lit a lamp, then she beckoned him toward the single rear room, shading the light with one hand and inviting him silently to peer over her shoulder.

The surprise of what he saw struck McGill dumb, for there in a crib lay the tiny lass who had befriended him that afternoon. Her lips were pouting sweetly, her face was flushed with dreams, one plump little arm was outside the covers, and just below the doubled fist McGill saw the deep dimpled bracelet of babyhood. Her presence made of these squalid surroundings a place of purity; the room became suddenly a shrine.

"The son-of-a-gun!" said McGill, inanely, then his face darkened once more. "I know her," he

THE BRAND

announced, grimly. "What are *you* doing with that kid—in this hell-hole?"

From the alleyways near by came a burst of ribaldry, but the woman's face was shining when she answered:

"Why, she's mine—my baby. We have no other home."

He did not—could not—speak, so she said, simply:

"Now you see why I must leave Barclay, and—all this."

"*Your* baby!" McGill's eyes dropped to the index finger of his right hand, then he touched his lips curiously.

"Barclay won't let me run straight. I've always wanted to, and now I must, for the baby's sake." When this brought no response she continued, with growing intensity, but in a lowered tone. "She'll begin to understand things before long. She'll hear about him—and me. Then what? She'll think for herself, and she'll never forget a thing like that, never. How can she grow up to be good if she learns the truth? It wouldn't let her. Nobody could stay good around Barclay. Even I couldn't, and I was a woman when I met him. I'm decent, inside, McGill. Honestly I am, and I've been sorry every day since you left. Oh, I've paid for what I did! And I'll pay more, if I have to, but she mustn't be part of the price. No! You've got to help me. Don't you see?"

373

THE BRAND

She mistook his gesture of bewilderment for one of refusal, then hurried to one final, frenzied appeal, although at a fearful cost to herself. It was this which had come to her in the dance-hall; it was this that she had led up to without allowing herself time in which to weaken.

"Listen! She shouldn't stay with me, even if I get away; it wouldn't be good for her; besides, Barclay would find us some time; or, if he didn't, I'm too sick to last much longer. Then she'd be alone. You're rich, McGill. You're John Daniels. You'll have to take her—not for my sake, understand, but—"

"*I?*" The man started. "I take Barclay's baby? Great God!"

There was a moment of silence during which the wife strove to steady herself, then she said:

"She's not his—she's yours—ours."

McGill uttered a great cry. It issued from the depths of his being and racked him dreadfully. He swung ponderously toward the rear room, then fell to trembling so that he could not proceed. He stared at the woman, lifted his hands, then dropped them; his lips shook. A fretful, sleepy complaint issued from the chamber, at which the mother raised a warning finger, and the necessity for silence calmed him more quickly than anything else could have done.

"*My—baby!*" he whispered, while he felt something melt within him and was filled with such an aching joy that he sobbed with the agony of it.

THE BRAND

His wife's punishment overflowed when he breathed, fiercely:

"Then give her to me. You can't keep her. You can't touch her. You ain't fit."

She bowed her head in assent, although his torture was nothing as compared with hers.

"You'll help me get away from Barclay, won't you?" she asked, supporting herself unsteadily.

"Barclay! I forgot him! He's the one that did all this, ain't he? He brought you to—this; and my baby, too. He made her live among women like these. He raised her in slime—" The speaker's face became slowly, frightfully distorted.

His wife went swiftly to him; she struggled to fend him away from the door, but he moved irresistibly. They wrestled breathlessly so as not to awaken the child, while she begged him in the baby's name not to go, not to bring blood upon her; but he plucked her arms from around him and went out, closing the door softly.

When he had gone Mrs. McGill stood motionless, her eyes closed, her palms pressed over her ears as if to shut out a sound she dreaded.

Barclay was dealing "bank" in one of the saloons when McGill entered and came toward him down the full length of the room. They recognized each other as their eyes met, and the former sat back stiffly in his chair, feeling that the dead had risen. What he saw written in the face of the bearded man drove the blood from his cheeks, for it was something he had dreaded in his dreams. He knew himself to be cornered, and fear set his nerves to jumping so uncontrollably that when he snatched the Colt's from its drawer and fired blindly, he missed. The place was crowded, and it broke into a frightful confusion at the first shot.

None of those present told the same tale of what immediately followed, but the stories agreed in this, that John Daniels neither hesitated nor quickened his approach, although Barclay emptied his gun so swiftly that the echoes blended, then snapped it on a spent cartridge as the two clinched. Curious ones later searched out the bullet-marks in wall and ceiling which showed beyond doubt the nervous panic under which the gambler had gone to pieces, and so long as the building stood they remained objects of great interest.

Now McGill—or Daniels, as he was known to the onlookers—never went armed, having yet to feel the need of other weapons than his hands. He tore the gun from his victim's grasp, then mauled him with it so fearfully that men shouted at him and hid their faces. Meanwhile he was speaking, growling something into Barclay's ears. No one understood what it was he said until the confusion died and they heard these words:

"—And you'll go with my brand on you where everybody 'll read it and know you're a rat."

Next he did something that a great many had heard of but few, even of the old-timers, had witnessed. He gun-branded his enemy. Barclay was little more than a pulp by this time; he lay face up across the faro-table with McGill's fingers at his throat. They thought the older man was about to brain him, but instead he turned the revolver in his hand and drew the thin, sharp-edged sight across Barclay's forehead from temple to temple, then from forelock to bridge of nose. A stream of blood followed as the sight ripped through to the skull like a dull scalpel, leaving a ragged disfiguring cross above the gambler's eyes; it scarred the bone; it formed a hideous mutilation that would last as long as the fellow lived, and constitute a brand of infamy to single him out from ten thousand, telling the story of his dishonor.

When he had finished, McGill raised the wretch bodily and flung him half across the room as if he were unclean, then, without a glance to right or left, he went forth as he had come.

His wife was waiting with her ears covered, but she saw the blood on his hands when she opened her eyes, and cried out.

"It's his," he told her, roughly. "I don't think I killed him. I tried not to, for her sake." He inclined his head toward the inner door. "But it was hard to hold in, after all this time. He'll never trouble you again."

"When do you—mean to take the baby?" she whispered.

"Now— She—"

"No, no! Not yet. Let her stay here a little while—till I'm strong enough to let her go. Just

377

a little while, McGill. You're a good man. Don't you understand?" She was palsied, incoherent with dread; in her eyes was a look of death.

But he held out his empty arms, crying, hoarsely, "Let me have my kiddie!"

So she went in and gathered up the sleeping babe.

It may have been the father's heart-beats that awakened the little one when she lay against his breast; at any rate the blue eyes opened and stared up at him gravely. Astonishment, alarm gave way to recognition; she smiled drowsily and her lids closed again, then a tiny hand curled about one of McGill's fingers.

His face was wet when he raised it to the stricken woman and said, gently, "We'll go now, if you're ready, Alice."

"What do you—?" She stared at him wildly. "You don't want *me*, McGill; not after all I've done, all I—am?"

"I've always wanted you," he told her, simply. "You'll have to come, for *she* needs you." Holding the baby close with one arm, he extended the other to his wife, but she drew back, choking.

"Not yet!" she managed to say through her tears. "Not until you know I'm not all bad— only weak."

He took her hand and together they went out, walking slowly so as not to awaken the child.

THE END